BLOODJACKER

A Bellers Tale

T.D. EDGE

Lucky Bat Books

Bloodjacker
A Bellers Tale

Copyright ©2013 T.D. Edge
Cover Art by Ben Baldwin

Published by
Lucky Bat Books
LuckyBatBooks.com

10 9 8 7 6 5 4 3 2 1

To Kim for your amazing and enduring support

ACKNOWLEDGEMENTS

Thanks to Cindie Geddes and Judith Harlan at Lucky Bat Books. Cindie for her invaluable comments on an early draft, and for constant cheerleading on writing what you love to write. Judith for a lot of patient hand-holding with websites and all sorts of other technical stuff, and for doing a great job on formatting this book.

Contents

ONE

The Princess and the Girl at the Astro

A CRISPY AUTUMN EVENING in Whitechapel, and in my three-houses-in-one gaff the butterflies in my stomach tap-danced faster than Fred Astaire on Viagra. I sat in my big Superman bath robe, sipping tea and staring out the window at the middle garden, the one Mum had worked so hard on when she was still alive. Rose bushes nodded at me in the rapidly ageing golden sunlight and the jasmine arch seemed full of her presence right then, mouthing at me, "It's just a *girl*, Jack Stapleton; she won't bite yer."

The gardens either side weren't much to look at but I couldn't knock them all into one, of course, on account of the satellites. Inside, it was another story—well, one big, long, storey, I suppose—except that right then, all me gizmos, weapons, robotics and the such, just seemed so *blokey*. Which was why I'd shut off Hilary, the house comms system, to be alone with my thoughts for once.

I tried to concentrate on my wardrobe and what, specifically, I could remove from it that would endear me to Ms Sandra Hollins, barmaid at The Astrolabe and Firkin—or at least she would be until closing time tonight. That's when she'd clock off forever and be lost to me in the mists of Whatever She Done Next.

I'd 'just happened' to drop in at the Astro several times over the past few weeks, trying to look casual while propping up the bar, when in reality I'd had to juggle dozens of doohicky jobs, Bellers' commitments, and even the odd social event just to get there.

Not that I told Sandra any of that. I didn't want her knowing I was a Beller. She was around thirty, about ten years younger than me, with light brown hair, green eyes and a great figure. What I really liked about her was the fact she didn't chuck her intelligence around, preferring to sit behind it and watch the world do its thing. Occasionally, we'd share a small smile at a comment some regular would make, that showed him to be a Grandmaster Pillock of the Bleedin' Obvious or whatever. Of course, I hoped those smiles also contained a bit of cautious need for yours truly.

And now she was leaving her job at the Astro. Oh, with my Beller connections I could no doubt get hold of her address and go knock at her door one night, but I'm a firm believer in the power of open declaration. Which in this case meant putting on me best threads, trundling along to the Astro and showing her what I felt, and all before last orders.

I carried on watching the light fade from the garden for a bit longer, trying to summon the courage; and blow me down if at the very moment I stood up, ready to have a heart to heart chat with me shirt collection, there wasn't a knock on the middle front door.

Well, not just any knock—an *official* knock. I could always tell: three firm raps and a heavy presence oozing through the letterbox.

Bleedin' duty called.

I opened the door to see two agent rozzers dressed in regulation black suits and slightly worried-looking visages.

"Oh, bloody 'ell, what is it this time?" I said.

"Jack Stapleton?" said this kid with a shaved head and pimply face.

I leaned forward to peer at him closely. "Are you telling me you don't know, son?"

He reddened a bit. The other one—who looked at least old enough to order a pint—said, "I'm Agent Lee; this is Agent Morris. May we come in, sir?"

There was no sign of their car on the street, so I figured they wasn't quite as stupid as they looked. Then again, black suits and square shoulders ain't going to fool no one in Whitechapel.

I stood back and waved them in, pleased to see the younger one unable to stop his eyes widening at all the techy hardware on view.

"Take a seat, gents, if you can find one."

"We apologise for coming here," said Lee, "but you didn't answer our calls, and you don't have an assistant."

We gathered around a work table, perched on stools. I cleared some drawings away, then Morris said, "There's been an incident."

I had to laugh. "I didn't think you was here to admire me roses. Whatever you want, fellas, my arse has to be back here by ten-thirty the latest when I have what will hopefully be a life-changing engagement."

And I was indeed being hopeful here, since the little favours His Majesty's Government asked of us Bellers often involved a few days' worth of travel, fisticuffs and general unfortunateness.

Lee took a glossy photograph out of his folder and put it on the table. "They're going to kill her," he said. "Happened just half an hour ago; it'll be all over the news any second now."

"Strewth . . ."

As soon as the rozzers left, I slapped my thumb against the personalised pad on the kitchen wall, dropped through the floor hatch, stripped off my bath-robe and flung it aside. I climbed down into the pod, which wobbled with my weight, lay naked on my back and took a steadying breath.

All I wanted to do right then was leave it to someone else for once and go prepare for meeting Sandra. But then there weren't really anybody else.

"Bellers' HQ, and step on it," I said.

"I take it you don't mean that literally, sir," said Jeeves 2.0, the Bellers' comms system. "Since you didn't see fit to provide me with feet."

"I ain't got time for banter, Jeeves. Just make this thing go very fast."

"Vroom, vroom it is, sir."

The black organo-steel Bellers suit wrapped itself around my body, a not unpleasant experience it has to be said. I felt a dozen or so electric ripples over my skin as the parallel nerve channels powered up; my face gently massaged by the black mask with its one-way visor.

The hovering pod sealed itself then dropped rapidly down its chute until it reached the horizontal tube forty feet below.

The pod shot forward into total darkness. But given HQ was just a quarter mile away, my stomach barely had time to catch up with the rest of me before it stopped again then ascended.

I stepped out of the hatch into a subterranean world of shiny black tiles, orgone lighting and the constant jabbering and flashing of the TV news spread across the walls—but with little chance of seeing what the rozzers had said would soon hit the nation's screens, because when I say 'the news', I'm being generous to my guys here. Let's just say their idea of current events was keeping up with the latest dog-racing odds and how long Tommy Cole's ankle injury would keep him out of the Hammers' attack.

I paced along the welcome corridor—which would have sprayed me with anything from tranquiliser gas to dismembering lasers by way of saying "Hi!" if Jeeves' scanners hadn't detected that this suit and bloke inside was seriously kosher.

Most of the boys would be here at HQ, mainly because that's where they normally spent their time. Their wives, girlfriends and boyfriends had been sworn to secrecy about their affiliation with the Bellers, not to mention their better half's particular special ability. And few ever asked what they actually did at HQ, which was probably just as well.

I stuck me eyeball in front of the retinal scanner at the end of the corridor and the metre-thick steel doors swung inwards. Then I was hit by heavy cigar smoke and a medley of geezer noises from a few dozen Bellers with too much time and large government grants on their hands.

Not seeing the two I was after, I made my way as niftily as possible to the bar, nodding and saying, "Watcha!" or "'Ow's it going?" to any Beller whose gaze I caught.

Behind the counter, Young Eric juggled several orders at once, his bow tie still admirably well-starched despite the ongoing pressure of a couple of dozen permanently parched clientele. I sometimes wondered if he wasn't a Beller himself, with super-patience as his speciality.

"Evening, Jack," he said. "It *is* evening outside, ain't it?"

"Quite a pleasant one, as it happens," I replied. "Mum's roses are like burnished gold in the softening twilight. In fact, I'd love to write a bleedin' poem about them but right now I need those two wasters, Sam and Pete."

He nodded behind him, in the direction of the private reccy rooms. "One's talking in tongues, the other's virtual bonking."

The boys insisted they needed the reccy rooms as tension relievers. I'd never used them, but then I guess my tension reliever was designing and building gizmos. Whatever, I kicked in the door marked 'Knights of Passion' and yelled, "Suit up, Sir Bangalot; your country needs you!"

Sam jumped to his feet, his goggles failing to hide his blushing bald bonce. On the big wall screen, a virtual naked dusky maiden continued to writhe and moan as she rode his trusty virtual charger. "Bleedin' 'ell, Jack," he said, hands cupped around his passion lance. "You coulda knocked first."

I got my suit to turn up the room's lighting, exposing all the decidedly naff red velvet cushions, couches, rose-scented plasma candles, film of rising flocks of doves, and so on. I also vanished said maiden whose face had remained contorted in Sammy-induced sexual ecstasy, her being unaware of course that she'd been rudely dislodged from his heraldic todger.

"Babs not enough for you?" I said.

He breathed hard, fighting the anger that would transform him. Good: I needed him focussed.

"None of this is real," he said. "You know that, Jack. So it's not like I'm being unfaithful or nothing."

"So Babs knows all about it, does she?"

He turned away, opening the battered canvas bag that never left his side. In moments, he'd flicked out his Bellers' suit and stepped into it, looking most mission-like. Only his slightly bonkers stare and sweaty head marked him out as one seriously naffed-off berk. But then Babs was always his soft spot, even if he hardly saw her these days.

"What's the job?" he said.

"I'll tell you in the tube," I replied, turning away. "Just need to pick up Pete."

"Oh, is it crazy Muslims again, then?"

"Nope, this time it's crazy Scots."

Pete seemed to be in a trance, standing in the centre of a circle of screens, each showing a talking head. Several different languages came at him all at once, yet his outstretched fingers seemed to be weaving all them alien words into some sort of Pete-sense tapestry.

Ecstatic though he appeared, I didn't hesitate in switching off all that babble. Where Sam got belligerent and explosive when cut off from his recreational needs, Pete just looked bemused. He shook his long black hair, opened his pale blue eyes and said, "What do you need, Jack?"

"A bit of Gaelic, as it happens," I said. "See you in the pods."

Lying in our separate pods, head to toe, hurtling north through a tube at four hundred miles per hour, I filled them in over the comms.

"A bunch of new Scots national extremists has kidnapped Princess Marion and is holding her in a castle on the west coast near Oban," I said.

Sam said, "'Ow the 'ell did they get her away from her secret service goons?"

"Seems they was a little slack. As she was opening a new community centre near the harbour, the nationalist nutters shot two rozzers dead, wounded two more, then grabbed her. They drove to the castle and took it over. Place has been evacuated, surrounded by cops and goons but they daren't burst in because the terrorists will kill her if they do."

Pete said, "What do they want?"

"Search me. So far, they've just been spouting some old rubbish about Scots independence."

"Yeah," said Sam, "but not from bleedin' English subsidies, no doubt."

"That's a big word for you, Sam," I said. "Good to know you've been keeping up with the political news."

"Bollocks."

I went through my plan of action then left them to their own thoughts for the few remaining minutes of our journey.

There was a quite a bit of malarkey in this semi-international event that I couldn't quite get my noodle around. Marion's title was Princess of Scotland, not that she spoke the language or even went there much. She was next in line to the throne, ever since her older brother died of the big C two years back, despite the best medical treatment the peasants' taxes could buy. The current king, Harold, was also said to be near croaking, so Marion could be parking her perky young butt on the royal divan any time now.

No doubt, though, the royal establishment would much prefer her younger sister, Beatrice, to be taking over the crown jewels. Marion, you see, was a rarity among royals, possessing something that hadn't been seen in more than a handful of 'em since Elizabeth the First, namely a mind of her own. But where Good Queen Bess had held and used real power, Marion didn't appear to see much call for the monarchy these days.

Breaking all the protocols, she'd given interviews to the media in which she criticised the vast sums of public dosh stumped up to keep the royals in the manner expected. She held no truck with the argument that royal bods brought tourists to the UK, arguing that the French had offed their toffs yonks ago and plenty of visitors were happy enough to spend their Euros there.

Needless to say, there had been much speculation about whether Marion would ever take the throne when it came up for occupation. It was easy to see why royals normally did so, being mostly thick and ugly. But Marion was beautiful and brainy. She could do *any*thing, most like.

If she lived long enough to, that is.

Our three pods rose side by side to hover under the hatch in the Bellers' Glasgow base, although when I say 'Glasgow', I mean in a hillside about ten miles from the city proper.

We exited the hatch, ran to the mini-stealth flying car, also designed by yours truly, and jumped in with me at the controls. I started the hydrogen engines, which in turn activated the tunnel lights, then we accelerated toward the stone wall one hundred yards ahead.

"Woo-ee!" shouted Sam, as the wall fell away and we hurtled into the evening air, toward the setting sun, Glasgow a dark huddled mass below us.

I took no chances, throwing the anti-radar screen around the car and gearing the engines to near silence. This meant the loss of around 30 mph but I figured it was more important the ultra-Jocks didn't detect us approaching. While in the pod, I'd commed Agent Lee to prepare the police and rozzers to not yell or point when they saw us land on the castle roof, but they could of course do nothing about the public's reactions, not to mention the media's.

"We have to hit 'em fast, guys," I said.

I had Jeeves throw up a 3D image of the castle, complete with our route through the roof door, then down two flights to the main hall where the Princess was being held.

"Memorise this in case we lose Jeeves," I said, tersely.

"Hey, Jack," said Sam; "what's got your Y-fronts in a twist?"

"I just need to be home by ten-thirty the latest, so why don't we save the royal bint sharpish then get the hell away from here."

"You really should get out more, mate," said Sam. "Living on your own has made you all sort of Horlicksified."

I didn't respond, my gaze fixed on the rapidly approaching castle, and behind it the great sweep of the ocean, deep blue in the evening light.

"Okay, Pete," I said, "we're in probe range now, so get your suit to listen in on the Jocks who apparently are speaking in Gaelic."

He was silent for a minute or two, then said, "They're discussing breaking away from the EU once they're independent but—I don't know—it doesn't quite make sense."

"Neither does haggis," said Sam, "unless you're Scottish."

I sighed. "What doesn't make sense, Pete?"

"It's like they're trying a bit too hard to convince themselves."

"Well," I said, "let's worry about it later, 'cos we're about to land."

I'd taken the car up high, before dropping quickly on to the castle's roof. But even though the car's chameleo-paint matched the colour of the evening sky, we still heard several shouts and cries from the crowd below.

"Pete?" I said, as we scrambled out of the car.

"They've seen us on the TV," he said, "and they're shouting to each other, to take up defensive positions."

"Sod it," I said; then to Sam: "we'll have to crash them."

His teeth gleamed in the twilight. "Excellent!"

We ran for the roof door, then down spiral stairs to the top floor. We followed a pulsing yellow line along the corridor, displayed in our visors, swerved right at a set of stairs.

Pete and I carried two guns each, left hand set to 'stun', right to 'kill'. Sam, of course, didn't need no guns.

We sprinted down some marble steps to the ground floor, then raced along the virtual yellow line, on to a huge pair of wooden doors. I waved the others to a halt.

We listened on our comms to the terrorists frantically radioing the police. They spoke English now, yelling that they'd kill the Princess if we didn't leave the hall immediately.

I nodded at Sam. "Do it."

Pete and I stepped back as Sam raised his arms, fists clenched. He growled like a gathering thunderstorm. His body shook violently, expanding in all directions. His suit and visor fell apart, as designed to do, leaving him naked, save for the curling dragon tattoo on his hairy back. His skin took on a flinty sheen, and his muscles knotted like some over-blown Renaissance statue's.

He lowered his head, yelled, "Geroni-bleedin'-mo!" and charged the doors.

Wood shrieked as it splintered, Sam running through the flying shards. We heard the crack of rifles and outraged shouts. I held up my hand to Pete on the other side of the ruined door frame: wait, wait, wait—no more rifle shots, Sam would be down. We needed to hold for just a few more seconds, to the point they began to wonder if he'd acted alone.

"Go!" I said, and we peeled into the hall, knelt and raised our guns. I felt pain in my right thigh, glanced quickly down to see blood seep through a slight bullet tear in my uniform, but nothing serious. We'd had to sacrifice some of the suit's resistance on the bits of our bodies that needed more mobility and I could live with the odd nick.

Eight terrorists ringed the hall, their rifles still trained on Sam's prone body. It would take them only a second or two to realise there should have been blood around it, and to focus on us.

At the far end of the room, on a raised dais, under a large modern tapestry showing some dippy artist's idea of being Scottish—wearing designer kilts and working in IT industries, apparently—the chief terrorist sat, relatively calm, with the Princess kneeling between his legs. He held a gun to her head, and I had just enough time to note the admirable fury in her eyes and to predict that Sandra would look the same in a similar position, before shouting "Fire!" to Pete.

Of course, the great advantage of a sonic gun is that you can sweep it in an arc and take out any flesh in its path. And that's what we did, all eight of them falling before they could fire at us.

"Keep an eye on them," I said, moving toward the dais.

I hoped Pete could use his other gun if need be. Because if any of these geezers happened to come round and raise a weapon, he'd have to off them.

The chief terrorist made an urgent gesture with his gun at the Princess' head and I stopped advancing.

This was when negotiations should take place. The terrorists were beaten and, although the chief could threaten the Princess, he knew he'd never leave the place alive if he killed her.

Then I recalled something Pete had said earlier and put two and two together. I glanced at the Princess who mouthed something at me and, although I couldn't make out her actual words, it was clear she wanted me to act, regardless of her safety.

I extrapolated fast, raised my right arm and shot. Invisible, razor-edged sound zipped into the chief's forehead. He jerked backward, gun firing by reflex but fortunately no longer pointed at Marion.

Regrettable to kill him, but I couldn't risk just a stun. I turned to Pete. "We need to leave—fast!"

He looked shocked at my action but the Beller in him jumped to help me pick up Sam.

We turned him over, several bullets falling from his unbroken body, plinking on to the stone floor. I slapped his face and his eyes had just fluttered open as the Princess appeared beside us.

"I saw him shot!" she said.

"I guess us East Enders must have thick skins, ma'am," I said.

Recognition widened her gaze. "You're the Bellers, aren't you? Daddy told me about you but I thought he was making it up."

We didn't reply. Fortunately, Sam had shrunk to his normal build so Pete and I could shoulder him between us. As we left the hall, I picked up Sam's discarded uniform.

"How can I thank you?" said Marion, and you know what, she sounded like she really meant it.

"Just take the throne when it's your turn, ma'am," I said; "this country could do with your spirit."

Pete and I pulled Sam up the stairs, on to the roof and into the car.

We flew over a chaos of media types and the excited public, in amongst which uniforms and goons radioed around, trying to work out what had just happened.

In the air, I sent a message to London, then, during the fifty minute pod journey back to town, filled in the other two on what I'd deduced had really gone on in the castle.

"Fascinating but predictable," said Pete, after I'd finished.

"Who gives a monkey's," said Sam, now recovered from head-butting duty. "It's all politics at the end of the day. Tell you what, though—I couldn't 'alf do with a shag."

"Shall I call Babs and tell her you're on your way?" I said.

"Bastard; but, yeah, I reckon that's a good idea of yours for once—boss."

I left them at the junction to my gaff then, just below my hatch, impatiently stepped out of my suit and back into my bathrobe.

I'd already opened the front door remotely, so stormed out of the hatch, practically yelling at Morris and Lee as they stepped cautiously into the house.

"You arseholes set us up, didn't you?"

Morris looked shifty but Lee maintained an admirably straight face. "What are you talking about, Mr Stapleton?" he said. "His Majesty's Government is extremely grateful to the Bellers for rescuing the Princess."

"Cut the crap: you wanted her dead. Your Jock stooge was meant to get me negotiating then shoot her as he made his escape, so the public blame would be laid at the Bellers' door."

"But the public doesn't know the Bellers exist," he said.

"One day it will. You've always hated asking us to help and this would be future security to keep us in line."

"We wouldn't endanger the Princess' life, just to—"

Noticing the time, I interrupted him. "Out!" I shouted. "Out!"

They scuttled through the door, muttering more phoney thanks and guaranteeing me a larger government grant in the new financial year.

I slammed shut the door then ran upstairs to change, part of my mind trying to tie up the loose ends of the case. But there were just too many vague facts to go on so far. All I knew was that Pete's instincts had been right. They weren't real terrorists who'd kidnapped Marion, just some Gaelic-speaking grunts acting the part, the whole shebang maybe intended to draw the Bellers into making the kind of mistake that'd have us uppity Cockneys more subservient to the Man in future.

Once in me best kecks and white cotton shirt, I ran downstairs and into the night, heart thudding in fear I'd be too late. But, hell, it was only eleven-fifteen and Sandra should still be clearing up in the Astro.

But as I ran into the pub, my spirits slumped. Being a Monday, the place was near-empty. Desperate, I asked the landlord if Sandra was still in the building.

"No, mate," he said, "I let her off a bit early, being her last night and—"

I ran back into the night, through the quiet streets, in the direction I hoped she'd taken.

Round one street corner—nothing; oh, bugger, bugger, bugger; why had I wasted a precious few minutes bollocking those two goons?

Round another corner—there she was! I'd recognise that proud gait anywhere: fast, too, her being no doubt aware that speed deters perverts.

I was about to sprint after her nevertheless but stopped, full of sudden doubts.

I thought about Sam and Babs, and all the other Bellers who rarely saw their partners. I'd always assumed they just preferred to bloke it up at HQ. But maybe it was more to do with fear of getting too close to anyone you may have to leave, forever.

After all, several Bellers had died on missions since Bow Bells rang that fateful day, of their own accord it seemed, changing the genes of any Cockney lad currently forming up in his mum's womb, turning us into something different. So was it even fair to shack up with someone?

I'd just turned around, ready to go home, when I seemed to hear Mum's voice again.

"It's just a *girl*, Jack Stapleton."

I smiled and turned again, shouting, "Hey, Sandra! Wait up—it's Jack!"

Two Gaffs Jack

NEXT DAY, I TOOK THE TUBE (the public version) to Westminster, on my way to MI5's headquarters.

I had a head full of aggravation over the shoot-up in Scotland, and fully intended to dump it on the committee. But, I don't know, maybe the brilliant sunshine of a clear autumn day sparking the Parliament buildings and making Big Ben look kind of fatherly—that and pleasant thoughts of Sandra—softened my anger a bit.

Whatever, I actually smiled at the passing commuters, ignoring their "Must be a looney" expressions and even stopped for a quick chat with the grubby old bloke who'd been camping in Parliament Square for years, protesting about the government's general lack of compassion for anyone who didn't wear Union Jack underpants.

"I reckon you're very brave, mate," I said, "living here, taking a risk every time you fall asleep, that the rozzers will just carry you off."

"Who says I sleep?" he said, smiling in a pretty strange way, like he knew who I was. "I hear and see a lot of stuff most people miss. And something bad is definitely on the way, make no mistake. You'll need to be at your best to survive it, young man."

I had me mouth open to question him more but he slipped back inside his tent like a ferret up a greasy trouser leg and I moved on.

MI5's centre was a huge, naff-looking pile of bricks with square cut windows on the south bank of the Thames. As the rozzers themselves knew only too well though, appearances can be deceptive.

The Bow Bells' Genetic Advancement Investigation Working Group met in a large room right at the centre of the building. No windows but a lot of artificial light, not to mention the quiet hum of several different types of monitoring devices hidden in the beige walls, most of 'em designed by me.

In the early days of the Working Group, proceedings had been somewhat hampered by the total absence of the main object of study: the Bellers themselves. Being blokes of a somewhat pragmatic approach, the idea of spending several hours sat in a corporation chair listening to rozzers and boffins droning on, had about as much appeal to a Beller as jellied eel flavoured ice cream.

But I started attending a few years back, mainly to keep an eye on the Man, even if I knew deep down it was a hopeless task. Some of the Bellers' ironically called me 'boss' as a result.

Today, I definitely wanted to be present when the suits got to discussing the latest Bellers' intervention. I wanted answers; like what they'd so far extracted from the terrorists we'd stunned back in Scotland.

I entered the meeting room, scanning the faces already present, clocking those who smiled openly as soon as they saw me, those who delayed before smiling and those what didn't smile at all. I shook hands, poured myself a coffee then chose a central spot around the long oval table to show I weren't hiding nothing.

Professor Paul Sandford took the seat to my left. Unlike most rozzers, he didn't wear a tie, just a snazzy black, collarless shirt. His head as usual was shaved and unlike the others he didn't have a notebook and pen or laptop with him.

"Hello Jack," he said, "how's your love life?"

I groaned. "Don't say you're spying on me too."

He laughed. "No, just that you don't look as fierce as normal for one of these meetings, so I wondered if you'd finally found a woman."

I should have laughed back at this but instead just shook my head in a non-committal way. Thing was, it bothered me the Prof could read me that easy, even if he did know more about the Bellers than anyone.

"Nah," I said, "it's just that the 'Ammers actually won a match last Saturday."

By now, around a dozen suits had taken their chairs, including the two rozzer agents, Lee and Morris, who looked somewhat uncomfortable. But then that might be just what I wanted to see.

There was nothing shifty about their boss, mind: Lucilla Hammond-Parker. Lucy—as she definitely didn't like to be called—stood at the head of the table, looking very important in a dark blue suit and just the tiniest bit of mascara, no doubt to make her eyes appear more focussed. The very fact she was here today, when she'd not been seen at the Working Party since I was first in long trousers, said much.

"You'll have seen the newspapers," she said. "It seems most reporters have decided the attack on the Princess was carried out by some lunatic Scottish national fringe group. And we aren't completely sure yet that isn't the truth—something funny, Mr Stapleton?"

I never read the papers, given they was always full of excitable crap by hacks trying to make a name for themselves. But the reason I'd been grinning right then was because I still believed the rozzers had set up the attack in the first place.

"Why don't you just issue a public statement," I said. "Tell the world about the Bellers and make sure everyone knows you aren't responsible for our behaviour. Ma'am."

She sighed. "Morris and Lee briefed me that you believe we created this attack to discredit the Bow Bellers. But we didn't; it's—"

"Oh, come on," I interrupted. "Yeah, you don't want to dump any bad press on the Muslims, but do you really think anyone's going to take it seriously, the Scots getting that uppity?"

Lucille drew in a breath, ready to reply, but to my surprise, Prof Paul spoke first.

"You're right, Jack," he said, "this does have all the signs of a set-up. I've reviewed the tapes of the interrogations and the men you stunned show the classic symptoms of being hired to order. They speak Gaelic, and they hate the English, but they don't know anything else, except they'd get paid a lot of cash if the ransom on the Princess ever appeared. But, believe me, it wasn't MI5 who hired them."

I fought back an argument. If Lucy had given me this line, I'd never have believed it but Paul had always been straight with the Bellers.

"So, if not you lot," I said, "then who?"

An interesting silence followed. Lucy, for once, looked straight at me. "We don't know, but we think whoever orchestrated the kidnap wasn't really interested in the Princess."

"Me and the boys?" I said.

She nodded. "We think they wanted to draw you out, to test your abilities."

While the suits continued debating the rights and wrongs of yesterday's events, I found myself thinking about the Princess, the kidnappers and for some reason even the protest bloke in Parliament Square. I could sniff the edges of a pattern but didn't push too hard to make it appear, guessing I needed a lot more pieces of the puzzle first.

Lucy's voice brought me back to the present. "Jack? Do you agree?"

"Agree to what?" I said.

"To having a live-in assistant."

"What—like some bloke with a posh voice who does me washing, cooks good solid meals and always has the answers to my life problems?"

She smiled: nice teeth; she should do it more often. "The fact is," she said, "agents Lee and Morris tried unsuccessfully to phone you yesterday, and you didn't answer your emergency bleeper. Which meant we wasted valuable minutes with them having to personally visit you. And you're the only point of contact the Bellers will allow us. You and I talked about this a year ago, and you said you'd sort it out."

Well, I was thinking about Sandra yesterday, wasn't I? And didn't want to be interrupted.

"So, while it won't be a personal butler, we will send you someone who can at least answer emergency calls and also help with your research work."

"And spy on me, too?"

"Yes, all right: spy on you too. Satisfied?"

"Okay, I agree—but on one condition."

"What?"

"I need another gaff—another apartment. Nothing too fancy but near the river'd be good, and off the radar, especially yours. Somewhere I can chill out and just *think*."

I didn't have to look at the Prof to feel him grinning, guessing what my sudden desire for a new doss pad was really all about.

One thing about Lucy—she decided fast. "Very well, but with one condition of mine: you *don't* switch off your phone and bleeper while you're there."

"Done."

After the meeting, I followed the Prof back to his office. Unlike my place, his was gizmo-free; just a couple of chairs, a few plants and a coffee machine.

"Lucy wasn't telling the whole truth," I said.

"How do you know; are you a body language expert now, too? Should I give up my day job?"

I waggled my left arm in the air, showing him what looked like an ordinary wrist watch. "New invention: reads all them tiny body reactions we try to hide, matches them against the Bellers' database then pricks me in the wrist if someone's telling porkies. And these little red dots say Lucy wasn't coming clean about the prisoners."

"No, but then I don't blame her. None of them had anything to say, mainly because they don't know anything. They were just hired to do a job. But the main man—"

"The one I shot?"

"We did a complete check on the body. Nothing out of the ordinary. But then we ran some tests on his blood and found some weird traces in it of, well, we aren't sure yet. But there are indications of independent neural configurations which may have continued to transmit piezoelectric signals for some time after the host was dead."

"Signals with patterns."

"We weren't able to translate them before they stopped. But my hunch, Jack, is that something's after the Bellers, and believe me it's not the government."

I stood up and walked to his window, looked down on the lunch time workers rushing about with sandwiches and polystyrene cups of coffee, busy and oblivious.

"I better get my arse over to our HQ," I said, "see if any of the lads can put together a feasible prognosis."

"Really?"

"Well, I might have to force the issue a bit," I said. "The guys aren't crazy on theories."

He sighed. "I've heard rumours there's no paperwork at Bellers' HQ."

I smiled. "Just don't tell the Treasury."

» THREE «

Man Marking

MOSTLY, I LOVED BEING a female agent in MI5. Having a job where you're made to think and learn new things is the reason I turned down the private sector. Even if Mum and Dad thought I was throwing my life away. But sometimes, it was hard to accept that the main price you paid for being an agent was that you had to follow orders.

I was in the gym when Lucilla Hammond-Parker came to give me new orders. My line manager had put me on a hand-to-hand combat course a couple of months previously. He didn't explain why and I didn't ask. Today, I'd been working with weights, so sweat poured down my back and sprang from my forehead as I waited for the head of MI5 to tell me what she wanted.

"Meera Nath?" she asked. The fact she hadn't sent an assistant indicated she wanted to keep this conversation between us.

"Yes, ma'am," I said. "Excuse me if I don't shake your hand but it's rather clammy at the moment."

She smiled, checking my body like a horse buyer. "Let's sit and talk," she said, gesturing at a bench by the wall.

For the first time, I noticed that the gym was empty.

"I've been very impressed with your progress, Meera," she said. "You work harder than any Level 6 agent I've ever known and yet you appear quite normal."

I risked an ironic smile. "I wish you'd tell my parents that, ma'am. They think I should be married by now and supporting a man with a proper job."

"They went back to Pakistan, didn't they?"

I nodded, playing the game of pretending I didn't know that she'd almost certainly read my parents' file before this conversation. "Dad's job at Ford's in Dagenham got cut five years ago and he decided to use the compensation money to set up a call centre in Punjab. He's doing okay but Mum wasn't too happy about going back. I guess she misses her kids."

She waited a few moments, to show me the polite conversation was over, then said, "I have a job for you, Meera."

"I wondered what the combat training was for, ma'am."

"Well, I hope you won't actually need it where I'm sending you."

"Am I going overseas?"

"I'm afraid not. Only over the river—to Whitechapel. I'm posting you to be the live-in assistant to Jack Stapleton."

Frantically, I rummaged my memory but the name didn't sound familiar. "Ma'am?"

"Stapleton is our main contact with the Bow Bellers."

I'm sure she watched the thoughts scurrying around my mind. Of course, I'd heard of the Bellers, although no agent was allowed to mention them outside official work. But I knew very little about them. There were rumours about special powers and them doing favours for the agency from time to time, but if anything their existence irritated me somewhat. I mean, I'd worked hard to progress in the agency, whereas from what I heard, the Bellers just did what they felt like, which a lot of the time apparently involved drinking, whoring and gambling.

"I've sent some confidential data to your machine, on Stapleton and the Bellers," she went on. "I'm afraid you'll have to read it quickly; I want you to start as soon as possible."

"If you don't mind me asking, ma'am: why now?"

"Firstly, Mr Stapleton is under the illusion that he can live a normal life. He's asked a local woman on a date. It will of course end badly, and we need someone there to help pick up the pieces. Secondly, it looks as if the Bellers are about to face their first really serious threat. Which means they need a fully concentrated Jack Stapleton to lead them. Even if they don't have leaders."

"How long is the job for?" I said.

"That depends on you and your loyalties, Agent Nath."

There are loads of different ways into Bellers' HQ. Although the guys each had tube links under their home gaffs, we could access the place through other, more direct, routes.

A popular way in was via the loo at The Lord Kitchener, a cosy little boozer down a side street off Commercial Road. This afternoon, I had a lot on me mind, so didn't take as much care as normal. The proper approach was to buy half a bitter, drink it then head for the bog situated between the Lounge Bar and the main door.

But today, I walked straight into the bar, just nodded at Big Trev behind the counter, not even checking who else was in the place, then backed out again, not acknowledging his startled glare. Unfortunately, this error, caused by me still having the hump with Lucy, would cost us plenty later, for I had failed to notice a strange but apparently watchful face in the bar.

In the toilet, I headed for the middle cubicle and locked the door behind me. Then I waited until I heard the grinding of small motors on the other side of the wall, activated by Trev's secret switch under the counter. The back wall turned away, leaving a dark space which I walked into, slipping past the cistern. There was a moment of utter darkness before the lights came on, then I paced along the sloping steel-walled corridor, to the spiral stairs that would take me down to HQ.

I got the guys together in the Moose Hall. Unlike most of HQ, we'd let just the one bloke design our main meeting room: Stewey Redbridge. We'd figured this would result in a less rozzer-like place to get our noodles together. Which it certainly had. Stewey went for the horn and hide look: leather sofas the size of buffalos, walls creaking with stag heads, wooden floor humpy with bearskins. He said he'd got the inspiration from an episode of The Flintstones, where Fred and Barney apparently caused mayhem in the Moose Masons or whatever stone age businessmen called themselves.

Funny thing—despite the smell of tanned leather and the wood smoke from the genuine log fire (an engineering wonder sixty feet underground, if I do say so myself)—the place felt like *us*.

Twenty-nine Bellers deported themselves around the lamp-lit, gold and amber shadowed room, the remaining seven away on minor missions or actually spending time at home with their families for once.

I stood in front of the fire, ignoring the heat on the backs of my legs, fingering the hand-held recorder in my jacket pocket. But then I let it go, deciding this was not a meeting we should have any note of lying around.

I told them all about yesterday's mission in Scotland, then brought them up to date on the MI5 meeting, ignoring the theatrical yawns this produced in some.

For a bunch of Cockneys all exactly the same age, we was a diverse looking bunch of gentlemen geezers. Chunky baldies sat next to long-haired beanpoles; and, out of the Bellers' suits, our attire ranged across jacket and tie, West Ham shirt, dungarees . . . well, it didn't matter what we wore, I suppose, since we knew each other better than our own parents, given we all had the same mystery swimming in our blood.

Sometimes my voice fought the chinking of ice in whisky glasses, but I understood why so many of them drank. Basically, unlike toffs and their centuries old social and political structures, there was no one for us to turn to.

"You look worried, Jackie," said Tony G after I'd finished. "Rozzers put the willies up yer with this personal assistant shit?"

"Maybe he's worried he might want to put his willy up the personal assistant," said Sam, glowing with Babs' residue, I was pleased to see.

"Thing is," I said, "we've been running missions for twelve years now, ever since we did a deal with the Man. But so far it's all been kind of ad hoc—sort a few kidnappers here, rescue the crew of a fishing boat there."

"Not so bleedin' ad hoc we didn't lose a few, Jack," said Al Noel, his burnt ochre skin shining with the often agonising empathy that was his special ability, and of course his curse.

"I ain't forgot 'em, Al" I said. "What I'm trying to say is that for the first time today, the head rozzer looked worried. I just know she ain't telling us everything. That, and the fact the Jocks were just hired guns, adds up to a queasy feeling in me gut that something's going on. You guys noticed any odd stuff happening lately?"

"Yeah," said Malcolm. "Herby's sartorial elegance has transcended several bleedin' levels with the recent addition of a fetching set of gold lycra nut-huggers to go with his illuminated cycle clips."

"Oi!" said Herby, "my nuts don't need no hugging, thank you very much."

"Voice sounds a bit high-pitched there, Herb," said Sam.

I was about to call an end to the meeting, given they obviously knew nothing, when Pete spoke up, so quietly at first, I had to ask them to stop guffawing at Herby's cycle gear and bleedin' well listen.

"I've noticed a change in the language matrix," Pete said. "Nothing dramatic but the sort of new pattern that ain't appeared since the late 60s and early 70s."

Guys who'd been shaking their heads or grinning at Pete's esoteric bent suddenly stopped, the significance of this period not lost on them.

"What sort of change?" I said.

"The sort that created us," he said. "The sort that also turned a lot of folk into dreamers and mystics."

"But we ain't seeing a bleedin' hippy revival or nothing at the moment," said Vince.

Pete stared at no one in particular, his mind once again away from the here and now. "It's more contained this time," he said. "Not wasted on the general public."

He didn't say any more and I guessed he wanted to get back to decoding this new pattern. I ended the meeting and made for the intel hub, needing to make a call or two before going home and getting ready for my date with Sandra later that night.

Jeeves 2.0 connected himself to my earpiece as soon as I sat in front of a bank of screens. I put my hands on the talk ball, feeling for the dial-up pits, waited for my fingerprints to lock in, then pushed in Frank's number.

"Jack? What's the problem, mate?" he said.

One of the screens lit up, showing me pretty much what Frank could see— a busy docks area near Manchester.

"Nothing, mate. Just checking you're okay."

"Bit bored, truth be told. Looking for people traffickers, from China, but ain't discovered none yet."

"Okay, mate. Ta-ta for now."

I checked all the others. Nothing out of the ordinary, apart from the fact Brian Deen's comms didn't register and him on follow-up duty in Oban, too. I thought about trying his personal mobile to give him a bollocking but decided to leave it for a bit. It was quite possible he'd just decided nothing more was happening and sneaked off home to spend a bit of time with the wife, and I always figured the guys could do with fitting up their families more.

So I took the tube back to my gaff and would have put in some more thinking time, while gazing out at Mum's roses again, except something still bothered me.

Pete's warning about language . . . the guys not quite as sparky as normal . . . Brian Deen out of comms reach. But, nah, I was probably just diverting me attention from the real task at hand: coming across to Sandra like a bloke worth getting to know.

I had a shower, trimmed some unsightly nose hairs, selected a deodorant to kill sweat but not make me smell like a trainee eunuch, then had a long conversation with me wardrobe.

Most of my stuff was casual, of course, given that I spent the majority of the day fiddling with screwdrivers and soldering irons. I had a few occasions suits, mostly black, and several smart/casual shirts, mostly white. But what I lacked was what those TV fashion twats called a 'statement of my personality'.

Then I got angry with said twats, not to mention the whole damn world what seemed to care more about what you wore than what you thought, and just put on a pair of jeans and a black T-shirt.

But then I realised tonight was not about said twats nor the rest of the world; it was about me and Sandra. So, I sat and stared at me gear for another half hour, this time trying to work out what I actually wanted to look like on a date with her.

Finally, I let my instinct decide and took out a blue shirt and black trousers. I'd just ironed the shirt and put it on when a knock at the door surprised me.

"Rozzers?" I asked Hilary, now back online.

"Female rozzer," said Hilary. "Her badge is authentic: Meera Nath's her name. No one from the agency called to tell you she was coming today."

"Damn. She must be my new assistant. Lucy probably didn't call ahead because she thought I'd make an excuse not to be home . . . Okay, let her in."

"It'd be a pleasure, Jack. For you, that is."

I sighed. Probably because I'd been a sad single bloke for so long, I'd allowed Hilary a degree of unrestricted personality. "What's that supposed to mean?" I said.

"Just that she's obviously—oh, never mind. You can find out for yourself."

The door was half way open and I didn't want this Meera bird to hear me arguing with my own house, so I stayed schtum.

"Mr Stapleton?"

In the doorway stood an Asian woman, about thirty; long, shiny hair, dark eyes, dressed in smart black trousers and jacket. And while the intelligent, curious gaze she threw around my gaff and at me was not unexpected, given Lucy obviously wanted her to spy on me, what wasn't so predictable was her sheer blinding beauty.

I took Sandra to a Turkish restaurant I'd heard good things about but where no one knew me. Fortunately, the place buzzed with chatter, the air was stuffed with the aromas of barbecued meat and fish, and general good vibes flashed between the clientele and the waiters.

"Good choice," she said after we'd chinked wine glasses. "I'd have worried if you'd gone for something too posh on our first date."

"So, this *is* a date, then?"

She just smiled. And for the first time in ages, I relaxed. She wore a real pretty silky red skirt and white lace shirt. One side of her hair was pinned back with a turquoise slide, the other falling across her eye from time to time in a right attractive manner.

She told me about her new job, working with social services, but then stopped talking to eye me thoughtfully.

"What's up?" I said.

"You're listening just a bit too hard."

"I'm showing you my caring, sensitive side."

"Maybe. But I reckon you're also taking the opportunity not to tell me what you do."

The evening back-tracked a little to my normal reality then. But I'd known I'd have to tell her about myself at some point. Up to now, I'd been pretty vague and got away with it through a bit of cheek and blarney, or so I'd thought.

Thing was, I didn't want to lie to her.

"I work for the government," I said, which was true enough; at least, they paid my bills and were, right about then I hoped, doing a deal on my second gaff.

She frowned. "Filing papers or driving a car with machine guns in the headlights?"

"Actually, I'm more like M. You may not believe it, but I'm a boffin. I invent things."

"Such as?"

It'd had been a great meal and I really wanted to see her again. So I took off my watch and put it on her wrist.

"It's a lie-detector," I said. "Test it out: ask me how old I am?"

She put it on. "How old are you, Jack?"

"Twenty-one."

"Oh! It tingles! Like a bunch of needle points digging at me skin."

"Now ask me what my full name is."

"What's your full name, Mr Jack Stapleton?"

"Jack Winston Stapleton."

She shook her wrist. "Nothing. Blimey—'Winston'?"

"My dad was a big Churchill fan."

"I've got another question for you."

"Oh-oh."

"What do you look for in a woman?"

It wasn't just the presence of my watch on her wrist what had me answer truthfully right then. I wanted to anyway.

"Someone who's honest and brave and independent-minded."

She nodded thoughtfully. "I know we don't have any candles here, but is there anything, I don't know, less worthy you look for too?"

"Green eyes, a great figure and freckles." I nodded at the watch. "Nothing?"

"You're a strange one, Jack Winston Stapleton."

"Because I'm an inventor?"

"No, because there's always something going on in your eyes; like part of your mind's on important other stuff. It's okay—I'm just deciding if I can live with that."

At that moment, the rozzers' bleeper in my trouser pocket thrummed against my thigh.

Bugger it.

I had my mouth open, ready to make up some excuse to leave but instead I reached into my pocket and, holding Sandra's gaze, switched it off.

"So, is Mr Stapleton always going on dates, Hilary?" I said.

I'd found what looked like a spare bedroom upstairs and unpacked. Then I'd managed to find teabags and a kettle, and a seat not covered in bits of machinery. But I didn't really want to make myself at home until he'd told me to, so I figured I'd fill the time by talking to his house.

"You do realise, Ms Nath," she said, "that my loyalty is to Jack, by programming and by the degree of autonomy he has allowed me to develop. However, the answer to your question is no, this is the first time he's taken out more than a screwdriver in three years or more."

"Has he ever had a serious relationship?"

"Only with the Bellers."

"But most of them have partners, don't they?"

"Jack believes that the majority of the Bellers with partners should spend more time with them."

"Ah."

"He's always avoided making a commitment to a woman because he doesn't think he could honour it fully."

"So, is this woman he's seeing tonight just a fling?"

"Jack doesn't do flings. Perhaps his biological clock is winding down. He's got a teenage nephew so, who knows, maybe he's worried his sap is going to dry out before he can spring a sprog."

"But his profile doesn't indicate—"

Three hard knocks on the front door interrupted me.

"Two of yours," said Hilary. "What do you want me to do?"

I resisted commenting on the irony that only a few minutes after I'd arrived to be available to answer Jack's phone, MI5 had sent two agents in person.

"It must be important, Hilary," I said. "Let them in."

I walked Sandra to her flat and we agreed to meet again. I wasn't confident enough to kiss her right then; either that, or I felt guilty about the bleeper.

I jogged back to my gaff and opened the door to find Meera with agents Lee and Morris, all three looking somewhat stressed.

"Why didn't you answer the call?" said Meera.

"What's up?" I said.

Morris glanced at Lee before replying. "Brian Deen's been murdered," he said. "By a vampire."

FOUR

Not the Same Hole and Not the Same Head

"OH, COME ON FELLAS," I said. "Don't joke about a Beller getting killed. There ain't no vampires any more."

Lee and Morris swapped a look, then Lee spread out some pictures on a work top.

I'd seen dead bodies before, but looking at Bri's cold white face made me feel right woozy. "Has anyone spoken to Julie Deen yet?" I said.

"No," said Lee, "we thought, well, that you might want to."

I nodded, looking at the close-up shots of Bri's neck: sure enough, a circle of teeth marks, with two of them deeper than the others.

"So, how do you know it ain't some sicko would-be vamp who's watched too many Dracula movies?"

"Because there have been others," said Meera, pointedly ignoring Lee shaking his head at her. "Five murders in the past week: all by vampires. I've only just found out myself."

At this point, I wanted to lash out at all of them, at the Man, even the Prof. They'd sat smiling at me just this morning, not one of them with the decency to warn me about this, and maybe give us the chance to have saved Bri's life.

But instead, I took a deep breath. "Bri had the power to turn invisible, so how did this blood sucker see him?"

"We don't know," said Morris. "Maybe—" He stopped, seeing Lee frown at him.

"Look, son," I said. "One of my brothers has just been murdered. I suggest you impart whatever knowledge you have before yours truly starts to build a gizmo that will zero in on any rozzers' arses I care to target and give them a permanent hard kicking."

"It's not that we don't want to tell you," said Lee. "We're just not sure yet. But initial analysis of the details in the pathologist's report on Brian Deen suggests these vampires may have the ability to neutralise the enzyme grouping that anchors a Beller's special ability."

"All right. What about these other five they offed?"

"All ordinary, working people; nothing was stolen."

"But Brian Deen wasn't ordinary. Strewth—it's hard to see a pattern here. How come none of this has got into the press?"

Morris said, "We thought it better to keep it quiet for now."

"Yeah, well, I suppose the victims ain't that important anyway, right?" Anger bubbled away at the pit of my stomach like a bad curry. "Gents—I'd like you to leave now. I've got some thinking to do."

They was only too pleased to scoot, of course, mumbling about how they'd keep me informed. Just as they reached the front door, I said, "Hold on a sec—what have you done with the bodies: you know, vampires rising from the dead and all that?"

Lee took a deep breath. "We don't know if that isn't just a myth but all the bodies are in secure morgues under constant surveillance. So far, they're just dead bodies."

"Brian Deen was 'just' a friend of mine, agent Lee."

"I'm sorry," he said, "I only meant we want to make sure they stay at peace."

I didn't have to ask him about crosses, stakes, garlic—the rozzers were always if nothing else prepared.

After they'd gone, I poured two brandies, handed one to Meera. She frowned as if mentally checking the rozzers' guide to fraternising with the subject under surveillance, but took the glass anyway.

We sat in the little rest area I just about managed to keep clear of soldering irons, computers and assorted spy toys. I sipped my brandy, eyes closed, trying to think.

"I take it you ain't married," I said.

"It's too early in my career to think about marriage."

I nodded. "Have you got everything you need upstairs?"

"Yes, thank you. I took the main bedroom in the middle house—what *was* the middle house."

"That used to be Mum's room."

"Oh, I'm sorry. I'll move my things out."

"No, it's okay. After she died, I got the agency to buy the houses either side of here and decided to clear everything of hers out. Bit like a new life, I suppose. The only thing I ain't changed is her garden."

Thinking of Mum's stuff reminded me of all her royal nick-nacks, which of course reminded me of Marion, and her being held round the neck by that Jock terrorist—

"Bleedin' 'ell!" I banged down the glass and jumped out of me chair.

"What is it, Mr Stapleton?"

"I've got to go check something, pronto."

I raced for the hatch to the tube. "You'd better look away!" I shouted, stripping off my clothes.

"What do I tell the agency?"

"I said, look away!"

Naked, I activated the hatch lid and paused, wondering whether or not to tell her the truth.

Not this time.

"Tell them I'm finding out if I'm dead right about something."

In the pod, I instructed Jeeves to make sure our transmissions couldn't be tapped by the rozzers, then headed north once more.

At the Glasgow base, I took a conventional car and headed for the town, after getting Jeeves to tell me where to find the morgue. It was something of a long shot, relying on them not yet having connected up all the dots.

I parked half a street away, then threw a raincoat over my Beller's uniform and strolled along as if my hobby was checking out body banks. The place was locked up for the night which suited me fine.

I took my computerised universal shimmy pick from my pocket and wangled open the door. Then it was down into the vaults, checking the drawers of stiffs until I found a label reading 'Unidentified Possible Terrorist, shot dead' with the date we rescued the Princess.

I pulled open the drawer, half expecting it to be empty but there was a cold slab of body in there all right. With a huge hole in its forehead where it had been shot. So far so normal.

What I'd just remembered from the fight was a couple of glints of white pointed teeth when the chief terrorist had been yelling at me. I pulled back the stiff's lips but already knew I'd find nothing. If he really did have vampire fangs, the rozzers would know and there'd be no way this body wouldn't be deep under MI5, worked over by their special pathologists.

Sure enough, he had nothing but normal pearlies. But then I noticed something else: the hole in his head had been made by a bullet not a sonic blast, and it looked like it had been fired at closer range than my shot.

Okay, things had happened fast and the light wasn't great in the castle hall but blow me if this bloke was the same one I shot. He might *look* like him, but someone else had killed this fella.

And if that was true, what had happened to the bloke I actually *did* shoot, the one with a set of teeth that could open a beer can?

I already knew there was no film of the actual fight, because the terrorists had shot out the cameras. But there was something else I could try.

Just over an hour later, I climbed back out of the hatch in my kitchen and hung my Bellers suit above the central work bench, reaching for me dressing gown.

"Does it need washing?" said Meera.

"No, it needs extrapolating, as a matter of fact."

She must have been ready to go to bed, dressed in a white cotton wrap, her hair wild around her bare shoulders.

"Mind if I watch?" She sat in an easy chair, arms folded.

I used a keyboard to fire up the base unit under the suit and within a few seconds, a million strands of blue intellilight spun around it, in and out of the fabric.

"I'm using intelligent light to analyse the movements of the suit over the past few days. The fibres it's made of have a kind of delayed memory. The computer matches millions of stored movements and builds them into a picture of what the suit actually encountered."

After a few minutes, the light strands retracted into the computer and I set it to the date and time I'd faced the terrorist chief.

"It's a long shot," I said. "The computer's extrapolating the shape, features and blood patterns of the terrorist I killed—*thought* I'd killed—then it'll match it against its database of just about everyone in the damn country. Here it comes . . ."

I switched output to the big plasma screen against the back wall.

Insufficient information to complete task read the message across it.

"Bollocks," I said.

"Wait a minute," said Meera. "Princess Marion was being held by the terrorist, wasn't she? Can you factor her in to the readings too? Maybe her struggling caused him to project more personal information her way."

"That's not a half bad idea, Ms Nath."

I programmed in Marion's stats, along with what the suit had read of her, then we waited an agonising half minute or so while the computer decided if it could gob out anything worthwhile.

"Something's coming," I said.

On the screen we saw a photograph of a right handsome geezer: around thirty-five—short black hair, bright green eyes and a smile me dear old mum would have called 'de-bleedin'-lightful'.

Under the photo was a name: Lord Alain Santonaga.

» FIVE «

Home is Wherever You Hang Your Pasta Pan

I SPENT MOST OF THE NEXT morning researching Santonaga. Meera kept her distance, probably doing her own checking on his lordship, for the rozzers.

Mind you, there weren't that much to go on. Apparently, he had a huge country pile in the Highlands that had been in the family for generations of toffs. Their unusual surname came from Portuguese ancestors who, reading between the aristocrat-sponsored lines, had made their dosh from piracy. They settled in Blighty and carried on robbing the poor to give to the rich, only now under the respectable authority of the monarchy, for the most part at least. Like all toff families, they'd fallen out with royalty from time to time, but overall they'd managed to keep their fortune and their heads.

The latest Santonaga wasn't hitched. There were loads of pictures of him turning up at charity bashes and the like, always with some female beauty or other, but his expression each time suggested he didn't respect them very much.

The only indication that he might be shy of the sun was the fact every photo showed him at night. Then again, charity bashes aren't much known for taking place during the day.

Overall, the most suspicious thing about him was just how average his life seemed to be, for a filthy rich tim-boy at least.

Then again, maybe the very fact I couldn't find a single unusual detail about him, or any record of him ever letting off steam—no kiss and tells, no drunken orgies—suggested someone being *too* careful to cover his tracks.

Around lunch time, I decided to go for egg and chips in the caff. I asked Meera if she wanted to come but, as I suspected, greasy spoons weren't exactly her idea of fine dining.

"How's it going, Jack?" said Steve, surrounded by steam from the hot water pipe frothing up my instant coffee.

"Not too good, mate, as it happens. I'm trying to develop a normal relationship with this really nice woman but business keeps getting in the way."

"The usual?"

"Well, I wouldn't say it's the usual, exactly. 'Cos at the very same time I've also had this assistant forced on me, and just to complicate matters further, she's a right good-looking woman."

"No, mate, I meant the usual double egg and chips with a crusty slice."

"Sounds good. Is *your* life complicated, Steve?"

He raised one dark eyebrow, which was particularly emphatic, given his bald head and large face. "Only because I'm a man. Women don't understand that we have feelings too, so we have to bottle 'em up and the result is the current economic crisis."

"You're wasted here, mate, you really are."

"Chips and philosophy with everything, that's my motto."

So I sat in Steve's caff for an hour or so, trying to figure an angle on Santonaga before the rozzers did. Rather than be seen talking to meself, I used my phone to instruct Jeeves to buzz all the Bellers with Santonaga's details and get them searching on the creep too.

I just *knew* he was the leader of the vamps, and therefore responsible for Bri's death. Once I'd thought about it, I wasn't really so phased to hear there was vampires about again. Probably hadn't surprised the rozzers, neither. Vamps had been big news back in medieval times, had even nearly taken over, especially in Europe. My research this morning reminded me that the combined forces of the Catholic Church and European nation states had done for 'em. Mind you, it'd ended the Catholic religion too, in that the Pope at the time had turned out to be the head vamp. His exposure, by none other than Sir Francis Drake, caused the whole caboodle to collapse like a pack of marked cards. Turned out the Vatican had been riddled by vampire cells for centuries, everything building to that outbreak, when they thought they'd win the world.

It stood to reason they might not have all been wiped out back then. But what exactly had brought them out into the open now? And why did they think they stood a chance of winning this time?

I didn't know yet no for sure why Santonaga had tried to kidnap the Princess. But at least his being a vamp explained why my sonic gun hadn't actually killed him, not when I'd set it to lance-mode. If I'd known he was a vamp, I'd have set it to explode on contact with brain tissue. Seems as if he'd used make-up to look like some poor sod he'd killed. He must have had the body nearby and swapped it for his when the rozzers weren't looking. But that raised more questions, like why he'd expect to be 'killed' in the first place.

When I started to wonder if he'd had an inside rozzer help with the switch, I turned off my brain for a bit. It's strange how satisfying the sensation of egg on white bread can be. Mum used to make me soft boiled eggs and soldiers. Steve made the best chips: crispy on the outside, soft on the inside. And his coffee—a spoonful of instant heaped on to whipped-up milky foam was the most disgusting but also the most comforting brew in East London.

"Seconds, Jack?" he said, collecting the plates from me table.

"No thanks, mate," I said. "How's Jennie?"

"She's great. Now the kids 'ave left home, she's taken up Tae-bloody-kwen-do, can you believe. If she asks me to make her a cup of tea, I jump to it, otherwise I'd get kicked in the 'ead."

When he'd returned to the counter, I called Sandra.

"Hi," I said. "Still on for tonight?"

"Yes, what are you cooking?"

Oh, bugger. I'd forgotten I'd offered to rustle up a meal at my new gaff; me, whose culinary skills extended about as far as knowing how long to dunk a Hobnob in me tea before the soggy bit falls in.

"Um. Any ideas?"

"Tell you what: why don't I cook? I'll pick up some stuff on the way over."

"Are you sure? I mean, I feel I'm being a bit obvious blokey here, acting dumb so you'll do the womanly thing."

"I'd rather do the womanly thing than eat burnt beans on toast."

"Okay, then. You want me to pick you up?"

"No, just give me the address and I'll come over to you. Around seven okay?"

"Fine. But can I phone you back in two secs?"

"Another call?"

"Sort of."

I couldn't remember the address of me new gaff, could I? After checking it with Meera, I rang Sandra back and gave it to her.

After ending the call, I decided I'd better actually check out said new gaff.

The rozzers had bought me a place in Docklands, far enough away from my proper pad but still within bothering distance of course, for although I'd stipulated no contact systems here, they still had my mobile and bleeper numbers.

I pulled up in the car park under the new set of apartment buildings, all glass and steel, right on a bend in the river. The key got me into the reception area as well as called the lift which I took to the fifth floor.

I won't say I felt like a kid at Christmas about to open his presents but there was a bit of a thrill in me gut as I pushed on the door. Unlike most of the boys, I'd always been pretty frugal with the government's money. They got plenty out of me, by way of new technology and the such, but I didn't like being in anyone's debt. Consequently, I'd taken very little off the taxpayer over the years. Now, I hoped they'd understand why I needed a bit of privacy.

"Bloody 'ell . . ."

I was at the top of the building, in one of the 'loft' apartments. Only my idea of a loft was a wooden platform covered with straw and old packing cases. This one was half the size of St Paul's cathedral, the far end all glass with just the river flowing black in the night outside.

The rozzers had furnished the place straight out of a modern art coffee table book. There was red couches with yellow cushions, standing lamps looking like giant praying mantises, glass tables, and just about everything else that would give a minimalist a wet dream.

Sandra was due in an hour so I set about humanising the place. But then I stopped again. Short of ripping up the cushions and throwing some dirt around the place, there weren't really much I could do to make the place more homely in the short time left.

And about then I experienced the first inevitable sinking feeling; that 'Who am I kidding?' sensation.

But I fought on; went into the kitchen and spent fifteen minutes working out how to switch on the kettle, then made meself a cup of coffee using the Fair Trade Organic variety the rozzers had thoughtfully left in the food cupboard, along with a packet of sugar and not much else. Oddly enough, they'd given me a pretty well stacked wine rack. Now, why would Lucy want me to get pissed?

I stood sipping coffee and watching the Thames, letting the events of the past few days do their thing in my mind. And I guess the main thought that crept up on me, as welcome as a tax inspector, was to do with the Bellers needing to up our game. We didn't know much about these vampires yet, but my instinct was they had a master plan. This was just the early, shake 'em up and see, phase.

And how had the Bellers responded so far? Well, we'd saved Marion but hadn't noticed that the kidnapping was really just a diversion. We'd lost Brian; the lads upset about it but a long way from co-ordinated in how to respond. And the rozzers had a hundred secrets up their sleeves which we were too fat and happy to extract.

Bollocks and double bollocks.

The doorbell ringing was a welcome distraction from all these rickety thoughts. I switched on the reception camera, checked it was Sandra then told her to come on up.

Mind you, opening me front door was not so easy.

"Where's the damn handle?" I said to myself, staring at the plain, opaque glass slab in front of me.

"Hang on!" I shouted.

"Jack?"

"I'm having a senior moment," I shouted. "Can't remember how to open the bleedin' door."

Then I recalled the touch screen and jabbed a porky at it; a panel lit up showing the helpful option of OPEN in glowing green letters. I jabbed at that too and thankfully the door slid back.

"Hey!" I said, sounding more relieved than I should have.

Sandra looked right nice in white shirt, black skirt and black tights.

She smiled and frowned at the same time. "You sound as if you just won the lottery."

"Well, that's how I feel, seeing you."

I blushed at this blatant schmaltz and she shook her head sadly. But at least she came inside, handing me a bottle of red. She also carried a bag of what I guessed must be the dinner stuff.

"Wow!" she said, gazing around at my swanky pad. "Not what I'd have seen you living in at all."

I led her to the kitchen, took her bag then felt stupid not knowing where to put it, so she took it off me again and stood it on a marble counter next to the black glass-topped cooker.

"What sort of gaff did you think I'd have?" I said.

"Something a bit more personal, I suppose," she said.

"You have to admit, it's modern."

"Yeah, but I didn't get the impression *you* was particularly modern, Jack."

Thing was, once she got into organising my kitchen and putting on pans, chopping onions, and so on, all that mattered was the natter. I guess kitchens are good for that. Mind you, I was right relieved she knew how to use all the oven gizmos the rozzers had given me, since my techy instincts tended to draw a blank when it came to domestic devices.

"You obviously don't do much cooking," Sandra said at one point. "Everything in here's too clean."

"That's why I'm watching and learning now."

And so it went on. She naturally commanding the place and me real happy she felt comfortable enough to do that. The meal was simple and superb: spaghetti with bolognaise sauce, proper grated parmesan and hot garlic bread. That and a couple of bottles of wine had me believing for a while that I really could run a separate, reasonably normal life here on the river, surrounded by city slickers without a thought in their heads except when they could afford the penthouse suite at the top of the block.

But then Sandra said it.

"I'm having a right nice time, Jack," she said. "You're just the kind of bloke I never thought I'd meet."

"But?"

"It's not really a but, more a why. Why ain't you more *in* this place? I mean, it's real smart and clean, but there ain't no photographs of your family, or football shirts in glass cases, or even any car mags. It's like you don't really *live* here."

And that's when I realised I couldn't ever hope to fool a clever woman like this into believing that I was up for a normal life. I'd have to actually *have* a such a bleedin' life to convince her.

I thought about telling her the whole truth instead. Then she could decide if instead of me changing to Jolly Jack Normal, she wanted to become Super-supporter Sandra instead.

Who *was* I kidding? I didn't know much about this woman, but her whole manner shouted that she'd only ever settle for a partner she was equal to. Not that I felt superior; it's just that my bleedin' job would never let us line up snug together.

And the clincher? I remembered what Meera said, about it being too early in her career for marriage. She was about the same age as Sandra. And I could tell that what she actually meant was that she wouldn't get married at all if duty came first. Just like me.

"Let's go out on the balcony," I said. I didn't want to tell her, surrounded by rozzer fluff.

So we opened the huge glass doors and stepped on to the planking out-side, with the big wide view of the Thames, silky black, dotted with smeared balls of reflected light from all the promenade lamps and the apartments either side. A couple of restaurant boats zipped past, sending waves slurping against the wall below. Drunken shouts and laughs tippled across the water from their tarty decks like faint echoes of another, happily ignorant world.

"Sandra, I need to tell you something."

She looked at me, then into the sky, giving me space to compose meself.

"You see, I ain't exactly been completely honest with you—"

"Jack: what's that?"

I followed the direction of her pointing finger, squinting at the blue-black sky. A dark shape came toward us, jerky in flight.

"Some sort of bird?" I said.

"Looks too big."

In the moment it took me to guess the truth, it was too late. A huge bundle of wings knocked us both to the decking, accompanied by screeching so loud my eardrums rang with pain.

My combat training with the rozzers kicked in and I rolled away from the tangle of bodies, reaching for the small gun in a holster strapped to my ankle. I leapt to my feet, pointing it, only to find my worse fears confirmed.

A man-bat shape, features shadowed by a cowl, had Sandra in a tight grip, holding his own gun to her head.

"You can't win, Jack Stapleton," he said, voice full of icy triumphalism.

Sandra's expression, by contrast, was a heart-breaking mixture of shock and betrayal. My gun, and the fact this monster knew my name, told her nearly as much as I'd intended to.

What I could see of his face seemed a little pale but not as much as vampire legend demanded. What bothered me most was the twin glints of white at the corners of his mouth when he'd spoken. That and Sandra's exposed neck.

Now at this point, I was supposed to ask him what he wanted. But I'd learned it's best to act just before you're expected to speak, because that's about the only advantage you'll ever get.

So, I shot. But he was quick; moved his head marginally so the bullet only clipped his ear.

I expected some sort of crowing speech here but in fact he did something even worse: just smiled briefly then took to the air with Sandra in his arms.

I rushed to the balcony pointing the gun but couldn't shoot, not with them so entwined.

Through fury and frustration, my heart drained at the thought that if vampire lore was right, Sandra now faced one of two options, both horrific. Either he'd turn her into a vamp too, or simply drain her of blood and leave her for dead.

SIX

Singeing Ducks and Rollers

I RAN OUT OF THAT APARTMENT, fully intending to never return. If I'd been honest with Sandra from the start, we'd have been eating dinner in my real gaff tonight, and I could have at least let her down with her eyes wide open. Because, even if Santonaga—and it must have been him—knew its location, he'd never have dared attack me surrounded by enough hardware and weaponry to fry his icy arse. How he knew the location of my brand new one was something I didn't want to think about right then.

I drove without due care and attention through Docklands, on to the East End. I overtook in queues, used the wrong side of the road, jumped red lights and finally left the car on double yellow lines at the end of my road.

I yelled at Hilary—"It's me, Jack, open up!"—and the door swung inwards, she bleating, "Is it too much to expect you to use the code, Mr Stapleton?"

Meera looked up from a laptop, slightly guiltily I thought.

"You promised me a secure gaff!" I shouted at her.

"What are you talking about, Jack—what's happened?"

I stood close, staring into her eyes, looking for deception. She didn't flinch, so I said, "I invited Sandra Hollins to the new place for dinner. When we was standing out on the balcony, admiring the view, Santonaga flew down, grabbed her and disappeared again. I had one chance to shoot him but missed."

"God, I'm really sorry, Jack. But there's no way Santonaga could have known your new address."

"So, how did he find it?"

She glanced at the screen, then back to me again. "I've been doing some more research on vampires. It was said that once they have the smell of someone's blood, they can trace them anywhere."

"Shit, I got a slight scratch in the Jock raid. He must have sniffed me out."

Maybe it was just chance, then, that he found me at my new gaff and not the old one.

"I'll alert the agency. We'll do our utmost to find her, Jack."

"Thanks, but it's time the Bellers got their act together too."

I clapped my hands in a pre-determined sequence and a wire with a simple red button fixed to its end dropped from the ceiling. I slammed it between my palms.

"Call to arms," I said, noting Meera's frown. "Ain't used it in years. No Beller can refuse to respond, so all those not already at HQ will be on their way immediately."

I ran to the kitchen. "Don't look!" I shouted, stripping off.

Naked, I was about to drop through the hatch when a hand grabbed my arm.

"I'm coming too," said Meera.

"Are you nuts?" I said, covering mine with me other hand.

"This is an emergency, Jack. I'm not going to sit around babysitting your home, sorry 'gaff'. I can be useful."

"But the Bellers are all blokes!" I said, not very convincingly, I have to admit. Being naked in front of a determined woman was not conducive to brilliant repartee.

She just shook her head and started stripping off too. Not wanting to argue, I jumped into the hatch and let the pod take me.

Being a rozzer, she must have known another pod would immediately fill its place, that I always had a spare ready, in case another Beller happened to be at my gaff and we both needed to get to HQ pronto.

I got Jeeves to programme in Meera's details to our defence system, then jumped out of the pod at HQ, helping her out of hers, on to the steel docking platform. My spare uniform fit her real tight and if we'd had more time, I'd have advised her to throw a coat over it or something, given she'd soon be meeting a bunch of men not known for their chaste ways.

Having said that, the gleam in her eye and the strong set of her chin as she stared right back at me, was convincing enough evidence that she really could help.

"Follow me," I said, "and don't wander off anywhere until we're right inside."

We ran past the betting screens, me hoping stupidly that she wouldn't notice, and I irised the entrance door. Oddly enough, I found meself worried that she'd be disappointed at finding so many super-Cockneys in the bar, pissed, full of cigar smoke and yakking about women in generally less than diversity-enhancing ways.

But the bar was empty, just Young Eric behind the counter, clearing glasses away. He frowned when he saw Meera but being a sensitive lad said nothing about it, assuming I'd okayed her presence.

"They're in the Moose Hall, Jack," he said.

That was a good sign at least. I figured around eight of us would still be on their way, which meant twenty should be waiting for me to spill the beans.

I threw back the big oak doors and stomped inside. Meera followed but then stood back, probably on account of facing so many quizzical blokes in their own den.

"It's time we got our arses in gear, fellas," I said, turning to face them all from in front of the log fire. "These vampires are taking the piss and we need to stop them."

I filled them in on everything I knew, including the part about Sandra getting kidnapped. Okay, I hadn't told any of them about her before, and I knew some of them at least would assume I was running on revenge right now, but it didn't matter.

In the event, something about my serious demeanour must have convinced them because the only question when I'd finished was from Sam. "So, what do you want us to do, Jack?" he said.

And then a funny thing happened. My mind had been racing with anger and unshaped determination to damn well *do* something, but with not much actual planning, it has to be said. I was about to say that I didn't have a bleedin' clue, what do you suggest? when I looked toward the back of the room and caught Meera's gaze. Her dark brown steady look, folded arms, body taught and ready, slowed down my thoughts and within seconds I knew what to say.

I fired off instructions to everyone with an ability that was immediately useful. To Sam, for instance, I told him to get whatever he needed and go catch a vampire. He was the only one who could, given that in his heightened physical state, the most powerful incisors in the world could not penetrate his skin.

I told Pete to monitor transmissions from anywhere he could get them. I figured the vampires' powers stopped short of telepathy and so they'd need to use mobile phones or radios just like the rest of us.

By the time I'd finished, every Beller had a task, even if it was as simple as getting round the country, following leads, picking up hints about where the vamps were shacked up and where they might strike next.

What I didn't realise, and should have, was that we needed to up our game even further. As we found out too late, everything we decided that night, he'd already anticipated, so all we'd really done by dispersing was play into his hands.

The lads skedaddled and just me and Meera were left in the Moose Hall. "Nice work," she said, looking around. "Not sure about the stag heads though."

"I'm not sure about anything the lads get up to here, truth be told, but they move pretty sharpish when they know the game's on."

"You didn't give yourself a task."

"Oh, I've got a task all right."

"You're going after Santonaga, aren't you?"

"Jeeves'll see that you get home okay."

She shook her head. "I'm coming with you. At the very least, you'll need someone to drive a stake through your heart after he bites you."

"You're very uppity for a house sitter, you know."

But I didn't argue and she kept pace with me as I scarpered from the hall, heading for the tube.

We dropped into pods and I told Jeeves to take us to the jet hanger under Rainham Marshes. The journey only took a few minutes but that was long enough for me to twist and turn with rage. I couldn't believe how naive I'd been in letting Sandra get kidnapped.

I'd been sleeping, basically, while still awake. We all had. The odd rescue here, a show of force there, but nothing had ever really stretched us before. Suddenly, we didn't have a damn clue what was happening or why.

I jumped out of the pod and ran up the concrete corridor to the jet hanger. Jeeves had already warmed the engines and blasted the warning hooter over our sealed-off area above, just in case any tourists or mallards had been dumb enough to wander in.

The two government guys on duty met us in the briefing room but I weren't in the mood for conversation, simply told them we was heading north immediately. Meera pacified them with some sort of rozzer double-talk but I wasn't listening, just rammed on me helmet and parachute then ran into the hanger. I climbed the retractable ladder, pausing at the top to jerk a thumb at the seat behind me for Meera's benefit.

As soon as the hatch dropped into place, I fired the jets and even wearing padded helmets, the roar shook the fillings out of our teeth.

"Come on!" I yelled, partly to the guys in the control room but mostly to myself, then let out the throttle. We surged forward, surrounded by clouds of exhaust, the concrete tunnel reverberating with the incredible din of the engines.

The doors opened under an overhang of mud and marsh, protected not just by the surrounding fence but also by a large pond. I'd designed the jet to reach maximum lift thrust at just the moment we hurtled out of the exit.

"Hang on!" I said into the helmet mic, then pulled back the throttle. We reached a hundred and fifty miles per hour before getting to the door at the end.

The rozzers always did their best to keep wildlife off the pond, but there was still a mad flurry of wings lifting into the night air as we crashed out of the bank.

If I was with one of the guys and in a better mood, I'd have shouted, "Roast duck for lunch!" or some such nonsense, but instead I concentrated on lifting us as quickly as possible into the sky.

Of course, everyone and his Aunt Jemima knew this was some sort of secret government related lift-off station, and most of them had seen the jets in person. But we reckoned people warmed to a bit of Thunderbirds gizmology, even at some risk to the local wildlife.

In seconds, I banked to the right, re-crossing the wide, light-smeared Thames, lining us up for a trip north that would take about thirty five minutes, hitting mach 3 on the way. The fact it was faster than taking the tube weren't the only reason for flying, mind you.

We hurtled over East London, to the Essex coast, where I banked left slightly.

I'd almost forgotten about Meera when her voice suddenly flicked into my ears.

"I'm using the onboard computer to look for more info about Santonaga."

"Good luck," I said. "But I've already tried and there ain't much beyond the usual 'Who's Who' gubbins."

"I'm going to add stuff the agency has, too."

I bit back my irritation. Just like the rozzers to not give us everything they had.

The plane's computers locked on to course and dealt automatically with the various authorities' air spaces we cracked through.

I started to slow down over Glasgow.

"Does this thing have anti-radar?" said Meera.

"Nope."

"So are we going to land and travel by road to avoid detection?"

"No, we're going to hover right above his bleedin' gaff, down thrust exhausts filling his gaff with noxious gases."

"That doesn't sound like a very intelligent plan."

"Got a better one?"

"No, but putting together the intel you and we have, I'm sensing something really interesting."

Beneath us the Highlands swelled up, all dark purples against the black night sky, as we dropped and slowed toward the bastard's country estate. If this wasn't a hit and run mission, I might have risked boasting to Meera about my patented heli-jet engines that allowed this bird to slow right down in flight and hover just like a helicopter. Instead, I said, "Hit me."

I hoped she didn't know how to read the plane's monitors as I pushed the sequence to bring the weapons system online.

"I don't think Santonaga and his followers are real vampires, at least not like the sixteenth century variety," she said.

"'Course they are. Otherwise 'ow do you explain turning himself into a giant bat and flying off with Sandra into the big black beyond, *and* you said he sniffed me out."

"I don't mean they don't bite and fly and sniff."

"What, you think they're bleedin' copy-cats—copy-bats?"

She sighed impatiently and I felt anger flood my throat. Who the 'ell was she to get ratchety with me, simply for asking reasonable questions. I was about to blast her for it when she said, "I don't know, Jack; it's just a hunch at the moment," and I eased back, realising she'd just been getting short with herself.

I brought the plane to a hover, thirty yards above and just in front of a huge pile of house: arc lights lit up the turrets and terraces, throwing glints across the private lake nearby. How jolly spiffing.

"But one thing I'm sure of," she continued, "is we won't find out the truth by levelling this place."

I hesitated then hit the trigger anyway, sending two rockets streaming at Santonaga's ancestral pile.

"Jack!"

I didn't reply, just let her see that I'd aimed for the swimming pool to one side of the main building and the tennis courts at the other. The pool erupted in a spray of orange-yellow flames and shattered tiles and water, sun loungers lifting into the air like dead seagulls. And the tennis courts blew up in a most satisfying tangle of fire, tarmac and netting.

"I'm just flushing him out," I said.

Within seconds, the various doors of the mansion flew open and assorted servants, maids and maintenance staff poured out, most in nightwear, some holding their arms over their heads—as if that would protect them from the giant black raven hanging above.

"I don't see his lordship," I said.

"Well, why *would* you?" Meera sounded angry. "He's not going to be so stupid as to just step out and make himself a sitting target, is he? If he's here at all, he'll be snug in some deep bunker your rockets can't reach. And I know you don't want to hear this, but you're not going to find Sandra by charging in there."

I was about to argue with her, my fingers twitching on the triggers. But she was right. Santonaga might not care if his staff got blasted to smithereens but he'd make sure number one got out alive. Also, he must have suspected I'd come flying at his main base, so that was the last place he'd hide Sandra.

I took the plane up a hundred feet higher and turned her round. Just before heading back south, though, I dipped the nose toward a set of garages with glass show-walls. A collection of classic Bentleys, Rolls, Ferraris and the such shone under spotlamps. A couple of mechanics got my drift and ran for the main house, just as I let off two more rockets. Bits of very expensive automobiles flew into the air, and the garages erupted into fountains of glass, stone, tiles, oil, tyres and what-not.

"Oh, Jack," said Meera, "that was just plain childish."

"You're right," I said, but boy did it feel *good*.

SEVEN

Some Things there Ain't no Gizmo for

BACK IN WHITECHAPEL, I was too angry to speak to Jack at first. Not angry with *him* entirely, even though I really couldn't see Santonaga loosing much sleep over such a schoolboy attack on his property. If vampires sleep, that is.

I think I was also mad with Britain as a whole, with our stupid half-baked ways of doing things. Oh, I was patriotic enough; that's why I worked for the agency. But we let ourselves down by being so tight-lipped all the time.

I mean, Lucilla had to be careful with what she told staff, but for God's sake, she could have prepared me better for vampires, of all things.

And *why* did the Bellers have to remain a secret? Because they had super-powers and that might scare the public? Well, the public was going to be terrified when they found out no one's neck was safe anymore.

And I *was* mad with Jack, too. All right, I'd not been here long and he was busy chasing a girl. But the point was, I could help. Yes, he'd picked up my signal in the Bellers' den and got his act together. But then he'd jetted off to shoot up a swimming pool and scare a few servants. He needed to tell me more about what went on in his head, even if the only other woman he was used to sharing his feelings with was just a bunch of circuits and chips that lived in the walls.

Meera wouldn't talk to me at first. She got on with some work in the rest area and any attempt by me to discuss events was met by a one-syllable response.

So, being a bloke and still too full of adrenaline to go to bed, I shrugged me shoulders and retired to the far end of the workshop to put in some time on a new device which, once working, would enable its wearer to instantly translate the body language of anyone in range.

I also checked on the boys.

Plenty of info came in, and they'd done well to spread wide around the country. But precious little hard facts about the vamps, or even fake vamps, hit my screen. Either they really could disappear into thin air or they was a lot more organised than we'd previously thought.

Sam had charged about town, staring into suspicious characters' faces, most of whom had then called the police, but eventually he'd realised he needed help in detecting the damn things.

I made two cups of tea and took them to Meera's space.

"Peace offering?" I said.

She looked at me for a second or two then sat back from her computer to fold her arms.

"I've been thinking," she said.

"And?"

"There's something just a bit too obvious about these attacks Santonaga's making, as if he's trying to divert our attention from his real plans."

"Can't you rozzers just arrest him?"

"Even if we could find him, we don't have any hard evidence. I know you saw him in Scotland and again here, but if we brought him in now his lawyers would enjoy themselves driving holes through our lack of evidence."

"Hmm, that's real interesting."

"Jack, what are you doing?"

"Nothing; just listening—wah!"

She'd reached forward real quick to snatch the mini-screen out of my hand.

"What's this? *The subject—Meera Nath—began feeling closed-off to your presence then, as you engaged her in conversation which she found interesting, she relaxed and became more open to you. But then she closed off again upon discovering this device.* Oh, for God's sake . . ."

She threw it back to me.

"Well, you wasn't talking, was you?"

"That's because you weren't listening. Look, I know you're upset about Sandra, but jetting over to Santonaga's place with your chest puffed out like an indignant Pearly King didn't help. It just showed him he could get you riled."

I switched off the body language reader.

"Good move," she said. "And it won't work anyway against someone with training anyway." She deliberately folded her arms and inclined her head to one side, smiling sarcastically. "You need to go beyond the surface."

I sat, holding up my hands by way of surrender. "Fair enough. In that case, and 'cos we're both too wired to sleep, how about you tell me why you joined the agency."

She sipped her tea for a few moments. "After I left college, I went to Pakistan for three years. My parents had already gone back to Punjab so Dad could start a business, and there's loads more of the family there. I worked for the World Health Organisation, building irrigation ditches and trying to get local leaders to adopt better farming practices. I might have stayed longer, except the more traditional side of my family tried to force me to marry a cousin one day. Drugged my coffee and kidnapped me. If I hadn't had my mobile and fired off a call to colleagues to rescue me, I could be chained to a clay kitchen in Lahore now, making chapattis with a dozen children round my ankles."

"I can't see that somehow."

"After that, I decided to return to Britain. And I joined the agency because I believe it's the best way for me to make a difference in the world."

"But how are you going to do that, babysitting me?"

She snorted. "I naively believe you have the ability to make a *real* difference, by cutting through all the red tape we get dragged down by. But I've seen now why that bureaucracy exists: to stop mavericks from shooting up the citizenry just because they can't think their way out of a paper bag."

"Wow, you don't pull any punches, do you?"

"Neither does Santonaga. We're going to have to be much smarter and faster than this, Jack."

"So, what have you come up with so far?"

"Let's start at the beginning: July 13th, 1970."

"The day Bow Bells rang of their own accord."

"Yes, sending out a series of sonic patterns that somehow affected the genes of around three dozen male embryos all at exactly the same stage of development in their mothers' wombs. We don't know why only boys were affected; maybe it's because male embryos are more vulnerable to outside influences. Whatever, six months later you were all born and your parents gradually realised their children had strange and special abilities."

"Some earlier than others. Sam's folks, for instance, discovered their kid could turn into a giant ball of stubborn granite the first time his mum tried to take her nipple out of his mouth. Whereas Pete's ability didn't really show until he got to speaking age. Then of course, he surprised his folks by saying his first word in nine different languages."

"The government tried to take you all away, didn't they?"

"Typical knee-jerk reaction from the pen-pushers. But our folks rallied together and refused to hand us over. Figured the last thing kids with weird powers needed was to be dumped in an institute somewhere."

"But you still needed the government's help."

"Well, yeah, but we didn't take no more than was necessary. They gave us a special school of our own so we could all stick together and have a fairly normal life. Even had our own school footy team; won the East London Cup in our fifth year, as a matter of fact."

"And you didn't cheat, just a little bit?"

"Only so far as we had Brian Deen turn invisible and slip into their dressing room at half time to listen in on their tactical talk. God rest his soul."

"But as you all got older, you *did* take more of the government's money."

"Yes, but it's been a fair deal, I reckon. You've had plenty of my gizmos for a start, and together the boys have done a great job on the rescue side of things. Remember, the flood which took out half of Winchester and—"

"I wasn't questioning the validity of the Bellers, Jack. Just trying to get a grip on why they came into being in the first place."

"That's something I've often tried to find out meself. The government insists it doesn't have a clue what happened."

"Or, perhaps more importantly, why."

"Why create a bunch of super-heroes?"

"Why create a bunch of *working-class* super-heroes."

"Why *not*?"

"I'm not insulting your background, Jack. But you have to admit it's the upper classes that generally have control of everything in this country. Working class people traditionally get excluded from the clubs and societies and institutions that really rule."

"Maybe that's exactly the reason we was chosen: about the only conspiracy theory you can throw at Cockneys is rhyming slang, and you can cop that off Wikipedia these days anyway."

"You could be right. Perhaps whoever created the Bellers wanted them to operate free of the old school tie system."

"Except it seems we've now got super-toffs on the loose."

"Just what I was thinking."

I stood up and paced for a bit. Outside a car passed. Machinery hummed around me, screens flashed. In the garden, Mum's roses had faded into the night.

Meera said nothing but I felt her watchful gaze.

I was used to pushing my brain into visualising circuits and digital patterns, ideas that could be confirmed by silicone, circuits and a few dollops of computer software. Whenever human patterns nudged themselves into my mind, I tended to let them slip away, not happy about the rough edges and non-confirmable elements.

But that was part of the Bellers' problem, I reckoned. We all stayed with what we was good at. Okay, I attended rozzer meetings but like the other lads, I only really pushed my mind at immediate problems I knew I could solve. I'd been sensing a pattern behind all the recent madness, for instance, but hadn't really tried to crack it yet.

"The greatest trick the ruling classes pulled on the workers," I said, "was to create conditions where they would have to concentrate only on what was to hand. If you're working in the docks or down a coal mine, all you can think about is the swing of your bleedin' pick or making sure some crane don't drop a pile of pallets on your head.

"That guy who camps out in Parliament Square—he told me something bad was on the way, even though I was a complete stranger to him. I mean, he's free from the usual binds and maybe his instinct is picking up on these vamps. Which reminds me, what you said back in the plane, about Santonaga and his crew not being real vampires: what did you mean?"

"Well, there's the obvious fact there are absolutely no records of any vampire attacks since the sixteenth century. Also, Santonaga is in his late thirties, so if he's a vampire, what's he been drinking up to now?"

"Maybe he's just been bumping off the help and keeping it quiet."

"Come on—there's no way he could have been necking his lunch without some evidence of it getting out."

"You really think he's only become a vamp recent-like?"

She sighed, looked exhausted. "I really don't know. It's late; I suggest we sleep on it."

"Okay. I'd offer to hang some garlic around your window but I ain't got none. Will a packet of cheese and onion crisps do?"

EIGHT

Just Call Me Uncle Normal

"WAKE UP, JACK. It's Sunday morning and you have to be at Danny's footy match in an hour."

"Thanks, Hilary, but I wasn't asleep, as it happens."

"Well, if you improved my visual and audio detection systems, I might have noticed."

"I would but then I'd have two women in the house getting on me back."

There was a pause before she replied which, if I hadn't invented her me-self, I could have sworn was for dramatic effect. "Ms Nath is already up and about—as it happens."

Thing was, I hadn't slept much because of the gaping hole in me guts. I'd been responsible for a monster kidnapping an innocent person who had no idea she was even in any danger. I should have been honest from the start. I should have told her what I was before even asking her on a date. I should have been more of a man.

Dad had his faults, not least buggering off and leaving Mum with two kids—one of them with special needs, as they say today in educational cir-cles—to bring up on her own. But at least he was always himself. He figured the government would take care of us so he was free to set up in Spain as a 'private consultant'. His consultancy work got him a very nice lifestyle for a while—swimming pools, young bits of female fluff hanging on his every flash of bling, extra rashers of bacon and his copy of The Sun ironed for him every morning at his ex-pat caff on the harbour. Of course, his consultancy skills was bound to cross over one day with those of the local Spanish con-sultants and that's when he disappeared. Probably permanently consulting the foundations of one of them new villas springing up everywhere in Spain these days.

I pushed some buttons on my bedside console. The window blinds retracted, bathing me in bright sunlight; I heard the shower start to hiss in the ensuite bathroom, and the rumble of voices from the waterproof TV screen in there permanently tuned to Bellers' comms.

While washing, I listened to reports and bulletins, some of it the standard stuff which most of the boys never bothered tuning in to. There were also a couple of reports from the lads, but nothing substantial. It seemed like the vampire toffs either had a remarkable ability to stay out of detection range, or they had help staying hidden. Or both.

In the kitchen, I noted a washed cereal bowl on the draining board, along with a mug, so figured Meera didn't need any breakfast. I put some bread in the toaster and made coffee. I spread peanut butter on the toast and took me breakfast into the middle section of the house.

"Morning," I said.

"Hi," said Meera, looking up from her laptop. "I'm not having much luck."

"You ain't the only one. The lads are drawing blanks everywhere, too."

"Smells good. Mmm, peanut butter. Wish I could have some."

I held out the plate. "Take a slice. I can make more."

"No thanks. I have to be careful what I eat."

"Oh, don't tell me you're one of these 'does my bum look big?' types."

"Actually, I have a peanut allergy. But does it?"

"Look," I said, "I have to go watch my nephew play footy this morning, on Hackney Marshes. Would you mind coming, too? I'm concerned I might get followed and I don't want to put my sister and her kid in danger."

"You want me to be look out?"

"Yeah."

"But, surely . . . no, that's fine; I'm happy to do it. Let me just send a quick message to the office."

I guessed why she'd hesitated; probably thinking that if the bad guys wanted to nab Sarah and Dan, they could find out easy enough where they lived anyway. Which I couldn't do nothing much about, but it would be even worse if they got taken because I'd led someone direct to them.

We walked around a couple of street corners until we reached my car.

"Impressively sensible," said Meera.

"No need to be sarky. The Nissan Micra, I'll have you know, is the most reliable motor on the market. It's also the most unobtrusive, which is what we need to be."

We climbed in and I pulled away from the curb. Meera made a big show of pushing buttons on the dash, looking for special features.

"Yes, this motor is gizmo-free," I said. "It is intended to stand out from the crowd about as much as a tin of baked beans in Sainsbury's. Besides, ain't you supposed to be watching the road?"

She straightened up. "I am. No one followed us to the car and no cars have pulled out behind us."

"Okay. I don't suppose you've been to 'Ackney Marshes before, have you?"

"I'm guessing it's not an area of designated scientific interest, full of rare birds."

"Oh, they'll be a few birds there, but a bit more on the common side. There'll also be hundreds of blokes, of all shapes and sizes with just one thing uniting them all: hatred for the little man in black."

"Do the Bellers still have a team?"

"Nah, we decided it was too conspicuous as we got older. A few of the lads play five-a-side games in our gym, and I join in sometimes but me knees aren't what they used to be."

"So, now you play vicariously through your nephew."

We headed up Commercial Road, past the colourful shops full of exotic fruit and veg, or hanging with bright silk saris, the odd caff with steamed up windows between.

"*I* don't, but prepare yourself for those what do."

At the Marshes, we took a long walk past the dozens of footy pitches, alive with heavily puffing pub teams and slender whippet-like youth outfits, the air ringing with the exasperated cries of those who really shouldn't be behind at this stage, or the bellows of triumph from those who clearly believed it was their right to be ahead. I scanned the straggling lines of spectators, but didn't see nothing that wasn't normal—parents, girlfriends, the odd pro scout trying to look inconspicuous but failing on account of him not hurling his tonsils to the heavens like the rest of them.

"But they're just terrifying their kids," said Meera. "They keep shouting at them to do it this way, not that way, and look, they're all too scared to perform."

"Yeah, but it won't affect the really good ones. They learned at an early age that their parents ain't got a clue about the game, and so they just zone them out."

"All the same, you'd think they'd realise nothing's gained by all that shouting."

I smiled. "I reckon you'd be a pretty good mother."

She snorted. "Just as long as my kids don't want to play football."

We made it to Dan's pitch a couple of minutes before kick-off. He was standing with his team, getting the low-down from their coach, but he smiled and raised his head slightly when he saw me.

Sarah stood on the touchline, swaddled in a big West Ham scarf and thick overcoat. Although it was a bright spring day, the wind was more than a little nippy. I wore a thick donkey jacket and Meera a maroon coat with black jumper.

"Hey, sis!" I gave her a big hug and she smiled warmly but I noted her taking in Meera too. She stood back with a blank but proper expression on her face, inviting me to make the introductions.

"Sarah, this is Meera, my new assistant."

Sarah put our her hand and Meera shook it. "You don't look like nobody's assistant, Meera," she said. "Is he getting too uppity again?"

"Yes, but to be fair, he's had some trouble to deal with lately."

On the way over, I'd informed Meera that Sarah obviously knew about me being a Beller, but we'd kept it from Dan. The idea was he should lead a normal life with a normal uncle, except for the small fact he was never able to visit his uncle's gaff.

Sarah looked concerned. But then she'd always been a worrier. "It must be very tough for you," she said.

I was about to manfully say I'd cope when I realised she meant Meera. As the teams lined up for the kick-off, Sarah took Meera by the arm and steered her along the touch-line, out of earshot of yours truly, for one of them girly chats, no doubt the gist of which I'd have about as much chance of getting out of them later as Dan did of scoring today.

Which ain't to say Dan was a bad player, just that his position was centre-back and he took defending mighty seriously. Uncomfortable when going up for corners, unlike the modern multi-tasking defender, he was a big lad and a brilliant tackler, but he also knew his limits, and racing back from a mucked-up corner, trying to catch the usually smaller but faster opposing forwards was something he got the horrors about.

Unlike his uncle, he knew his limits and stuck to them. Which was why, ten minutes into the game, the opposition hadn't had a single shot on our goal. Sarah and Meera continued their chat, disconcertingly laughing my way every so often, and I stood back, quietly watching the play, ignoring all the dad-the-lads around me labouring under the delusion they should actually be managing the 'Ammers, such was their constant stream of effusive, somewhat colourfully put, but ultimately useless advice.

At half-time, Danny trotted over to say hello. He looked to have grown another inch since I'd last seen him.

"Nice use of the offside trap," I said.

He smiled and blushed, pleased I'd noticed him marshalling his back four so well.

"Yeah, but we ain't done nothin' up their end yet, Uncle Jack."

"Your lad on the left wing looks pretty useful. Can't you get the ball to him more?"

"He does better when he's 'ungry, as a matter of fact. So we sort of wait till the last ten minutes before we give him a lot of the ball."

I nodded to show he was a better judge of his team than me, and he ran to join the others for their half time team talk.

Which was when I noticed the man in the black coat and hat on the other side of the pitch, looking our way. He could be a scout, of course, but I didn't want to take any chances. So I strolled over to Sarah and Meera as casually as I could and stood with me back to said bloke.

"Sorry, Sarah," I said, "but we need to go. There's a meeting me and Meera have to be at in half an hour's time."

Meera watched me closely and must have read in my face that I had good reason, for she stayed schtum.

Sarah grimaced but said, "Okay, Jack." Then she turned to Meera, squeezed her arm. "Really nice meeting you, Meera. And don't forget what I said." She gave a slight nod in my direction.

Meera looked directly at me. "Thanks for the info."

As we walked away, I waved at Dan, said to Meera, "See the bloke on the other side of the pitch in the hat? I think he's watching us."

"He should be. He's one of us. I asked the agency to provide cover."

"Why didn't you tell me? I could have stayed for the rest of the game; can't go back now, Sarah'll be freaked."

"Sorry, I thought you might be mad if you knew."

"Is he going to cover Sarah and Danny for a bit longer?"

"Do you want him to?"

I thought for a moment, against a background symphony of Sunday morning punts, shouts and whistles. I never wanted Dan to grow up anything other than normal. Before, it hadn't seemed necessary to consider providing him and his mum with protection.

"Yeah, thanks."

She took out her mobile and said, "Hi!" in a big, casual voice, then spoke what must have been code for 'keep an eye on Jack's family'—"I've booked two more for the restaurant tonight, darling . . . No, you can cancel the other two. Bye!"

We'd just reached my car when my mobile rang. It was Pete at HQ.

"What did he say?" said Meera after I hung up, no doubt concerned at my expression.

"We just had a call from your lot at MI5. Police at Marylebone handed them a woman who'd wandered in there, disorientated, not knowing her name nor nothin'. All she could tell them was she'd been kidnapped by a vampire."

NINE

Blood Like a Beller's

MEERA ASKED ME TO DROP her at a taxi rank, intending to travel back to Whitechapel; said she needed to do some more research on vampires. I drove into London, thankful it was a Sunday and the traffic didn't amount to much. I parked around the corner from MI5 then scooted in to reception. They made me wait a few minutes before Prof Sandford came to pick me up.

"Hello, Jack," he said, shaking my hand, then leading me to the elevator. "We've got her in the basement. She fits the description you gave us of Sandra Hollins, but this woman doesn't respond to that name. She doesn't appear to remember anything about herself at the moment."

"Shock?"

"There are bite wounds on her neck, I'm afraid. The lab is still testing her blood; we should have the results any minute."

The Prof led us into what on the surface looked a nice, cosy rest area, with sofas, cushions, tasteful lamps and so on. But I'd noted the heavy steel door and the fact there were obviously no windows here in the basement.

Sandra sat on one of the sofas with her eyes closed, a female rozzer in a chair by her side. An intravenous drip ran from Sandra's arm to the bag on a stand next to her.

"Agent Noland," said the Prof, "this is Jack Stapleton."

Noland looked to be in her 50s, eyes full of experience. She shook my hand but didn't bother with pleasantries.

"Ms Hollins has been asleep for the last hour," she said. "She's exhausted and undernourished."

"Thanks, Agent Noland. Is it okay if I try to talk to her?"

Noland nodded and I joined Sandra on the sofa. The sight of her thin white complexion and the dark circles under her eyes, not to mention the surgical robe the rozzers had put her in, didn't exactly lessen my feelings of guilt.

I suppose I should have been suspicious that Santonaga had apparently returned her. Maybe he just wanted to show me and the Bellers that he had reach.

I took her hand in mine, flinching at the coldness of her limp fingers. "Sandra?"

Maybe everything would be all right, once she'd been restored to health and got her full memory back.

"Sandra. It's Jack."

Her eyes flicked open and for a moment I looked into the abyss. Then she focussed and hate exploded into her gaze. She screeched, hands bent into claws that ripped at my throat. I just got an arm between us in time, but she pounded and smashed me with her supposedly weakened body.

Just as I decided I'd have to fight back, she went limp and fell back against the sofa.

Agent Noland held a syringe, the Prof by her side.

"What *was* that?" I said.

The Prof took me by the arm, led me toward the door. "Come on, Jack, let's grab a coffee."

I took one last look at her, eyes closed again, body at rest.

"Jesus, is she a vamp now, too?"

In a rest area, the Prof made coffee and left a small hand-held computer switched on where I could see it.

"We'll know her status when the lab results come through," he said, nodding at the computer.

I took a sip of coffee, trying not to stare at the screen.

The Prof said, "All the deaths have been by some sort of poison injected through the bite marks in the neck area. Also, a pint or two of blood has been consumed in each case, but I suppose that's what you'd expect."

The screen stayed blank. "And none of the dead have, you know, revived yet?" I said.

"No. We have them all in secure cells, monitored around the clock, including the one Santonaga replaced in Glasgow. But so far, they've stayed dead, and if they get any more dead, there won't be enough body infrastructure to revive anyway."

"So, does that mean they ain't real vamps?"

"I don't know, Jack. They kill people by biting them, drink their blood and appear to change into bats when it suits them—sounds like vampires to me."

"Me and Meera was talking about it and she—"

"Meera?"

"My new assistant, remember?"

He smiled. "Oh, you mean Agent Nath. Brilliant student, if rather earnest about her work."

"Yeah, well, she's *good* at her work. We thought it must be significant that Santonaga and his gang ain't appeared to have done any vamping before now."

"We're not sure about that yet, actually. We're still checking records over the past thirty-five years. It could be they've been more discreet in the past. Which brings us back to the patterns in their current behaviour."

"I didn't think there were any."

"There's *almost* one. It's frustrating, as if they're taunting us to choose a final piece for the puzzle, knowing if we get it wrong, they win. But for now, we—"

"Prof," I interrupted, "incoming message."

He studied the handheld for a minute or so, me doing my best not to yank it out of his hands and read it direct.

"Well?" I said.

He frowned. "This is extraordinary—Sandra's blood has an uncommon extra constituent."

"What kind of constituent?"

"It's not a substance, more a tendency in the red cells toward a holding shape, the kind similar to that produced by sonic effects. There's nothing in her medical records to suggest this has always been present in her blood."

"Are you saying what I think you're saying?"

He nodded. "Somehow, her blood has the same properties as the Bellers."

By the time I'd finished filling in Meera back at my gaff, it was evening. At one point, it occurred to me that I seemed to be trusting the rozzers more than usual, by divulging any info I had to hand. Who knows, it might even be some super subtle plan of Lucilla's, knowing I was basically the trusting type and if she got one of hers inside my base, I'd eventually tell her everything. But, what the hell. The vamps might have gone quiet for a bit but we all knew they'd be back, and the more we worked together the better chance we'd have of not getting it in the neck. Literally.

"It seems strange," Meera said, "that Santonaga would apparently let Sandra escape; maybe she was supposed to be picked up by us—the easiest way to get to you."

"I'll need to think about that some more, but later," I said. "Fancy a snifter?"

She frowned. "You're not offering me drugs, are you?"

"No, I'm offering to buy you a drink in the pub. That's short for 'public house', an establishment dedicated to supplying alcoholic beverages in an atmosphere conducive to social intercourse."

"A snifter *and* verbal sex? A girl should be so lucky."

"I'll take that as a yes. We'll need to go mufti, mind."

"That one I *do* understand: my dad was in the army in Pakistan."

She went upstairs to change and I took the opportunity to check the lads again; but there still weren't nothing new coming in.

I heard footsteps on the stairs. "Hey, that's some mufti."

Meera did a little twirl, her shortish, black skirt flaring around her black tights. She also wore a blue silk shirt cut impeccably to show her figure to its full advantage, and a tasteful silver necklace with a small cross at its centre.

She saw me looking at this and said, "Well, you can't be too careful."

We put on our coats and I had me hand on the doorknob when she said, "The Astrolabe and Firkin is where Sandra worked, isn't it?"

Now, I knew damn well I hadn't told anyone about my trips to the Astro, so I guessed this was Meera telling me I'd been watched there by the rozzers. Which was no great surprise in itself, but the fact she'd fessed up said a great deal.

"Hilary," I said, "we're popping down the boozer for an hour or two."

"Good for you," said my house, "be sure to bring me back a bag of virtual pork scratchings."

≈

I took Meera to The Holly Bush, a tiny little boozer a few streets away where the landlord knew me well enough to leave us alone.

Meera smiled as we sat at a little corner table, my pint and her G & T wobbling slightly on the buckled beer mats.

"This place is very much you," she said. "No music, fruit machines or games."

"Ah, that's only because I spend all day with gizmos and electronics; good to get away from all that for a while."

"But you don't, really. You invent stuff and keep in touch with the Bellers via comms, yet you spend most of your time with it all switched off."

I started to protest but then realised she was right. "Funny," I said, "I'd always assumed me and my gift was inseparable. But maybe the inventions are more like a symptom of something else."

"Or even a side-track."

"What do you mean?"

She surprised me by downing her drink in one visit. "I need another," she said, standing. "You?"

"Glenfiddich with ice, please."

While she was at the bar, I looked around the room, listening to the shapes of the conversations but not quite divining their essence. Once again, I saw that I was in the habit of only pushing so far in understanding what lay beneath the surface.

Meera seemed to pick up my on my thoughts, or lack of them, after she came back with the drinks.

"The Bellers have never had a focussed enemy before," she said. "You've run separate missions enough times, but no one's come at you in a co-ordinated way. So, you're not prepared."

"We're not used to looking for deeper patterns."

"But you're going to have to. Santonaga is way ahead of us. We don't have a clue how or why he's murdering people, or why he kidnapped and returned Sandra, now with Bellers' type blood. But one thing I'm pretty sure of is that he does have a plan. These aren't the actions of a chaotic joker."

I sipped whisky, looked away; said, "I never wanted Sandra to be involved in all this malarkey. In fact, I was just about to tell her it wouldn't work when he nabbed her."

Meera said nothing. I wished she had, since that might have distracted me from making the next unwelcome step in this new chain of reason.

"Actually," I went on, "I reckon it was more that I wanted her to be part of a life outside all this—for me. *I* needed a normal gaff and a normal girlfriend and a normal life because . . . Well, let's just say I would never have asked for a new place if I hadn't sensed there was something big behind the Princess Marion caper."

"You were just following genetic tendencies, Jack."

"What the hell does that mean? Are you saying that at the first hint of big-time trouble, I revert to me working class roots and look to keep me 'ead down in domestic concerns until it all blows over?"

Boy, did that make me angry. And I got madder still when she didn't reply.

"Just because you've had a university education and talk posh," I said, "doesn't mean you understand *any*thing about the working class."

Head swarming with red mist, I ignored the small voice of sanity at the back of my mind trying to point out that Meera's family lived half a world away in a land where most folks prayed to have what our working class had; and that she'd had to sacrifice her own working class life to do what she did.

"We've been canon fodder in two world wars," I went on, "but you know what? There's more soul in a single Cockney household than in all the stately bleedin' homes and royal castles combined."

"Oh, come on, Jack," she said at last. "Don't give me that heart of gold, honest working people crap. What about the Krays? They were working class lads who loved their mother—in more ways than one, it seems. Everyone around them doffed their forelocks while they behaved as badly as any robber barons in the middle-ages. And what about the fact the BNP only ever wins elections in places like Barking, Dagenham and the East End? Try being black or Asian and living in one of those nice, cosy, family communities."

The argument went on for another ten minutes or so. Every reasonable point I put to her, she twisted somehow until I wondered if I even knew what I thought any more. Then, noticing the pub had gone quiet, I stood up, drained my whisky and said, "I suggest we take this outside."

She finished her drink and we left. Out in the cool, night street, she took the offensive.

"This has nothing to do with class, Jack."

"It has *everything* to do with class. It always does. Middle-class types like to go on about how class doesn't exist any more, but that's only because they've found themselves a nice, cushty nook between the two sharp ends of it."

Our footsteps echoed on the pavement. When she didn't reply, I thought I'd better make my point again.

"It's just that we get fed up with people *thinking* they understand us, when in fact—"

"Jack, will you please shut up! I meant *this* has nothing to do with class; not that there isn't a class problem in this country. But right now, you're using it as an excuse not to see the truth."

I didn't want to hear her. I wanted to tell her to go away, that she couldn't be my assistant any more, that she hadn't earned the right to tell me I was avoiding the truth.

We turned onto our street, silent, she with her arms folded, shoulders hunched.

I unlocked the door and Meera brushed past; threw her coat onto a table, just stood with her back to me.

Her presence reminded me that I was used to the atmosphere in the house being the way I wanted it. She shouldn't just stand there like that. Invading my space.

I took off my coat, threw it at a peg.

She turned to face me. Here, not going anywhere.

"Meera; I'm sorry for shouting."

She said nothing.

This wasn't what I wanted at all.

Heart thumping, I took a step forward, then another. I put my hands on her shoulders, feeling her still angry breath in the rise and fall of them.

I don't know what exactly in me decided to, but I kissed her, pressing my hands into her back, bringing her tight against my body. She kissed back, tongue searching out mine.

I couldn't remember ever needing anything so much. And maybe it was the pressure of the times, but I just switched off all my usual inner blockers and for once let my body do the talking.

I woke up in my room, without Jack. He'd looked a little hurt when I'd left his bed last night but I've always felt that sleeping with someone—actually *sleeping* with them—means a whole lot more than sex. Not that I didn't enjoy the sex. I guess both our sets of hormones were wound a whole lot tighter than we'd realised. All that arguing about class was just our subconsciouses trying to drive a wedge between us, to prevent the inevitable.

But right then, I didn't know where he and I were headed, if anywhere at all. The world had turned into an extraordinary and dangerous place, and we sat in the middle of it all somehow, with death just around the corner. So, yes, of course we were horny.

Then again, when he put his arms around me in the kitchen the next morning, and kissed me tenderly, eyes full of warmth, I nearly turned off that world and settled for a smaller, safer one.

Nearly.

I woke up to the memory of wide brown eyes looking into mine as she bounced on top of me, driving hard; me already gone but still wanting her to also, and her amazing grin of delight when she did; my hands on her breasts, she pushing her nipples between my fingers . . .

Of course, the pleasure-shock dissolved in a sting of guilt, 'cos what was I doing shagging Meera when Sandra lay in a rozzer hospital bed, sedated and fitted up to cold machines while they tried to figure out what Santonaga had done to her?

But then, I don't know, maybe it was the dodgy times we found ourselves in, but instead of indulging, I parked the guilt and went downstairs to kiss Meera as full on as I could, and I'm right pleased to say she kissed me back the same.

Soon after breakfast, she said she had to go to MI5 to pick up some files.

After she'd gone, I sat in me Superman dressing gown, feeling quite a lot more Man and not lacking in Steel either, truth be told.

"Shouldn't you be worrying about Santonaga, instead of practising for the Sickly Grin Olympics?" said Hilary.

"Shouldn't you be polishing the burglar alarm or something?"

A long silence followed which lulled me into a false sense of security, literally in this case. Then she said, "Actually, while you were testing the effectiveness of your memory foam mattress, I was testing a hypothesis or two about Santonaga."

"Aren't you supposed to stick to seeing off Jehovah's Witnesses and checking the gas man's credentials?"

"It's just a hunch but I think you should phone your sister, Jack."

Well, that wiped the grin of my face, not to mention taking the lead out of my pencil. I grabbed the phone and dialled Sarah.

"Hi, how are you?" I said when she answered, trying to sound like I always phoned her on a Sunday morning just to check in.

"Fine," she said, making it almost a question. "How are you?"

"Splendid, mostly."

"'Splendid'? Have you been listening to Radio 4 again?"

"How's Dan?"

"Okay, I suppose. For a teenager, he's suspiciously good-natured, only gets a strop on when 'is team loses."

"Can I have a word with him?"

"He's out at a mate's."

Damn. If I asked her who, she'd get suspicious.

"A girl?"

She snorted. "I bleedin' well hope not. I ain't had The Talk with him yet, for one thing."

"Don't they do that at school these days?"

"Well, they give them the biological details, but they tend to be a bit light on the 'phwoar!' factor."

I blushed. "Can I give him a ring where he is? Just wanted to apologise again for missing the end of his match yesterday."

"He's round Tommy Hannigan's place; hang on . . ."

While she searched for the number, I nodded at Hilary's camera eye and a screen dropped before me, already loading up with details about the Hannigans.

I said goodbye to Sarah then got dressed while listening to directions and details from Hilary.

"You don't honestly think Santonaga would snatch Dan, do you?" I said.

"He snatched Sandra. Sorry, Jack. I think I'm just getting jittery because Jeeves hasn't checked in with me today."

"He's probably busy with the lads' reports."

"I don't know: I just sense something bad's about to happen. Sorry—what I mean is that I extrapolated from the absence of normal data that there is an increased probability that an emergency event has transpired."

"Okay, well I ain't got time to follow up your hunches right this minute, Hil. Just page Jeeves if you get any more details."

I left the house, drove in the Nissan to the Hannigan's place in Chigwell. I parked near the end of a right pleasant cul-de-sac, showing that Tommy's folks obviously had a bob or two to their name. And then I felt pretty stupid: I mean, what did I do? Walk up to the door and announce meself as Dan's concerned Uncle? Concerned about what—his school exam results, his acne, his worrying tendency to sometimes push his back four too quickly forward when trying to spring the offside trap?

And so I sat there like a confused suet pudding, for at least half an hour. I was about to leave when the Hannigan's door opened and Dan walked out, waving goodbye to Tommy.

As he moved alongside, I wound down the window. "Want a lift?"

"Uncle Jack? Bloody 'ell: I thought you was a perve. What are you doing here?"

He climbed in and I pulled away from the curb. "I ain't sure, exactly," I said. "Just wanted to see you."

I was glad I couldn't see his eyes because the sharp blast of air he rasped through his lips was expressive enough.

"Did you ask yourself if I wanted to see you?" he said.

"Well, not really, but—"

"Uncle Jack: you like to pretend to be me dad when it suits you—turning up at footy every now and then, sending me cool new phones for Christmas, even before they're in the shops. But you can't expect me to just jump when you feel like playing Happy Families."

"Dan," I said. "There's something about me you need to know. I reckon you're old enough now."

"Oh, no, you ain't gay, are you?"

"No, but would it matter if I was?"

"Well, not to me. But the lads in the team might take the piss a bit."

"But one in ten of the population's gay, which means at least one of your team probably is too."

"Nice maths, Uncle Jack, but us footy players prefer to leave our calculators at home when there's a big match on."

I drove to Whitechapel, parked, then led the way on foot to The Lord Kitchener. But as we turned the corner, my spirits sank at the sight of a whole posse of police cars, throwing orange flashing lights across the crowd gathered outside the pub.

So, at least Hilary's sense of doom didn't after all involve Dan. But given the location, there was a fair chance it involved others close to me instead. Jeeves had not been in contact, she'd said. Buggeration.

I showed me rozzer badge to the policeman standing guard.

"What happened, constable?" I said.

"Someone shot the barman. Locals said the gunman just walked in and popped him; went behind the bar, to nick something presumably, then walked out again before anyone could react. They've taken the barman to the hospital 'cos he's still breathing, but it looks bad."

"Have you caught the shooter yet?"

He shook his head. "All we know is he isn't in the pub."

It could be a coincidence, but I doubted it.

"I need to go in, mate," I said.

He looked me over, and Dan, then nodded. "I'll take care of the boy."

Dan's expression was encouragingly calm. "No, he can come with me," I said. "There's nothing much to see, right?"

He shrugged. "It's your funeral, mate."

I steered Dan through the crime scene tape, into the lobby of the pub.

"This way," I said, pushing him toward the Gents.

"You really need to pee?" he said.

I didn't answer, shoved open the door, throat pumping with dread. Inside, I opened the door of the central cubicle to find my worst fears confirmed: the door to Bellers' HQ wide open. I guessed the police hadn't actually opened this cubicle yet, just looked under the door and seen nothing other than darkness.

TEN

Undead or Jacked?

IF YOU ASKED ME AT WHAT exact point I'd become a man, I'm not sure I could tell you. Maybe the day Dad left home and the look in Mum's eyes said she needed someone to be strong for her. Or perhaps it was that fumble in the park I had with Sherry Bolton in the third form. Then again, burying Mum ranks right up there with the moment you realise it's just you and whatever God you got from now on.

But I'm pretty sure Dan would never forget his turning moment.

"Stay behind me," I said, ducking through the door.

We ran down the slope, everything too quiet. I glanced around, worried that no sensor lights were flashing. I stopped at the steel door blocking our way to the inner rooms. Normally, I'd have to press my eye to the scan patch but something told me it wouldn't be necessary.

I pushed lightly and it swung open.

I pulled a multi-factor gun from my jacket pocket.

"What *is* this place, Uncle Jack?"

The digital walls of the entry corridor were blank, just black marble dulling the light from the strip overhead.

"It's where my mates live. I hope."

We reached the far door which also should have been locked but I could see light rimming its edge. I pushed and it too swung back.

"Bloody hell . . ."

Tony G and Herby lay sprawled on the steel corridor, blood blooming around their heads. I thought about telling Dan to go back but couldn't be sure whatever did this wouldn't have circled back round.

I touched Herby's neck with my fingertips: no pulse; then I saw a ring of holes in the flesh. Santonaga's crew, then.

"Are they dead? Were they friends of yours?"

In amongst the shock in his eyes, anger flared.

"They was a lot more than that," I said.

I ran to the Moose Hall, pushed open the door and knelt, gun held out in front of me. But aside from the crackle of flaming logs, the room was silent. Just a pity it weren't empty of folk too, but scanning around, my heart sank at the sight of around a dozen more of the guys, all dead.

"Jeeves," I said, walking slowly into the carnage. "Play back what happened here."

"I'm afraid I was taken off line about fifty minutes ago, only just now able to re-boot, sir, along with all my sensors. I have no record of what happened during the attack."

"How many still alive in HQ right now?"

"Two, sir; just you and the boy."

"Any undead?"

"Sir?"

"Vampires."

"I have no reliable data regarding vampires but if they are as generally described in the sixteenth century, they should still register on my sensors: brain activity, corneal pressure, that kind of thing."

"How many Bellers dead?" I said.

"Seventeen I'm afraid, sir."

"How the hell did they get in here?"

"Excuse me a minute, while I extrapolate from the data pre- and post-attack."

Dan stood in the doorway, trembling; shock at last setting in.

I walked quickly to him, took him outside and closed the door. I led him to a guest room I was pretty sure would be empty, put him in an easy chair, gave him a coffee from the dispenser, then sat opposite, waiting for him to settle.

"He appears to have somehow turned his corneas into a replica of Brian Deen's," said Jeeves. "That got him inside, then he used Brian's handheld to get into my systems and shut down all my sensors and recording devices. He seems to have known I'd only be offline for just over half an hour, and he was gone before I regained consciousness. He left the building about fifteen minutes ago, took exit Five."

"*He*? There was only one attacker?"

"Apparently, sir; but I may have missed some data. There are traces of an unknown sonic effect. I suspect he paralysed the men with it before killing them. He would not have been able to tackle them single-handed otherwise, no matter how strong he may be. I should be able to analyse what he used and help the Professor to make an antidote."

I kept my gaze on Dan. "Good. Now, this what you have to do, Jeeves. Seal off The Lord Kitchener entrance. From now on only open the main doors to a Beller who passes your full body scan—yes, I know that'll take at least three minutes—or anyone I personally authorise. Call Professor Sandford, tell him what's happened and ask him to send a clean-up squad here."

"Very well, sir. Will you be phoning the families of the deceased?"

"Yes, please prepare the comms room with a video link."

Dan looked at me over his coffee mug, eyes full of dark.

"What *are* you, uncle?" he said.

"Until I was eight, I thought I was a kid just like you. Played footy, permanent scabs on me knees, joined the Wolf Cubs, dib dib bleedin' dib an' all that . . ."

Much as I wanted to, there was no point in rushing after Santonaga. Even with all me gizmos, I didn't reckon on finding a shape-shifter any time soon.

"It took a bit longer for the rozzers to find me than the others. Most of them showed their powers pretty early on, busting garden walls with their heads, that kind of thing, or turning invisible in the vicar's arms just as he was about to dunk the baby in the holy water. But I guess all I had to show was top marks every year in Science, which was balanced out by coming bottom at just about everything else."

"'These blokes had super-powers?'"

"We're the Bellers, Dan. Conceived at the same time and all changed when Bow Bells rang of their own accord one day. Something in the pattern of the sound worked on our genes and altered them big time."

"How did the rozzers finally find out you was one?"

"In the end, I couldn't have made it much more bleedin' obvious. I turned our Ford Anglia into a flying car, didn't I? Invented floating head flexi-jets for lift, thrust and so on. Then took it for a spin, right past the Houses of Parliament, on down the river, passed MI5's headquarters. Had three helicopters tracking me before I turned round at Greenwich."

Jesus, so many of the boys just blown away in an instant.

"Does Mum know?"

I nodded, guessing his next question. "And she ain't never told you because she and I wanted you to live as normal a life as possible."

"Fat chance of that now."

Right then, I realised just how inadequately prepared we'd been for a ruthless, powered attack like this. Oh, we'd spent the past couple of decades helping victims of crime and natural disasters, but only in-between a lot of puffing cigars and congratulating ourselves on being such right, royal Cockney super-geezers.

Now, half of us were dead and the other half scattered. Christ, I didn't even know what to do next. Where could I put Dan, Sarah and Meera so they'd be safe while I hunted down Santonaga and his gang?

"What killed your friends, uncle?"

"We ain't sure exactly. At first we thought they—it; we don't know how many—was a vampire but Meera reckons we could be looking at something different. In the meantime, it bites people in the neck and they're dead all right; so far, they ain't risen again."

All but one, at least.

He shivered. "And you wouldn't want that to happen to your mates."

"The rozzers will keep their bodies safe. But I think you and your mum need to stay here for a while. It'll be safe now. He caught us off guard but he won't get in again. And anyway, I reckon his work's done here."

Any other kid would have protested, I reckoned. But Dan seemed to take everything in and knew it was for the best.

Twenty minutes later, Professor Sandford, Lee and Morris turned up, along with a rozzer clean-up squad. They told me that Lucilla had promised no questions would be asked, no investigations made.

After filling them in with what I knew, I asked them to send a car for Sarah and wait with Dan until I got back. Then I ran to the tube and dropped into it.

Back at my gaff, Meera was waiting in the lounge. She put her arms around me and I lay my head on her shoulder.

"I'm so sorry, Jack."

I let the tears come then; great racking sobs.

Later, we sat together and I said, "I just don't know what we do next. We've got shape-shifting vampires who can get in anywhere and kill by biting folks in the neck. We know Santonaga has a plan, but don't have a clue what, only that it ain't going to be good and it's definitely going to be big."

"We also know," she said, "that in Sandra's case—and there could be more—his blood can lend great strength to those he infects, as well as apparently keeping them shackled to his will."

"But it don't make sense. Why would he kill some but power up others?"

I had the impression she was deciding whether or not to try me with something.

"Come on, Meera. Spill it."

"I found an old folk tale in the agency's archive."

"MI5 keeps folk stories?"

"You'd be surprised what we store, just in case. Don't forget, in past times it could be a death sentence for even a government agent to write a report on anything with magical connotations. So they sometimes put coded information into a kid's story or folk tale instead. I looked through all the material we had on vampires, and found a story about a medieval baron who had the power to turn others into vampires without killing them. The price they paid for not passing through death to gain their powers was that their will remained tied to his."

"So, he was like a vampire's vampire?"

"Except the story had another name for it: a *bloodjacker*. Someone who can bedevil the blood of others by spitting into their veins, tying them to him forever."

I shivered. "And you think Santonaga is a bloodjacker?"

"Maybe. Nearly all the victims we've found so far are just dead, so it seems as if their ability to become the undead is a myth."

"All the victims except one," I said. "Sandra."

"Yes, and there could well be others he's not actually killed, but turned his way instead. We need to find out more about vampires and the bloodjacker."

"At the British Museum?"

"No. The secret services down the centuries removed the darker aspects of British history from the public records. But there's one place they've never been allowed access to."

I smiled. "The Palace archives?"

She nodded. "Normally, it's impossible to get access. But don't the Bellers have a royal favour to call in?"

ELEVEN

Spitting Blood

IT SEEMED BIZARRE TO BE approaching the Shetland Isles in a stealth jet, on me way to look for a wizard at a music festival. At least the green spread of fields and moors below me, and the granite cliffs sparkling in the sunlight, felt reassuringly normal and ancient. But then I shivered, realising that Santonaga's influence would reach here too eventually, if we didn't stop him.

Somewhere over the North Sea, I'd arranged for the plane's chameleo-paint to turn her into an RAF bird. Then I'd radioed ahead using call signs Lee and Morris had given me. Now, as I prepared to make a vertical landing near the control tower of Lerwick's small airport, I just hoped they'd worked.

Three ground staff ran to meet me as soon as the engines died down. I climbed out of the cockpit and introduced myself to the one in the suit as Colonel Stapleton. He looked slightly sceptical at my Cockney accent but waved me through anyway.

I hired a car and drove to Lerwick proper, a grey granite town, kind of stern but cautiously welcoming. The rozzers had arranged for me to take over the apartment of a local officer who happened to be on leave. I let myself into a small ground-floor flat, tidy and sparse. One room had a couple of computer screens and various other gadgets in it; the living room contained a TV screen as wide as the wall, otherwise, just a small kitchen, bathroom and bedroom.

I unpacked then put on what I reckoned would blend in with the folksy crowd, namely jeans and baggy jumper. After a cup of tea and a quick call back to HQ to let them know I was okay, I headed for the folk festival centre.

Which turned out to be a local school, full of kids running around, people playing fiddles, and sausage roll smells.

I bought a ticket then found a place to stand at the back of the main hall. The rozzers told me that on the first day of the festival, every single act played one song in the centre. This gave everyone the chance to get an earful before deciding how to best spend their time between all the other venues. It also gave yours truly the chance to see if any of the performers had a hint of magic about them, and I don't mean as in groovy sounds.

The audience looked like a mixture of locals and out of town music lovers. Everyone seemed less than awed by the presence of so many folk stars coming in and out to do their turn. I guess this was a mix and match kind of event which should suit me purposes well.

I have to say, I'd never been much of a folky, thinking it meant a lot of beardy blokes sticking their fingers in their ears and hey nonny no-ing about the summer a-cumin in, and the such. So it was a surprise to hear flamenco bands from Spain, blues combos from the USA, dance band-ish English folk music, and of course plenty of Scottish. Not just Scottish, but Nova Scotia Scottish, since several bands had flown over from that part of Canada especially. What's more, to my uneducated ears at least, their music sounded in some ways even more authentically Scots than the Scots' own stuff. But that was one opinion I figured best kept to meself.

After the concert, I went for a walk, down to the sea, watching the waves and wondering what the hell I was doing so far north of the nearest pie and mash shop. Well, I knew what I was looking *for*: a retired court wizard named Ambrose. But although the Palace records had revealed the last sighting of him in the UK had been here, that was six years ago. He could have died or at least skedaddled by now.

Meera had reckoned I'd know if Ambrose was anywhere nearby because my blood would feel pulled to him. But so far, I hadn't felt anything other than the urge to tap me foot to some of the more jiggy bands I'd heard.

The whole question of magic was a vexed one, to say the least. Everyone knew that royalty and some rich families paid for magic retainers, usually called a 'wizard' when probably 'wish-hard' would be a better description. Magic may or may not have been as real to folk as religion a few centuries ago. But now, most people didn't believe a wizard could do anything without a very large pair of gadget-concealing sleeves.

And I might have thought the same if it weren't for Bow Bells and the contents of my blood.

I returned to my temporary gaff and made a bacon sandwich. Then I headed back to the festival centre to catch the evening's entertainment.

Lots of rooms were full of groups of serious-looking musicians jamming on what sounded like traditional ditties. The bar seemed as useful a place as any to hang out, so I got meself a pint of Old Kilt Droppings or the some such and squeezed into a corner table.

I tried to forget the country was only a haggis skin's width from being taken over by super-vampires and listened loosely to the conversations around me, letting my mind drift on them like a cork on the ocean.

I must have nearly dropped off to sleep because I jerked in my chair when a few words from the chat soup around me hit home.

An American-sounding accent: " . . . how musical sound patterns can have actual, physical effects . . ."

I zeroed in on the speaker—a young guy with bushy black hair a few tables away, talking to a blonde girl in black everything.

I picked up my pint and went over to them. "Mind if I join you?" I said. They both said no but the way you'd say you didn't mind your incontinent uncle tagging along. I didn't care; this could be the lead we needed.

"I'm Jack," I said. "Sorry to barge in but I heard you say something about sound having physical effects. I'm interested in that kind of thing, as it happens."

"I'm Nick," he said. "I'm not going to be able to help you much, though. I was just telling Cassandra what I'd heard a few guys talking about back home."

"Which is where?" I said.

"Halifax, Nova Scotia."

"Well, I didn't think you meant Halifax, Yorkshire, son, not with an accent like that."

Cassandra folded her arms and I figured I had about another two minutes before Nick realised he'd better off-load the old bugger fast if he wanted another crack at romance tonight.

"Can you remember anything else?" I said. "What the band was called, that sort of thing?"

"It's not really a band," he said. "More a small movement. I think they have a teacher, an old guy by all accounts."

"Can you recall his name?"

He shook his head. "I never actually heard it. But I think he's British."

Now I felt the tug in my blood.

"Give me a name, son. It's really important."

He frowned, obviously trying to figure out why a complete stranger should be so interested in a bit of gossip he'd picked up on the other side of the Atlantic.

"Sorry. But if you're ever in Halifax, ask for Jimbo in the Harbour Inn. He's a member of the group."

I stood. "Thanks. I'll give him your regards."

I left them frowning at each other, wondering if the crusty old geezer really was planning to go to Halifax, just on a rumour.

He was. The rumour plus the tug plus the complete absence of any other leads had me walking fast back to me lodgings and packing the bag I'd only just unloaded.

I drove to the airport, then had the somewhat surprised ground crew ready the jet.

The moon filled my windshield as I headed west of the Shetlands, skimming through the night air over the black and silver waters.

"Morris, Lee?" I said into comms.

A pause then, "Lee here, Mr Stapleton."

"I'm heading for Halifax, Nova Scotia, in the jet."

"And you won't have enough fuel to make it in one hit."

"Glad you know something about jets. I'm hoping you also know something about aircraft carriers and where I can hop on to one before I have to turn round and come back."

"Leave it with me, sir."

Sir? Well, that was new. Still, I liked that he was on the ball, and had no doubts he'd find me a carrier in mid-Atlantic.

"Oh, and Lee: best not to let the big wigs at the agency know what we're up to here."

"Understood," he said. "Rob and I don't know who we can trust here at the moment, to be honest. But the fact is, they'll find out anyway that you're heading for Canada."

"In which case, it's best I don't tell you why."

"Agreed."

I had a five hour flight to negotiate. I hadn't slept in over thirty hours and despite the adrenaline fix of scooting in a jet across the pond, my eyes felt as if they'd been rolled in cat litter.

I dialled a number on the jet's phone.

"Jack?" She sounded sleepy.

"Sorry, did I wake you?"

"I wasn't really asleep. Lee told me you're over the Atlantic."

I could picture that fierce furrow she got between the eyes when thinking real hard.

"Not much to go on. Just what some spotty kid said to a bird he was trying to impress."

"And you had to ruin his big moment."

I laughed. "Well, he can always go for a jig if he needs to work off any stored up sexual tension."

"Maybe I should go for a jig too."

Oh, now that got my blood tingling, and not as in pulling me west.

"Any news?"

"Not really," she said. "It's too quiet at the moment. No new bodies, which suggests he's now turning more than he's killing. You can sense him out there, forming up out of the shadows behind a new victim, taking their blood, leaving his hooks in, all the time getting closer to some sort of tipping point. The weird thing is that so far it's all stayed out of the news. And not because the agency's been leaning on the press. I reckon he's well connected, pulling the media strings, waiting for the right moment."

"How's Dan and Sarah?"

"Asleep, thankfully. They've been through a lot, but they don't complain. It's harder for them, not having our training."

"We never got trained to deal with a bloodjacker, Meera."

"I never got trained to deal with a Beller, either."

Lee came through nine minutes before I'd have to turn back to Blighty. A US navy carrier let me land and re-fuel without asking too many questions. The government had a pretty good relationship with the yanks, I guess. Whatever, I was pleased no one asked me any awkward questions.

I landed at Halifax airport around breakfast time. In another hired car, I drove the twenty-odd miles to town, where I booked in to a B & B and crashed out for a few hours.

Early afternoon, I headed down towards the water and found the Harbour Inn, a wooden building with posters in its windows of various bands and singers. I went in to the cool shadows of the main bar, half full with people having lunch. I ordered a beer at the bar and said to the girl who served me, "I'm looking for Jimbo."

"You a relative?"

"More a friend of a friend."

"Well, he's due behind the bar at seven tonight."

I thanked her and sipped my beer, thinking. Why is it that in the movies, no one has to hang around? If this was a bleedin' film, I'd have walked into the bar just as Jimbo was polishing his beer pump and we'd be off and running. Now, I had several hours to kill before I could get any closer to finding the wizard who according to the Palace, might have had a big hand in making me.

I spent the rest of the afternoon in my room, scanning the TV channels for what exactly I wasn't sure. The endless chit-chat of the studio talk shows; the smooth urgency of the news readers; the screeching cars and rattling guns, balls and bats and clubs swinging through the air, all seemed so utterly banal. Very soon they may no longer have their own minds, if they'd ever really had them in the first place, of course. Why didn't they ever sense anything beyond the too neat and tidy front garden fence of their immediate hungers and desires?

And then I let it go some, reminding myself of the booze, horses, reccy rooms and general hording of rats' arses that had made up the Bellers' world view not so long ago.

Just before seven, I headed out again. The Harbour Inn was fairly quiet, this early in the evening and with only one man behind the bar.

"Excuse me," I said, "are you Jimbo?"

He looked like a school kid to me—no wrinkles, curious gaze, wild hair—but also with an air of caution right then, as he took a few moments to assess me.

"Yeah, I'm James," he said. "What can I get you?"

"Draft Guinness, please."

I figured asking for the dark stuff would give me a few moments to think while he pulled it. Clearly, he'd spotted my London accent, and if Ambrose was some kind of teacher to him, he would probably be wary of any other Brits who already knew his name.

Then again, where events back home were concerned, I couldn't afford to be on Guinness time. If this kid knew anything, I had to get it out of him and fast.

He brought the glass over and I said, "My name's Jack and I hear you've been doing some work on sound dynamics."

"Well, I'm a musician, if that's what you mean."

I glanced at the miniature lie detector on my wrist: James was not giving me the full Monty.

"I understand why you don't want to say too much, son. But if you've got a neutral number I can call or something, it'd be much appreciated."

He frowned but reached under the counter for a pad and pen. "You can leave a message at this number," he said. "Then someone will phone you back. Or not."

"Cheers; appreciated." I put the paper in my jacket pocket then forced meself to take a little time finishing the drink; didn't want to freak him by rushing out straight away.

Back in my room, I unpacked the small host of gizmos I'd brought with me. I connected the laptop to the house wi-fi, then set up my communications extrapolator—a little device I hadn't bothered to give the rozzers yet. Didn't want them extrapolating me, for a start.

This gizmo needed three points of information in order to do its work. Basically, it built a tripod of ethermesh in which I let it use the same semi-intuitive software I'd given Hilary. This meant it could make anti-logic leaps across security systems. I reckoned Ambrose would have an untrackable mobile phone and I didn't even bother looking in the phone book under 'W' for Wizard.

I opened the Palace file I had on him and loaded it into the extrapolator, along with the number Jimbo had given me. My desire to find him made the third vector, I hoped. Then, knowing it would take a few minutes, I put the kettle on.

It had just switched itself off when the room phone rang. I picked it up, expecting to be asked if I needed a morning wake up call.

"Jack Stapleton."

It wasn't a question. Male, British well-educated accent, with a slight Canadian burr.

"Ambrose? How did you find me?"

"I've been tracking you since you first stepped off your jet. I have my technologies too."

Magic.

"I need to speak to you," I said.

"Face to face? I don't think so. Not unless you're prepared to come shorn of any of those monitoring devices I know you have a penchant for."

"Done. Provided you keep your spells in your pants, too."

He laughed. "Come to the address your little spy box is showing right about now."

I glanced at the laptop and sure enough a Halifax address sat on its screen.

"So, you don't want me to bring *any*thing?" I said.

"Just a bottle of good malt whisky."

After he hung up, I set about stripping meself of gadgets and gizmos, like the lie detector watch, the recording buttons on my belt, the satellite tracker in my boot heel, not to mention various guns and knives folded in tiny, flat packages. I'd heard enough in that call to know Ambrose was the real deal, and I didn't want him throwing me out before I got to ask some important questions just because my underwear was a Faraday cage designed to prevent any harmful em radiation messing with my internal organs.

Ambrose's address was only a few blocks from the B & B so I legged it there, stopping only at a liquor store on the way to pick up a bottle of Balvenie.

Then I found myself outside a modern apartment block, pushing the button for number 34.

"Balvenie's okay, but the 12 year old's smoother than the 10."

I didn't bother looking for a camera, mainly because the whisky bottle was hidden inside a brown paper bag.

The front door clicked and I pushed it open. In a neat, modern hallway I pressed the elevator button, smiling. Either Ambrose had viewing devices and informants of his own everywhere in town or he knew enough about me to work out what whisky I would choose.

I stepped out at the third floor, raised my fist to knock on his door but then it opened anyway. I walked inside, clocking the tiny camera above the transom and the motors on the hinges. So, maybe not all magic, then.

I suppose I half expected to find myself surrounded by glass tubes bubbling with multi-coloured magical goo, talking owls and dancing brooms. But in fact, Ambrose's pad looked to contain nothing more dangerous than a large wall-hung TV screen, a trendy white leather three-piece suite and a few potted plants. There wasn't even a book case.

Ambrose himself stood with his back to the huge window overlooking the town, the night ocean stretched across the horizon. A lamp in one corner threw his face into light and shadow which allowed me to see that, despite being an old man, he possessed strong features. He wore blue trousers and a plain white shirt, his chin and head smooth.

It was impossible to read his expression as I walked towards him, hand outstretched.

He took my hand and laughed as I flinched slightly, not entirely sure as I'd been that my fingers wouldn't burst into flames on contact.

"You can call me Daddy if you like," he said.

Uncertain how to reply, I gave him the bag and he took it, leading me into the kitchen, which was also clean and sparse.

He took two crystal glasses from a cupboard and half-filled them with whisky. "Water, ice?" he said.

"Just a little water, please."

He took a bottle from the fridge, added water to my glass, swirled both glasses then held them up to the light.

"You can't see it," he said, "but my voice is creating sonic patterns more quickly in your drink than mine."

"Because mine's slightly less dense?"

He nodded. "But when a pattern does establish itself in the denser medium, it holds together longer."

"Are you saying boys are denser than girls?"

"Not *in*side the womb."

He handed me a glass and we returned to the living room, where he sat on the sofa and I in a chair opposite.

"I've a ton of questions," I said.

"And you wouldn't be here unless things are getting desperate back home."

"Don't you know? You seem to see everything that goes on."

"My sensory spell ends five miles out of town. Inside it, I know most of what happens, but it reflects attention from its outer surface, so I've no idea what's going on in England, apart from what the news shows me. And all that's apparently happened since I left is that footballers now get paid silly money and reality TV is more real than most people's reality."

"But you must have known when Santonaga's blood was due to switch on."

He didn't flinch at that but his eyes dimmed ever so slightly. He sipped whisky, watching me closely for a few moments, then looked away at the night outside the window.

"Let's just say I've been working on a cure," he said.

Meera and I had figured that if Ambrose had a hand in creating the Bellers, he'd probably set up Santonaga, too. But the fact Santonaga had not vamped anyone until he was in his thirties suggested Ambrose had somehow delayed the activation of the lord's blood.

"You were forced to make him, weren't you?"

He nodded. "Afterwards, the Santonagas thought they'd killed me. Why didn't you think I was dead too?"

"There were reports you'd been seen here and there. Besides, I felt a tug in my blood."

"They used a team of wizards to hold me in their cellar; weakly-powered impostors but strong enough when connected to keep me trapped, especially since I'd had to use so much of my own power on the boy. Don't bother trying to find them, by the way; I killed them as soon as I rose from the pretend dead. Vile scum."

"What did the Santonagas want from a bloodjacker son?"

"Good, you've done your research. But that's not actually the right question to ask. Better to think about what the so-called upper classes want."

"Money, power, good-looking staff to roger?"

He smiled. "That's pretty much it, boring though it is. You know that old saying about how the devil's greatest trick was getting people to believe he doesn't exist? Well, the British ruling classes have managed to do the same thing by opening their stately homes to the public and allowing a few ramblers across their land. No one really believes any more that these are the same people, by genetics and inclination, who bled the country dry for centuries with no more justification than they believe they're born to it by right. And who would do it again at the drop of a hat."

"So the Santonagas wanted you to turn their son into a super blood-sucker, to restore the toffs' status quo?"

"More or less, except they had a new idea. Instead of stealing land and wealth, this time they figured stealing wills would be a much better way of keeping folks in line."

"But why did you go along with them? Couldn't you have refused, even if it meant taking a bullet?"

"Don't look so self-righteous, Jack. Yes, I could have taken a bullet, but for one thing: the shadow wizards in the Santonagas' pay had managed to unravel enough of my work in spell sonics to produce a mutant without me anyway."

"So, what did they need you for?"

"To make it safer. The shadows didn't have the full technology. Anyone they turned super might just explode or implode or just plain over-load. And before you ask why I didn't refuse, it was because they'd have gone ahead anyway. In which case, their mutant could have turned thousands of others into mad monsters. At least I could make sure that didn't happen; he'd still turn them, yes, but underneath the command in their blood to follow their master, their essential self would remain intact."

At that, hope flared in me chest. "You mean they can be turned back?"

He sighed, sipped more whisky, had his mouth open to answer the question when in the corner of my eye I noted a black shape heading for the—

—window shattered, glass shards flying everywhere, a body rolled on to the floor between me and Ambrose. I dropped my glass, reached for the gun normally in the back of my trouser waistband, cursed at finding nothing there, then jumped behind my chair as the black thing sprang upright.

Ambrose stood, winding his hands through the air, red light pulsing and flaring from his fingertips: hidden laser gun or magic?

Our attacker was completely concealed by a black fight suit and balaclava-like mask with shaded eye-holes. It flew at Ambrose before he'd finished conjuring, hands around his throat. I reached for the whisky bottle that had rolled to the floor, rushed to the fighting pair. But as I raised it, a whole bush of red fire flared around the black figure. It staggered backwards then fell flat on its back, smoke curling from its chest, the smell of burning rubber filling the air.

Ambrose turned to the shattered window and waved his hands as if plastering over the hole. Amazingly, the cold night breeze I'd felt since it broke, stopped.

He reached down and pulled off the attacker's mask.

"Friend of yours?" he said, no doubt noting the shock on my face.

"Bloody hell. Sandra Hollins. We went on a date recently; then Santonaga kidnapped her."

"She must have followed you here."

"Does that mean Santonaga now knows you're alive?"

He shrugged. "Once she comes round, he may sense what she's found here, or she may simply phone him with the news."

"She must have escaped from MI5. Those buggers never tell me anything. But how did she know where to find me, and how did she get here, all the way from England, when I came by jet?"

"Did you have sex with her on your date?"

"I don't think this is the right time to be filling you on my personal life, Ambrose."

"Did you?"

"No, but she might have thought that I wanted to, that I had strong feelings for her."

"Well, that explains how she knew where you were."

"Really? Do you mind explaining it to me."

"Jack, your blind spot is that you're a scientist, so you expect everything to have an entirely logical explanation, even though the Bellers were formed by largely magical processes."

"I'm not totally convinced about that. I mean, the Bellers' genes show signs of explainable, if unusual mutations which—"

"Sandra's heightened powers mean she can *taste* you, Jack. The tiniest trace of your feeling for her still in her systems acts like an emotional compass. She knows where you are pretty much round the clock."

"You don't think a simpler explanation is Santonaga has a double agent in MI5 who just *told* her where I was heading?"

"It's possible, I suppose."

It was possible but I didn't really believe it. Meera wouldn't betray me and the only other agent who knew I was in Halifax was Lee. And while my instinct for traitors wasn't perfect, I didn't figure Lee for anything other than a straight down the line rozzer.

"Even if you're right," I said, "it don't explain how she got here so fast."

"She'd have known as soon as you did that you were heading for Halifax. She probably just bought a plane ticket and flew here. You didn't contact me immediately, did you? So, she had time to catch up. A passenger jet flies pretty close to the speed of a private jet if it's not to burn up fuel too quickly. I guess you made one stop on the way over: aircraft carrier, right?"

"Yeah, the yanks did a favour for our rozzers." I walked to the window. "Tricky climb from down there."

I turned to look at Sandra, her face deathly pale, hair damp and raggedy around her head. Unconscious, she looked more like a barmaid without a care in the world again.

"So, can you turn her back?" I said. "What about that cure you mentioned?"

"It's not ready yet, and even if it was, Santonaga would know the moment we try it."

"So what?"

"Come on, Jack; think. If he knows Sandra's cured, he'll guess who's behind it and have me killed."

"You really don't want to take a bullet, do you?"

He sighed. "Okay: yes, if it's a choice between me and your girlfriend, I'd choose me. But that's not the point. We'll need to re-turn everyone else he's bitten, not to mention stop him from reaching critical mass. Which means I need to finish the cure, and I can't do that if I'm dead."

"But we can't just leave her tied to him like this."

"Sit down, Jack. Somewhere your arse won't get shredded."

He picked pieces of glass off the sofa and sat himself. "There's something else that might work," he said. "But if it does, she could be permanently damaged by it."

"But will she be herself?"

"Mostly, I think. What I'm about to show you would probably work fine on someone who's been prepared or trained in some way for these kind of changes. But for Sandra, who hasn't, the shock of being herself again could destroy her mind."

Hobson's Choice then. Leave Sandra as she was and we'd end up having to kill her like any other blood-sucking vamp. Save her and she could be a zombie for the rest of her life.

"Another alternative—and I can't be certain it will work—is to put Sandra in a holding state until I can finish the cure, then use it first on her."

"Do it," I said.

"Actually, *you* have to do it, Jack."

He took a scalpel from his jacket pocket. "With this, make a cut in her neck; draw blood, put your mouth on the wound and mix it with your saliva. Normally, you should do that for exactly a minute to fully re-turn her. But if my guess is right, holding it for thirty seconds will bridge her mind back to before she was turned. The result will be she won't remember Santonaga, which means he won't realise she's being re-turned, but she will still be linked to him so hopefully he won't suspect anything. "

"But don't that mean she'll still be a vampire, needing to drink blood an' all that?"

"Santonaga can choose if those he turns become vampires or not. It suits him to have the rich and powerful crave blood but for an agent like Sandra, who needs to range more freely, I suspect it's more convenient to keep her turned but human."

Before the sheer horror of the act could stop me, I kneeled, made a cut in Sandra's neck and put my mouth over it. Warm blood flowed over my lips as I pressed saliva into the wound. All the time, I concentrated hard on our last moment of normality together, chatting in my new gaff about all the silly bollocks of everyday life; trying to force that image into her mind. Then Ambrose tapped me on the shoulder to signal the half minute was up. I leaned back, took the napkin he held out, pushed it against the cut.

"How long before we know?" I said.

"The spell I used to put her out would hold a normal person for at least twelve hours. But with that much power in her blood, yours *and* Santonaga's, I'd expect it to be much—"

Sandra's eyes flicked open and her chest heaved as she broke back into consciousness. She sat up, pulled my hand away from her neck, checked her fingers, saw the blood.

"Jack? Where the hell am I, and why is me neck bleeding?"

Her gaze flicked around the room, taking in the broken glass, Ambrose, me, her black body suit.

"I'll get some tea," said Ambrose, heading for the kitchen.

Sandra leaned against the sofa, eyes flashing a dozen different lights.

"This ain't your flat, Jack; where are we?"

"Is that the last thing you remember; standing on the balcony, looking at the Thames?"

"Yes . . . no. Oh God, I thought they was *dreams*."

For a few minutes, I watched helplessly as shadows of understanding darkened her eyes. Every so often she focussed on me briefly, frowning, realising Jackie Stapleton was more than a bit mixed up with what had happened.

"We're in Halifax, Canada," I said.

Ambrose put a tray on the floor next to her. Absently, she poured milk into the tea, stirred it, sipped from the cup, her mind obviously struggling with the where and what, not to mention the bleedin' who.

"Where'd all this glass come from?" she said.

"I'll tell you about it later," I said. "But for now, if Ambrose don't mind, I reckon you need a shower."

I didn't say it but I also thought she should get out of the assassin's uniform, in case it fused her thoughts back into the original reason she'd come here.

"Yeah, that's not a bad idea," she said, putting down the cup. "I feel right dirty, for some reason."

Ambrose led her off to the bathroom. I found a dustpan and brush in the kitchen and swept up all the broken glass. Then I poured two more whiskies.

Ambrose returned to the living room, took the glass and sat again.

"The Bellers' influence seems to be stronger in her at the moment," he said. "She hasn't yet remembered anything to do with Santonaga. I suggest you keep it that way."

"Any tips on how?"

"You said she was kidnapped on a date with you. So, why don't you pick up where you left off? That'll help to keep her on the right side. Even better, have sex: the exchange of such energy will really boost her resistance to Santonaga. But no arguments or rows; the slightest weakness could have her snapping back to the shadow side. Don't give her any reason to doubt the way you feel about her, Jack."

TWELVE

Whoppa Count Rising

BUGGER, BUGGER, BUGGERING buggery with seconds of bugger. What was I supposed to *do*?

But by the time Sandra came out of the shower, swaddled in a big blue bathrobe, towelling off her hair and looking a lot more like herself at last, I'd decided.

"Hey," I said. "How about you get dressed then I take you out for a special meal?"

She smiled. "That'd be good. I know you have to explain about what's happened to me, Jack. But it'll make it easier if it's part of our next date."

While she dressed, I told Ambrose about Meera.

He shook his head slowly when I'd finished. "Tough one, Jack. I can't really help you. My love life has been pretty complicated, too."

"Because you're a wizard?"

"No, because I'm a perpetual bachelor boy who has commitment issues, according to the last woman I dated, anyway. Mind you, that was back when I was a young man of fifty-three."

"I hate lying to her."

"You already have. You didn't tell her about the Bellers, did you?"

"We'd only had one date!"

"I would have thought that was the perfect time to tell her: right at the start, before she'd formed any illusions about you being normal."

"Hey, I thought you couldn't help me?"

He nodded and I turned to see Sandra, red hair long and shining, looking a little lost in the baggy jeans and jumper Ambrose must have lent her.

"I need to get some clothes," she said.

There was an awkward silence which Ambrose broke by saying, "You two must be hungry. I know a very good fish restaurant on the harbour."

"Sounds great," she said. "Jack?"

"Yeah, great."

Ambrose held my gaze as he said, "But before you go, I need to have a quick word with Sandra in private."

I thought I knew what he wanted to do: put her under some kind of spell that would stop her asking me too many questions about what really happened between my balcony in London and here.

"Sure," I said. "I'll wait downstairs in the lobby."

About fifteen minutes later, Sandra joined me and we headed for the harbour. She skipped down the hill, me half-skipping, like kids half our age. Whatever Ambrose did to her, it seemed to have worked, even if that just increased my guilt at her having her mind messed with yet again.

Over a bottle of wine in the restaurant, we talked, and she remembered everything right up to the moment before she got yanked into the sky by Santonaga. She chatted away about my lie detector jape in the Turkish restaurant, and the spag bog she cooked in my new gaff, all the time avoiding anything more recent, like what the hell we were doing several thousand miles from home. So it seemed Ambrose's method must be holding.

"Penny for 'em?" she said after I'd gone quiet for a few moments.

"I'm not sure they're worth that much, actually."

"Tell me about your mum, when she was alive," she said.

"Well, she was pretty weird in a lot of ways," I said. "I mean, she loved me and all, but she believed in kids getting on with their lives, adults with theirs. So she gave me a great gift, really, which was the freedom to be meself. She didn't even interfere when the rozzers—well, that don't matter."

"When the rozzers what?"

"Caught me lifting a bit of copper pipe from a building site."

So there it was, the first of many whoppers to come, no doubt.

"What did she die of?"

"Officially, pneumonia, but I think it was really a broken heart. Dad decided to take his freedom to the ultimate and bunked off for a new life in Spain. Mum hardly said a word, just bottled it all up. You'd have thought she'd never even been married. But you know what I'll never forgive him for? Not just going but leaving her because he'd convinced himself she didn't care. He chose to mistake her generosity for indifference."

"How old were you when she died?"

"Twenty-eight, and I can tell by your expression you want to ask me how come I didn't move out of Mum's house."

She frowned. "But you obviously did. You've got your own place on the Thames."

Whopper number two. God, I was crap at this lying game.

"Well, yeah, I did eventually. But unlike most blokes, I wasn't in any rush to go it alone."

"But you don't strike me as a mummy's boy."

I leaned back to let the waiter place the main course on our table, asked him to fetch another bottle of wine, which in a way was another whoppa.

"Nah, I don't think I was. I guess the main reason I didn't strike out on me own early was that I never really related to other people my age." Bellers excepted, of course. "Besides, I spent a lot of time in me room, inventing stuff."

"Well, that's probably more useful than what most boys spend time in their rooms doing."

The food was good, the wine unwinding, the restaurant full of what the French call ambience and we Cockneys refer to as a bleedin' good time, and I don't know, maybe I just decided to let meself off the hook for a bit. So I asked her about her family, despite knowing that's a sure way to a girl's heart.

"My parents live in Norfolk, on a narrow boat, would you believe?" she said. "When Dad retired, they decided to sell the house and spend the rest of their lives pootling about the Broads . . ."

And so it went on. I heard about her friends and work colleagues, and what TV programmes she liked; somewhere in it all we had dessert and finished the wine, and had brandies.

She took my arm as we walked back up the hill and it wasn't until we reached the road with my B & B in that I realised I'd not thought about where she was going to stay.

"Sandra," I said, "I'm pretty sure Ambrose won't mind putting you up for the night."

Her face clouded briefly and I feared for the shadow returning, but then she nodded, and said, "Well, you know what they say about the third date."

I escorted her to Ambrose's apartment and fortunately the wine and general exhaustion convinced her to go straight to bed.

Ambrose had been writing as we came in and I asked him what about.

"You need to sleep too, Jack," he said. "Let's just say I'm accelerating my efforts to find a cure. I've even got my students working on it, too, but don't worry: they have no idea why."

"I forgot about your students. How did they come about?"

He shrugged. "If a man's learnt anything worth knowing, he has a duty to the universe to pass it on."

"Well, since you put it like that . . ."

I thanked him for looking after Sandra, said goodbye, but at the door, I turned to face him again. "You never said: why didn't you decide to do something about Santonaga before I came here?"

"I'm old, Jack. Maybe I didn't really care what happens back home any more. I've got my shield here; this is the last place on Earth Santonaga will try to take over and I'll be dead by the time he does."

"Nice story. But I don't believe you."

"Because I'm helping you now?"

"No, because wizards believe in life after death, and you wouldn't want to reincarnate in a world run by bloodjackers and quasi-vamps."

"Actually not all wizards believe in the after-life, Jack."

I left, the wine leading me toward bedsville and at least a few hours of happy oblivion before the whoppa count started rising again.

THIRTEEN

An Old-Fashioned Kind of Guy

BEFORE BREAKFAST THE NEXT morning, I phoned Meera on the secure line I'd set up before leaving London. I knew it was the middle of the night there but figured she'd still be awake.

"Hi."

"Jack? How are you?"

"Pretty good. I found Ambrose."

"Fantastic! Can he help?"

"He's working on a cure, but I think I'm going to be here for a few days at least. How are things there?"

"Not great. We need a weapon, a tactic, something we can tackle the bad guys with. Well, something we can *find* them with first. Everyone's putting on a brave face, but they're getting restless with nothing to do."

"Dan and Sarah?"

"They're fine. But they've had plenty to catch up with, especially Dan. He's at me all day long, wanting to know about the Bellers and the rozz—MI5."

"Meera; something's come up here."

I might have to lie to Sandra, but I could tell Meera the truth, most of it at least. So I went through the crashing window, the fight, the amnesia . . . but not the meal last night.

Meera was quiet for a long time after I'd finished, and all the while my guts churned worse than when I'd waited to hear if the rozzers were willing to fund my inventions, back when I left school and needed to find gainful employment.

"Jack? Here's what I think: you have to do whatever it takes to keep Sandra on the right side. If she reverts now, it won't just affect us, it'll be the end of Ambrose and he's the best chance the world has right now."

"*Any*thing?"

"Yes, anything."

So it was I spent breakfast not tasting much, talking to the landlady without knowing what I'd said, then walking to Ambrose's place with the sea wind whistling a vacuum through me mind.

Sandra looked real relaxed, on the sofa with the morning light flaring up her red hair. Ambrose sat opposite, so I settled down next to her. He said, "We've been chatting," just as if it was the most natural thing in the world for him to do.

"Really?" I said. "What about? The world economy? Philosophy? The effects of Christian fundamentalism on US politics in the late Twentieth Century?"

"No," said Sandra. "Just life and things."

"This is a wise woman, Jack. She understands you much better than you think."

Later, Sandra and I drove out to a rocky bit of coastline, then took a walk along the cliff top, the sea breeze making our flesh pimple.

Under an over-hanging rock, I put down a blanket I'd borrowed from Ambrose and we sat out of the wind, watching the gulls on the wave tops, waiting I suppose for the next part of the play to take place.

I put my arm around her shoulders and kissed her. And you know what? It felt good. *I* felt bad, but the kiss winged through my nervous system like a good will sirocco.

When we broke the kiss, she smiled. "I've been ready for that since my first glass of wine last night."

"I think I know what you mean. But I reckon you should wait a bit longer. Make sure you're strong enough."

"Okay. But I'm starting to remember more things: a room in a tower in a castle—but I don't recall ever staying in a castle, did I?"

What could I say? She'd probably been held at some private castle Santonaga owned. But the last thing I wanted to do was revive that kind of memory.

"Butlins in Clacton has a guest house in a mock castle tower, I've heard."

"I wouldn't be seen dead in Butlins . . . would I?"

"Good family fun and terrific value. Top class cabaret entertainment for the adults and an endless supply of chips and chicken nuggets to keep the kids soporific."

"O—*kay* . . . so maybe I saw an ad on the TV or something. Just promise me you never took me to a bleedin' holiday camp."

"Hey—look around."

"*Did* you bring me here, Jack?"

Naturally, this had me wondering if Ambrose's spell was weakening. On the other hand, she didn't seem too anxious, just curious.

"Let's just say you were compelled to follow me," I said.

"Well, I never could resist a good set of knobbly knees."

Another restaurant, another easy time. We drank a lot of wine again, in my case I admit to stop my mind from churning through its endless cycle of reason.

With the moon hanging in the black before us, we walked back up the hill but as I steered us toward Ambrose's, Sandra pulled us the other way.

"I'm ready, Jack."

In my room, I poured more wine, delaying, hoping even that she might drink too much and pass out. But it seemed that alcohol just made her more sensuous, which led to her smiling at one point, standing up and slowly taking off her dress.

"Wow . . ."

She must have gone shopping that morning, before I picked her up. Either that or Ambrose was a cross-dressing wizard. She wore lacy black bra, panties, stockings and suspenders.

"I figured you have old-fashioned tastes," she said, "and judging by that extra fold in your trousers, I'd say I was right."

Thing was, her sexiness was powered by her generosity. She was doing this for me, and getting off on that, expecting me to do the same for her. So, if I backed out now, all her giving would invert, and no doubt turn her back.

At least, that's what I told myself as I stood and put my arms around her, kissing her. Without taking her mouth from mine, she unbuttoned my shirt, then my trousers. Breaking away, I finished removing my clothes as she reached behind to unhook her bra. I stepped forward, slipped my hands under the lace, thrilling at the feel of her nipples.

On the bed, me on my back, her lifting herself up and down, my hands cupping her breasts, tickled by the curtain of red hair swinging between us, I reminded myself that this was necessary, that this would keep her essentially Sandra.

Then she climbed off me, on to her back, opening her legs. I knelt between them, suddenly wary. For now I had to lead.

"Fuck me, Jack," she said, and God help me but I swear a shadow flickered in the corners of her eyes.

I pushed into her and she raised her buttocks to improve the angle.

"More," she said.

Thing was, I didn't usually last very long and did my best then to let go as quick as possible, hoping she'd be disappointed. Although that would test the shadow, somehow it seemed the most honest option. So I didn't hold back, expecting it to be over in seconds.

But who'd have thought it? When I tried to go, blow me down if I didn't.

"God, Jack," she said, "that's amazing."

"Turn round," I said. That way always did for me.

She smiled, got on to her knees, and I rammed away but still couldn't finish. I wrapped her suspenders in my fingers and pulled, hoping that would finally set me off but I just kept thundering on like some Cockney porn star.

"Jack, I'm coming!"

Bloody hell, so was I, at last. The first time I'd ever coincided with a woman.

Wouldn't you just know it.

FOURTEEN

What Good's Audionic Harmony When Your Boyfriend's Bonking the Barmaid?

MY HEAD WAS SPINNING after the phone call with Jack. I'd told him to do what was necessary, and knew that he would. He'd put the world first. But he was a man. I tried to convince myself I didn't have time to think about it but all the same I was glad when Professor Blandford called a meeting in the Moose Hall.

We'd cleaned up the place in the few days Jack had been away. Seems odd that we would want to make everything spick and span, when people were being killed or having their souls or wills or whatever taken over by a phantom in their blood. But the remaining Bellers had brought their families inside and I suppose they wanted them to feel at home, as far as that was possible. All the same, I noticed they'd turned their attentions to the bar first, making sure it remained stocked and open. Young Trevor still served there. Santonaga had not bothered to kill him in the attack, but all the same he'd moved in permanently with the rest of us, just to be safe.

Of course, we'd also been using as many of M15's monitoring devices as we dared, trying desperately to track Santonaga, and to extrapolate how many more he may have turned. I was hoping the Professor might have more news on that front.

Just before the meeting began, I decided to look in on Jack's family. They'd made themselves at home in a two room suite near the armoury. Finding it empty, I went to the kitchens.

"Hi, Sarah," I said, "where's Dan?"

She sat at a large table, peeling onions, with various pots bubbling on the steel stoves behind her. The Bellers, of course, had a hi-tech kitchen and used to employ a couple of top chefs but they'd understandably resigned immediately after the attack.

Her auburn hair was tied back with a scarf, face ruddy from the kitchen's heat.

"Sam's helping him make hisself a Beller's suit. I could hardly object since it might save his life. But I ain't sure Sam's the best role model for that boy."

"Shouldn't you be getting a suit, too?"

She put down her knife. "Tell you what, Meera darlin'; I wouldn't mind getting me one of *you*. But there ain't time to get the training, not to mention the necessary physique. So, much as I know it looks like women's lib got put back forty years here, I reckon the best thing I can do is at least make sure we all get fed right."

"What are you making?"

"Shepherd's pie."

"Could you put some curry powder in it for me?"

"Um, I suppose . . ."

"I'm joking. Curry makes me fart."

She laughed. "How's Jack?"

I told her about the phone call with Jack and what I'd given him permission to do.

"I love Jack an' all," she said, "but he can be such a bleedin' idiot at times."

"But he *has* to keep Sandra thinking everything's okay."

"Yeah, maybe. But that don't stop him making sure you know how he feels, does it?"

"I'm not sure either of us has had time for too many feelings, actually."

I wished she hadn't looked at me with such kindness then.

Just about every current resident was present by the time I arrived at the Moose Hall: fifteen Bellers, three agents including myself, and the Professor. With a slight shock, I noticed Dan sitting on a sofa next to Sam, but I made myself smile encouragingly at him. He was too young for this in many ways but with what might be coming at us soon, I thought for once Sam probably had the right idea in including him.

The Professor cleared his throat. "Thank you all for coming," he said. "I wanted to make sure we're all up to date on events, then I think we have some important decisions to make."

He leaned against the mantelpiece, flames from the log fire throwing orange lights across his lower body. He took a sip from his coffee mug and continued.

"Agents Lee, Morris and I have spent the day trying without success to locate Santonaga. What makes it difficult is that so far there are very few ripples on the surface of his plans to focus our attention. It's weird, but while we barricade ourselves down here and struggle to find a way to save the country, the country is going its usual sweet way above without the slightest clue anything might be wrong.

"But at least our computers have collected enough data to work out Santonaga's likely plan. First, to recap, this is what we actually know about him: he's a bloodjacker. When he bites someone, he either kills them or activates his saliva to enslave their will. We're assuming one reason he killed people early on was to side-track us into believing we had a straightforward vampire on our hands. But the truth is, none of those he murdered has risen again, or shown any signs of doing so. As for those he has turned, we're pretty sure he's infected at least fifty so far."

"So what *is* his bleedin' plan?" said Malcolm.

"We believe he's building a blood-nerve sonic matrix. The computers have interrogated police and personal data, trying to spot patterns of altered behaviour and we suspect that those fifty are extremely well-connected people. Also, they have common genetic links: ideal for supplying resonance grids."

"Which means what exactly?" said Malcolm.

"Once it's built and he activates it, he'll have access to the minds of those who hold power in this country. He'll be in control, basically. We also suspect before that, he's going to try to turn the minds of the masses, too; to prime them for the power take-over. Then, he'll have *every*one under his influence. Maybe not directly, since he's going to need to farm out matrix points to an extent, but he'll be the one with the strings tied to his fingers."

He let that sink in for a few moments. I thought about asking *why* anyone would want that kind of control but the answer wasn't really important. Some people just lust after power, which is all you really need to know to stop them any way you can.

"Anyway, the good news, as such," said the Professor at last, "is that I think I've put together a blood sensor that can tell if a person is carrying Santonaga's taint. Which may give us a chance to poke some holes in his matrix, and at least buy us time until we come up with a better plan."

"Consider us all volunteers, Prof," said Stewey. "We're going stir crazy in here anyway."

"Don't forget, those who've been turned have developed powers too. They may be tormented by them, not having your training in how to handle the side effects, but that won't stop them lashing out if they sense you're on to them."

"Thanks for the warning, Prof," said Sam. "But then we know what his plans are going to be for the rest of us Bellers, since we're all pretty common, eh?"

The Professor sighed. "Sam, I'll do my best to get access to all the places you're likely to find his people. I don't know who's been turned at the agency, but I guess we'll just have to take a few risks."

"What about Uncle Jack?" said Dan, making my stomach trill.

"Meera?" said the Professor.

I thought for a moment about holding back, but then let my instinct decide that they all had the right to know.

"Jack's in Halifax, Nova Scotia," I said. "He's found Ambrose, the wizard who made the Bellers."

I waited while the Bellers swapped looks and all spoke at the same time.

"*And* who made Santonaga!" I shouted.

"So, we know what to do!" said Sam, face hopelessly excited.

I shook my head. "It's not that simple. Ambrose made Santonaga well; stopping him, I suspect, is going to take more than a magic formula or a few occult words. Having said that, Ambrose appears to be fairly confident of developing an antidote to the turned."

"Wait a minute," said Pete, the very fact he'd spoken up for once, grabbing everyone's attention. "Why should we trust Ambrose if he made Santonaga?"

"I think we just have to trust Jack," I said. "He told me that Ambrose was forced to make Santonaga what he is; but at least he built in a delaying factor, which gave you guys the time to develop powers that might stop him. Jack's convinced that Ambrose really does want to help."

"He didn't do much to stop half of us getting killed, did he?" said Sam.

I had no answer to that. I wasn't sure I trusted Ambrose either, but the fact was we didn't have much else going for us right then.

"So, when's Uncle Jack coming back?" said Dan.

"That's a little complicated," I said. "He was followed to Halifax by one of Santonaga's turned, directed to kill him. Fortunately, he and Ambrose managed to overpower her."

"Her?" said Sam.

"Sandra Hollins. Jack told you she got captured by Santonaga, remember?"

"Yeah, but I got the impression Sandra weren't no posh bird and didn't the Prof say Santonaga prefers to *kill* working class mongos?"

"Santonaga turned her," I said, "because Jack dated her and he wanted to firstly, hurt Jack and secondly, have an assassin who could catch him off guard when the time came to kill him."

The Professor said, "Sandra was dropped outside our headquarters, in a semi-comatose state. She appeared to have no memory of what had happened to her since Santonaga kidnapped her. But when Jack came to visit her, she leapt at him with intent to do serious damage, leading us to believe she was actually faking amnesia, probably to draw Jack in close before trying to kill him. Her attempt was stopped fairly easily but I now think that may have been intentional. Santonaga probably suspected Jack would track down Ambrose, so wanted him to live at least long enough to do so."

"Sandra now really doesn't remember what Santonaga did to her," I said. "Ambrose found a way to repress Santonaga's influence in her blood, but she's crucially balanced. And if she slips back into his mind-hold, he'll know for sure Ambrose is still alive and go after him."

"What's keeping her onside?" said Sam.

"Jack's taking her on dates, romancing her just as if the last few weeks never happened."

"Oh, great," said Sam, "so while he's bonking the barmaid, we're all putting our necks on the block."

"That's not fair, Sam," I said, even though I partly agreed with him. "If Santonaga gets Ambrose and thereby destroys the cure, there really isn't any hope."

The meeting wound up around ten-thirty which was too late for the Bellers to go looking for the turned. So they did what they always did and went to the bar. I went too, this time.

I got our table of four the first round of drinks then found myself next to Pete. I took a long swallow of lager, delighting in the sharp kick of it against my throat. He looked at his whisky and ice, as if not sure whether to drink it; then I sussed.

"You're listening to the ice cracking, aren't you?"

He smiled. "Anything put in a container, with time melting away at its very existence, quickly develops a language."

"What are the cubes saying?"

He listened for a few more moments, then said, "Drink, you Cockney bastard! Drink! Can't you see we're dissolving into bleedin' nothingness here."

He finished the drink in one go then stood. "Whisky?" he said.

It was funny, the first time I'd ever drank spirits was when Jack gave me brandy not so long ago. I'd always thought that road led to lack of self control which for Meera Nath, fast rising special agent, was worse than catching Asian flu.

"Double, please," I said.

After a few large whiskies, which clearly affected me more than Pete, he said, "I didn't want to say it in the meeting, but I reckon there's worse on the way."

"What do you mean?" I thought I said, but judging by his indulgent grin, must have sounded more like, "WACHAMEEN?"

"Any language is multi-faceted, no single level of which is the actual essence of it. Academics think the dictionary is the definer but it ain't; it's just the gravel bed. Poets think it's the rhythm of words, but it ain't that, either. Sam over there thinks it's what helps you put food on the table, and gets you laid. But actually the essence of a language is in the atmosphere it builds with other languages. It's the same for people but we've mostly lost the knowledge of that."

I'd like to say I was following all this but to be honest, my head felt like a helicopter with one blade shorter than the others. "Hey, Pete," I said. "I'm feeling a bit piddled, so do you think you could get to the point. No offence."

He laughed. "None bleedin' taken. What I'm trying to say is that I've been monitoring the atmosphere between the languages out there, and the changes in it. You can't turn even a dozen people's blood without it causing ripples in the language matrix. Hijacked blood affects voice boxes, which puts crosscurrents in the voice tides . . . I don't really know how to explain it, and it doesn't matter. What does, is that these ripples are building rapidly. I sense it only needs a few more people to be turned, then the effect can go exponential. So, I'm saying I agree with the Prof. Unfortunately."

"But shortly—surely—sound alone can't turn people's blood."

He smiled wryly, nodded around the room, and I blushed.

"It won't affect everyone," he said. "Same as Bow Bells didn't turn every embryo."

"That's a point: how come Santonaga can turn adults but Bow Bells only worked on babies?"

He shrugged. "Maybe the bells could have been made to work on adults, but that would be a corrupting influence. As babies, the Bellers could still develop their own free wills, even with their super . . ."

"Hmmm . . ."

My blood felt totally turned at that point. Pete smiled, took away my drink, stood and held out his arm. I grabbed on to it and he helped pull me to my feet.

Just outside my room, he said, "I'm sorry about Sandra. You and Jack have real audionic harmony."

"How dyaknow?" I said, although not really sure what he'd actually said.

"I listen to tapes of phone calls all the time; have them on in the background, the same way people do with music. I don't hear it unless something stands out. Your voice and Jack's are completely different, but the sonic waves fit together perfectly."

I thanked him for getting me back safely, pushed open the door, kicked it shut again, fell on to my bed and cursed Jack bloody Stapleton until I fell asleep.

Maybe it was the hangover, maybe it was still feeling angry at Jack, but I just had to get out of Bellers HQ the next morning.

"Jeeves," I said, walking out of the shower, "I need to get to MI5."

"The quickest route would be to take the Bellers' tube, ma'am."

"But I'm not a Beller."

"Indeed, ma'am. Which is why yesterday Mr Stapleton informed me you are now authorised to use the system."

I felt a swell of pride, but then caution had me say, "Are you sure it was Jack, and not someone impersonating him?"

I wasn't sure but thought I heard a sniff of disdain. "I have thirty-two check points for Mr Stapleton, Ms Nath, including speech patterns and voice resonance grids. There is no doubt as to his identity. Besides, he sounded a little guilty about something, and that is not a tone one would expect to find in an enemy, ma'am."

Guilty? Good. That should soften his yardstick somewhat.

I finished towelling then nude, walked to the wardrobe.

"Jeeves, are you still monitoring?"

"Forgive me, ma'am; I was. I thought Mr Stapleton might appreciate a picture or two."

I shook my head. "Look, I know you're a highly advanced A.I. but you can't just cater for the desires of your Beller masters without considering the feelings of—"

"Ma'am? The feelings of?"

On the other hand . . .

I sucked in my stomach, pushed out my chest and tried to pout without looking as if I'd just swallowed my own chin.

"Snap away, Jeeves," I said.

With any luck, they'd be waking up about now; maybe she'd even get to the phone before him.

"If I may say so, ma'am, comparing your dimensions to my somewhat extensive database of Beller males' anatomical preferences for the female form, you score at the exceedingly scorched end of 'Hot Babe.'"

"Thank you, Jeeves. It's a pity you're not embodied yourself."

"Oh, I don't know, ma'am. I shouldn't really care for all that excreting, perspiring and the overall decaying of flesh after puberty."

"Killjoy. Do I have to wear a suit to use the tube?"

"Yes. As soon as you drop into the shaft at the back of your rooms, I will arrange for a suit to join you."

"I've changed my mind, Jeeves: don't send those pictures to Jack."

"As you wish, ma'am. But I'll hold on to the copies, just in case."

I sipped coffee for a few minutes before leaving, trying to force a form to my thoughts. But in the end I decided the best approach for now was to wing it at the agency. My people had been helpful since the raid, but aside from Lee and Morris, not exactly pro-active. I figured this may just be old mistrust of the Bellers' more cavalier approach, but couldn't be sure.

I threw some clothes into a bag, then at the back of my room, pressed my thumb to the wall patch. The round steel cover slid back from the tube shaft.

Stomach fluttering at the thought the hard air fields may have been sabotaged, I threw in my bag and jumped after it.

To my relief, about ten metres down, my body slowed to a halt. The shaft walls glowed in pale blue light and a dark shroud separated from it to wrap around my body.

Once the suit was fitted, I dropped again, this time into a pod, lying on my back in darkness broken only by the soft lights of comms around my head.

"I'm ready, Jeeves," I said, and immediately the pod shot forward, into the black.

"Your journey will take a little over one minute, ma'am."

"How close to MI5 HQ does the tube take me?"

"It stops right under the building."

"But I didn't think the agency had access to the tube."

"It doesn't. And the Bellers would not use this route normally, either. But Mr Stapleton built it, with Professor Sandford's help, for emergency or priority use."

"I see."

"To anticipate your next question, ma'am, Mr Stapleton instructed me to send you on this route should you wish to visit your headquarters—for safety reasons."

"Did he now? It seems as if Mr Stapleton's guilty feelings have got my arse well and truly covered."

"And a very nice—"

"That's enough pre-programmed flannel, Jeeves." The pod slowed rapidly. "Are you still in range when I'm in the building?"

"I *could* be, ma'am, but if you contact me in there, it's very likely the agency's own comms will detect us."

It figured. I'd not been based at the agency's HQ long enough to be shown the more occult uses of the internal comms systems. But given we paid Jack for a lot of his amazing inventions, it seemed likely the agency could at least tap into any transmissions made from inside its own building.

The hard air mesh lifted me up the shaft under MI5, to a cover plate that slid aside at my touch. Cautiously, I poked my head above the entrance, to find myself in a small, dimly lit room full of beige storage boxes. I climbed out and smiled at the shaft cover plate, disguised to look just like another floor tile.

I replaced the plate then put on the nondescript skirt, blouse and jacket from the bag. Pinning on my agency pass, I took a deep breath, opened the door and stepped into the basement corridor. Because I hadn't entered by the front door, as soon as a camera picked me up, comms would know I'd breached security. I headed for the stairs, then moved quickly up to the fifth floor. There, I slipped onto the main corridor where cameras would definitely be watching me closely. I walked briskly to the mostly open plan area at the front of the building, and stopped by Lucilla's receptionist.

"Hi, is Lucilla in her office?" I said, casually.

No flicker of surprise in her eyes. Good. "Yes," she said, "you're?"

"Meera Nath."

She picked up the phone. "Agent Meera Nath wants to see you, ma'am."

She frowned slightly, as if not expecting the response she received, then nodded me through.

I'd never been in the boss's office before, and the Impressionistic paintings, bright, sunny colour of the walls and large green plants were unexpected. The rest of us in the building mostly kept our work areas clear and clean; at least, that's what we found helped us concentrate best on the job.

Lucilla smiled, rose from her desk and held out her hand.

"Hello, Meera," she said, "I was hoping we could have a chat, face-to-face, soon. Please, sit. Tea, coffee?"

"Hello, ma'am," I said, shaking her hand and sitting in the chair opposite. "Actually, water would be good."

While she poured two glasses from the table to one side of her chair, I studied her briefly: short, grey hair, a strong but undistinctive face; today dressed in white shirt and black trousers. I guess, most of our leaders looked as if they could pass muster in a Mormon bank. The best security is anonymity.

Yet Lucilla also seemed to have a spark in her eye today, as if she was actually enjoying herself. She handed me a glass then settled down to study me quite openly.

"Your reports on Jack Stapleton have grown somewhat less detailed lately," she said.

I wondered if I should ignore this and plunge into the reason I was here. But if I did that, she might just conclude I'd gone native with the Bellers.

"There's been a lot of clearing up to do since the raid, and I haven't seen much of him."

"Isn't he in Halifax?" she said, expression neutral.

Well, I'd expected her to know that. Just as I knew she'd next ask me why he'd gone there. And although I'd decided not to tell her everything, mainly because I agreed with the Bellers that we needed to believe that *any*one could have been turned, it still hurt to keep intel from my superior.

"Yes, he had some personal business to deal with there," I said, "wouldn't say much about it."

She no doubt concluded I was lying, and probably knew Jack and I had slept together. But I figured she'd believe on balance it was to the agency's advantage to let me handle him in my own way, at least for now.

"We aren't aware he had any family or associates in Canada."

"He thinks his father might be there," I said, hoping that if Jack had no real idea where his dad currently was, MI5 wouldn't either.

"He took a jet and used a US aircraft carrier to refuel, just to go say hello to his father?"

I began to panic, feeling out of my depth. How did I know that the Professor, Lee or Morris hadn't been keeping her fully informed about what was really going on with the Bellers and Jack? Well, it didn't matter anyway. The fact was, someone had to do *some*thing; and I'd decided it might as well be me. So, I ploughed on.

"I think it's more than that. He's hoping his father might know something about the Bellers' genes—anything that could help us beat Santonaga."

"Jack's father was a womanising gangster; seems unlikely he'd know anything intelligent about his son's biochemical origins."

I shrugged. "Actually, I think he also wanted to get away from town for a while. He feels responsible for the attack on the Bellers, and was getting frustrated at not coming up with any leads on the killers."

"Very interesting, Meera. So why isn't it all in your report?"

"Sorry, ma'am; I've got a little behind."

She nodded. "Well, I suppose the attack was a huge shock for Jack and the survivors, not to mention the families of those murdered."

"And how are we doing with regard to tracking down Santonaga?"

Her gaze flicked to the screen at her left, no doubt learning that I'd entered the building unconventionally. I had to speed this up.

"Not too well," she said. "Of course, it doesn't help that the Bellers won't allow us to give the bodies to our forensics team."

"Professor Paul has run some tests on the bodies and the surroundings, but it seems the attackers entered and left again clean."

"Speaking of entering clean: why didn't you take the front door like everyone else?"

"Honestly? Because I don't know who to trust. Santonaga has the power to turn people. Anyone in MI5 could be in his pocket."

"Including me?"

"If you'd been turned, ma'am, I think you'd have had me locked away by now."

Or let me go so she could have me followed.

She smiled. "Fair enough. All right, I won't ask you how you got in—although I think I can guess—but why did you come here today?"

"I need you to grant me gold clearance."

"No one below Director level has ever been given gold clearance. Why do you want it?"

"I'm going to find Santonaga."

"What makes you think you can do better than the agents already looking for him?"

"I have something he wants."

"Which is?"

"Access to Jack. Once he sniffs that I'm looking for him, he'll come for me."

"And how will you stop him capturing you?"

"I can't. Professor Paul and the Bellers have developed a chemical they believe can kill Santonaga. It just needs someone to get in close enough to inject him with it."

I was lying. My plan was to get close enough to shoot Santonaga in the head with an exploding bullet. He might have survived Jack's sonic lance but I figured even a vampire would have trouble recovering from having his brain blasted seven whichways.

"But why do you need *gold* clearance?"

"You probably know that Jack and I had sex," I said, and when she didn't change expression, continued. "I believe that Jack's sperm will have set up sonic ripples in my blood, which can be detected by Santonaga or those he's turned. All I need is access to the kinds of places they may inhabit."

Gold clearance meant I could go anywhere in the country—inside any government or royal building, no matter how secret. I didn't need to spell out to Lucilla that Santonaga was targeting the rich and powerful, and while she wouldn't want to grant access to their homes and institutions, equally she couldn't let him continue turning people until a point came when the country was his by default.

"I'm not at all convinced this plan will work," she said. "But I concede we have few other options at the moment. Very well. Go to Security and pick up the pass."

"Thank you," I said, standing.

"Meera, one more thing. It was expected that you and Jack Stapleton would bond, but your future with the government depends entirely on you knowing where the line is and not stepping over it."

"Yes, ma'am."

On the way to Security, I tried to relax. But the fact was, if Lucilla had been turned she may right that moment have been sending me to a lifetime in jail, or even direct to Santonaga, never mind my feelings for Jack. But someone had to take chances, or we'd never find him.

To my relief, Security simply took iris and fingerprint readings to confirm my identity, then with little more than a raised sceptical eyebrow or two, handed me the most powerful pass ever created in Britain.

I saw no reason not to leave by the main door, so soon was heading through the crowds to the public underground system.

It seemed strange that people looked so normal, unaware of the danger they were in. Or, then again, maybe the danger would simply engulf them at some point and change them without any visible difference to their lifestyles. They would still commute to work, eat egg mayonnaise sandwiches for lunch, fail to explain how they really felt to their bosses, go home and watch the television. The only difference—their wills tied to Santonaga instead of the general habit of life.

Which in many ways was just like life had been for the peasants back in the robber baron days. Their lives were ruled by routine, and the fact their Lord owned them made little difference, only that he had the lion's share of the wealth and could have them destroyed should they ever decide to think for themselves for once.

But that was it, what I'd signed on for with the agency: to protect people who for the most part didn't know they needed protecting and who would never know if you'd succeeded anyway. He wasn't an agent, but Jack had made the same promise.

I sat on the train to Whitechapel, surrounded by faces occupied with tiny issues, things that ultimately meant little to the universe, to God, or even to the world. Yet that was the covenant we all had with the divine: no person's trouble was more important than any other's.

Santonaga was wrong, simply because he believed his way should be everybody's way. Even if he made the trains run on time when he took control, lowered taxes, made us all immortal, he was wrong—because he wasn't God.

I smiled, bringing a cautious look from the man opposite. I didn't believe in God. But I damn well wanted my right to change my mind. Santonaga would remove that right.

So, fuck him.

Hilary let me into the house. I made a cup of tea, sat at a work bench and said, "Screen please."

"Of course," she said, "but only because Jack has programmed me to allow you access; not because of that gold pass in your pocket."

I didn't change expression. Instead of what I'd intended, I used the computer to order some CDs. Then I put my coat back on and left the house.

Hilary had just warned me that her systems had been breached. The only way she could know about my gold pass was if another system with that information on it had jacked hers. The most likely suspect was the agency, but Jack had told me he'd made Hilary rozzer-proof, as he put it. Which meant Santonaga or his agents had dug into our comms further than we'd thought.

I walked to the end of Jack's road, then a hundred yards along the main street to a cafe. Inside, I went to the counter to order a cheese sandwich and a cup of tea. As it was being made, I said, "Are you Steve?"

He looked up briefly from spreading butter on to the two white slices. "Guilty."

What had Jack told me to say?

"Do you reckon the Hammers will manage to hang on to their brightest young stars next season, mate?"

He finished the sandwich, put it on a plate, smiled. "Only if they can afford to pay 'em with more than jellied eels."

Oh, damn it; what came next?

Steve put the plate on the counter, expression blank.

Ah! "I always preferred a nice pot of winkles myself."

"Take a seat. I'll bring your tea over."

I sat and took a bite of sandwich although my stomach felt too nervous to really hold it down. Hammers, winkles? Did Jack realise how incongruous that made an Asian woman look?

Steve brought over a cup of tea, placing a napkin next to it, a slight bulge indicating it hid something. I waited till he returned to the counter, picked up the napkin, wiped my mouth with it, then dropped it and the keys it had been concealing on to my lap.

I made myself finish the sandwich and drink the tea before leaving the cafe, nodding to Steve as I went, in what I hoped was a normal customer's way. In the street, I took the keys out of my handbag, memorised the address on the label then removed it, to dispose of later.

Jack had told me to take the third street on the left, which matched the name on the label. Ordinary terraced houses lined the street, but about fifty yards down it, they gave way to a row of five garages. I went to the middle door and used one of the keys to unlock the heavy duty padlock which protected it. Knowing Jack, the padlock would be extra-resistant to attack, probably packed with nano-resistors. But it opened easily enough to the right key, and I swung up the door, slipped inside then pulled it down before anyone could see what the garage held.

I flicked on the light switch Jack had told me would be a yard to my right, and the utter blackness gave way to bright white light. In the middle of the otherwise empty garage, something sat under a large black sheet. All I knew was Jack said it could get me where I wanted to go fast, and that he'd programmed it to respond to my intuition, whatever that meant.

I pulled back the sheet and smiled: a red and white Honda 50 motor scooter. Innocuous, old-fashioned and no doubt modified beyond the wildest dreams of any pro motorcycle racer.

Yet, as I sat on the red leather seat and placed my hands on the rubber grips, everything looked normal enough. I put on the red helmet, pulled down the visor and turned the ignition key.

A reassuring rumble came from the engine. I climbed off, opened the door and wheeled the bike on to the street.

Intuition? Hmmm . . .

"Bike: take me to the home of Lord Stratton of Surrey."

» FIFTEEN «

Manorisms

FINE LINES OF YELLOW LIGHT moved across my visor, like a sensory net. I had the feeling it was reading my irises. A voice in my ear said, "Just put your hands on the grips; I'll direct you there immediately, Ms Nath."

"Jeeves 2.0?"

"Not even 1.0," he replied as we pulled away from the curb. "My name is Bertie and I am a completely independent version of the Bellers' comms identity. Mr Stapleton established me—turn right here please, ma'am—to be untraceable via Jeeves or any other system. I have one million data filters spread around the globe which continually cross cut each other, ensuring my detection is impossible by outside agencies."

"How far can we go on one tank of fuel, Bertie?"

"There is no fuel in the tank. This machine runs on solar power: every part of its surface is made of extremely sensitive light gathering prisms. Two hours in any kind of daylight provides another ten hours of travel. The engine sound you hear is generated by me, responding in harmony with the bike's manoeuvres."

"Weapons?"

"If we should be attacked, ma'am, just tell me where to aim and I'll do the rest."

We continued along the Embankment, following the river to Chelsea, then through Hammersmith, toward Surrey. All the while, Bertie provided me with a stream of information about Lord Stratton and his residence on the North side of Richmond Park.

"If I may ask, ma'am," he said, just as we turned into the royal park, "why Lord Stratton?"

"I saw him on television recently, talking about the House of Lords, and his eyes looked dead to me."

"I've heard the same charge made of many noble peers."

"Yes, but at the time, he was acting enthusiastically, arms waving around, that kind of thing. Yet his eyes just stayed still, black and lifeless."

He didn't reply, which just reminded me that it wasn't much to go on.

We passed a herd of deer, their coats flaring in the low sun. It would be dark soon.

Bertie had advised me to enter the stately home from the park side, rather than the main street. So I rode the bike beneath a large yew tree, growing close to the high brick wall dividing the Lord from the common man.

I climbed off and the engine stopped. The sky had darkened now and I figured the bike would be safe in the shadows, then I gasped as it disappeared.

"Copycat image resonator," said Bertie in my ear. "I suggest you keep the helmet on ma'am; you may need my comms resources."

"Sorry, Bertie; I'll feel too constrained in this. But I'll take any weapons you can give me."

The visor sent a tight beam of white light at the invisible bike, highlighting the luggage box on the back. I opened it and pulled out a spare Bellers' suit.

"The suit has weaponry that will respond to your body's bio-chemical signals, as well as to your more direct vocal commands."

I would have asked him to elaborate but decided to trust Jack instead. I took off the helmet and placed it on the bike where it promptly disappeared too. I stripped off my clothes, hid them in the bike's carrier. Naked, I stepped into the black suit and felt again that ridiculous tingle of pleasure as it tightened around my flesh.

The wall must have been twelve feet high. I put my hands on it and instantly the suit produced spikes from my fingertips, grasping the red stone. My toes did the same and soon I was pulling myself over the top, dropping down to the ground below.

I moved through some trees, to the edge of a long, wide lawn sweeping up toward a huge white stone house, fountains spraying in front of its arched windows. Because there was little cover, I decided to wait till the last of the day's light had gone. So I made myself comfortable, back against an oak tree, hidden from sight of the house.

I knew I shouldn't, but I thought about Jack. Plain and simple, I missed him. I'd never been close enough to a man to feel his absence and with a kind of low shock, I realised that I missed him on all sorts of levels: to talk to, to argue with, to make love to . . .

My body must have sent chemical triggers into my blood because the suit—the one Jack had made for me—tightened around my nipples and groin, massaging slowly.

This was ridiculous. I needed to be cold-headed. I was about to break into a powerful man's home and maybe confront him.

But then the suit varied its contractions . . . Oh, this was *good*. It speeded up, slowed down; my chest tingled with desire and my groin rippled with pleasure. Well, I had to do something while I waited, I reasoned.

Oh, *God* . . .

I forced my mind blank, waited without moving a muscle until the suit relaxed again. Much as I wanted to just let go, I couldn't step into a hostile environment with my legs trembling, all shagged out.

The sun finally dipped below the tree line and I crept out of cover, keeping close to the foliage until I reached the side of the house. I paused to consider how to enter but really had no idea; this whole escapade was instinct-driven, so I might as well stay with my gut feeling.

I ran across the pavement surrounding the fountain, water whispering in my ears. I made for the dark French doors furthest from the lighted window at the other end of the house. I remembered what Jack taught me and flicked the end of my forefinger with my thumb. Then I drew my gloved finger in a large circle around the lower glass panel of the door. I stretched the fingers of my left hand slowly three times then placed the palm of that glove on to the glass. As soon as the circle was complete, I pulled away the cut glass with my suctioned hand; laid it gently on the stone.

I climbed through the gap, relieved no alarm had sounded. I stood, waited for my eyes to adjust to the darkness. A strong smell of polish hit me and a faint trace of cigar smoke; a den, maybe. As my eyes cleared, I saw bookcases lining the walls, and fairly ornate furniture on a Persian carpet.

I ran lightly to the door, opened it, keeping out of the light of the wood-panelled corridor beyond. Where to go? I could head for the lighted room at the end of the corridor, or . . .

I made for a bare stone staircase winding down to the basement. At the bottom of the steps, a heavy wood door, light flickering under it, and music reaching my ears: *stripper* music.

I pushed but the door was locked. Carefully, I took Jack's universal pick from a pocket and worked it in the lock; the door opened and I slipped inside, crouching in the shadow of a large box. The basement was very long with exposed brick walls. Wine racks stretched along both sides for half its length. The rest of it opened into an area with a solitary chair facing a small, spot-lit stage.

A man sat with his back to me: grey hair and the straightness of his posture suggested this could be the Lord himself. On the stage a pretty young woman dressed as a maid danced to the music. Or, rather, the longer I watched the more it seemed she was *danced*.

As the music swelled and dipped, she peeled off a long black glove; then the other; twirled them stiffly then threw them to one side. She shook her hips, not quite in time with the music.

I stood up and moved quietly forward, not worried about the girl seeing me because her eyes were lifeless.

I paused, waiting for the moment Lord Stratton would be most distracted. The girl unbuttoned her blouse, her fumbling fingers confirming she was not in control of her movements.

Had Santonaga bitten her as a present to Stratton; seemed unlikely, but that would mean the Lord himself—

My thoughts were shattered as the chair clattered to one side, Stratton hurling himself at me in one smooth, impossibly fast movement.

I had no time to do anything but trust my automatic systems and Jack's suit. This frail-looking, grey-haired Lord flew at me, face exploding with hostility, teeth exposed, hands bent into claws. I suppose my very presence told him I knew what he'd become so he had no reason to bother hiding.

Just before he knocked me over, the suit hardened, stretched over my head and face. All the same, air was smashed out of my lungs and I could do nothing for those first few seconds of lying on my back. His mouth clamped around my neck, and I felt his sharp teeth pushing at the suit's fabric. The pain was so horrible I thought he must have punctured it. His breath smelt of piss.

I flexed the backs of my fingers then smashed my hardened fist against the side of his head. He fell off me, yelling in pain, and I rolled away to spring to my feet. He stood too, now studying me carefully although still with lust in various shades glinting his eyes.

"What are you?" he said.

I didn't answer. Instead, used the mask's visor to scan for old injuries to his body.

"Didn't realise the Bellers appeared in such comely shapes."

I let him approach slowly, shrugging off his tweed jacket, straightening up to presumably show me age didn't weaken him. He should have been unconscious after the blow I gave him but he didn't appear to even feel it now.

As he crept closer, with me deliberately frozen so as not to give him any clue to my intentions, I realised how difficult capturing him would be. Because that was my plan: to take a living specimen of the turned back to Bellers HQ where the Professor could hopefully work out a cure.

But as he leapt at me again, I had no time to do anything other than dip a shoulder and aim my fist at his weak heart. His hands closed around my throat and for a moment I thought their massive power would finish me. Then his eyes took on the look of a frightened boy's and he slipped to the floor, clutching at his chest.

I resisted the urge to go closer, in case he was faking; so waited until his chest stopped lifting with inhaled air. Even then, I turned first to the girl on the stage. She'd simply stopped all movement the moment he'd attacked me. Now, her limbs trembled and eyes flared with panic, as she came out of the trance.

"Are you all right?" I said, flicking away my face mask.

"Where am I; who are you?" she said.

"My name is Meera. You're in a country house in Surrey. Do you remember how you got here?"

"No . . ." Clearly, she didn't understand why she wore a maid's outfit but instinctively folded her arms as if horrified she'd been showing so much flesh. "The last thing I remember is sitting in a bar, waiting for a friend. This old bloke asked me the time and—oh, God: that's him; is he dead?"

Forgetting her own situation, she rushed to Stratton, knelt beside him. I waited, figuring she'd need a little time to come round. Big mistake.

In a flurry of violent movement, he overpowered her, sank his teeth into her neck, blood running on to her white maid's shirt. I raised my right arm, pressed the palm pad in the required sequence and fired a sonic laser from the duct on the back of my glove.

But he was fast, ducking behind the girl's head, causing me to throw up my arm as I fired, not wanting to hit her. He jumped to his feet and ran toward the door, faster than I could think. So I saw right then how unprepared we were for the raw power of these monsters. For he'd left me with a clear choice: tend to the girl or go after him.

I did a rapid calculation—the fact she'd performed to his requirements showed she'd already been bitten; to bite her again meant he'd killed her. I ran after him, feeling the suit's semi-intuitive nano-muscles giving more speed to my legs. I took the basement steps four at a time, up to the corridor, Stratton just ten yards ahead of me, glancing over his shoulder, not as frightened as he should have been.

Three strides from him I recalled that he'd kept his head at a careful angle while biting the girl, not getting blood on his clothes; then wiped his mouth with a handkerchief he'd discarded as he ran from the room.

He sidestepped smartly into a room and I followed, to find a small gathering of well-dressed people, drinking from crystal glasses. They looked up from their conversations to see Stratton composed, urbane, just rejoining his guests after a brief absence and—who on earth was that girl in the black lycra behind him?

Stratton advanced to the centre of the room, turned and said. "We have an intruder, everybody—who's been foolish enough to follow me into a gathering which includes a former Home Office Minister, a retired chief of police and two high court judges."

How many of them had been turned, I wondered, or were they completely innocent of what Stratton had become?

Then he made a mistake: nodded imperceptibly to me, indicating that I should take the opportunity to run.

Which told me that in fact not everyone in the room had been turned. And with me gone, he'd have time to dispose of the dead body in the basement.

But if I stayed, how could I convince the others of what he'd really become? Take them down to the basement? Fine, but if I couldn't persuade them, I'd be caught.

All these thoughts took only the time between his slight nod and the knowing smile he gave to the rest of his audience. Behind my back, I'd been sequencing my palm pad. Figuring he wouldn't expect me to shoot in such a public place, I whipped my hand forward and fired the sonic laser.

A high-pitched whine, a red light tracker beam and his right eyeball exploded, followed by a spray of blood and small shards of skull.

Screams from some of the guests, men rushing both toward me and the fallen Lord.

I jumped back to the doorway, turned, shouted: "He killed a maid in the basement; have his blood analysed; contact MI5 when you get the results."

Into the corridor, sprinting for the room I'd broken into earlier. Running over the moon-lit lawn, silver dew drops bouncing off my black leather boots, I realised I had no idea if Stratton could recover from a shot through the brain, of if the shock would finish off his weak heart anyway. But that wasn't the most worrying aspect of this raid. The real problem we now faced was the possibility that Santonaga's people might also be turning others. If so, how far did the chain already stretch?

My gut feeling told me Stratton at least could not change shape else he surely would have done so, to avoid me. Then again, perhaps he really believed he'd be safe surrounded by polite society. What a pity my family lives in a country where everyone talks at the same time and you can't even take a bath with any degree of privacy.

Through the wood, up the wall then I dropped lightly to my feet, back in Richmond Park. I was just about to reach for where I believed the moped to be when a flitting of black caught the corner of my eye. Before I could react, a gloved hand covered my nose and mouth and I lost consciousness.

SIXTEEN

Sharing the Old Guy's Sofa

THEY SAY WOMEN ARE BETTER actors than men. They say it's because women have a longer history of hiding the truth. They say—who the bleedin' 'ell are 'they' anyway? You know what, I reckon 'they' really means 'me'; only by saying 'they', I can go on believing it ain't yours truly who's having all these profoundly average thoughts; that it's really some group of boring farts out there, you know—the ones who write to the BBC to complain about swearing and too much sex on TV.

Which weren't the only place where too much sex was going on.

The neat and tidy nature of me hotel room just after breakfast, when we'd cleaned it up, was in strong contrast, let me tell you, to what it looked like before croissants and coffee: like a hurricane of lust had blown through it.

That morning, Sandra had gone straight out to buy some clothes and I'd sat at me laptop, trying to find the will to turn it on.

I felt like I'd built this Jack suit of armour around the real Jack. Not as in cold shiny metal and toff peacock plumes sprouting out the helmet; more as in touchy-very-feely, smiley-eyed protection. Trouble was, the more Sandra bought my passion and returned it, the worse I felt.

Sure, I could justify it by Ambrose telling me the game was up if Sandra returned to her dark self. But even if you're saving the world, it don't change the fact that pretending you love someone is going to bugger up her life when she finally finds out.

'Cos here was the thing: every time Sandra and I had sex, I thought about Meera. Every touch of Sandra's hand on my face or the shape of her smile aimed back at my smile, drove me deeper into where my heart really lay.

Oh, I suppose an analyst would tell me this was classic grass-is-always-greener syndrome; that I'd probably feel the same way about Sandra if I was with Meera.

But I knew the real score, 'cos Ambrose last night had asked me a very simple question: who did I see myself sharing a sofa with when I was an old guy? Leaving aside the distinct possibility I might not get the chance to find out, the answer popped in my head as soon as he asked it: Meera.

"You sure there isn't a bit of posh totty syndrome here?" he said when I told him. "Okay, she's Asian but she's also well-educated and talks proper."

"Hah!" I said, "if I was holding out for posh totty, why did I go romancing Sandra?"

He said nothing, the bastard, and didn't really need to. Because as soon as the question was out of me lips, I knew the answer. He topped up my glass and waited for me.

"Strewth," I said, "Sandra was the trigger."

He nodded. "I reckon you held back so long because you didn't want to face the fact that the East End family life was never going to be for you. By going out with Sandra, you showed you'd subconsciously reached the stage where you had to sort the problem or you'd never find a woman you could be with."

"Then Meera turned up. Talk about bad timing."

"Are you sure that's all it was?"

"Well, yeah; I mean, how was I to know MI5 would talk me into having an assistant."

"Why did they insist on it?"

"Because I'd developed the habit of switching off comms with them. Oh, bloody hell; this is really weird . . ."

An image flashed through my mind; something I'd completely forgotten about.

"What is it, Jack?"

"About a year ago, Lucy put the idea to me of having a live-in assistant. She got this file of agents' photos; asked me to go over them. I didn't want no assistant so I just flicked through the pages."

"But you paused slightly at one, didn't you, and Lucy noticed."

"Bugger me; she is one devious lady."

"Just doing her job. Like a good football manager, who picks wives for his players so he can keep an eye on them."

"I bet she even had my new gaff done out to suit Meera's taste. Bloody hell."

"Don't be too hard on yourself, Jack. Besides, it sounds like you and Meera have one thing in common at least: you're both outsiders who have decided to put your duties before a personal life."

"Sandra ain't likely to have a nice, normal life now, either."

"Are you so sure she really wants one?"

"Who knows? But I am starting to see that Santonaga has the edge on us because he don't have any doubts about what he wants. While I'm letting me subconscious take me all around the romantic houses, he's just getting in there, biting necks and planning to take over the whole country; and after that the rest of the world, no doubt."

I stood, yawned. "Thanks for the whisky, Ambrose. I'd better get back to Sandra; like you said, I'm a man who does his duty."

Which brought my thoughts back to the here and now, and I was about to call Bellers HQ when the door opened and Sandra came in, arms full of bags.

She threw them on the bed and smiled at me, eyes full of mischief.

"Fashion show?" she said.

The worse thing was she didn't know the shadow side of her was leeching into the light, influencing her decisions. So, for example, instead of going into the bathroom to change into one of the dresses she'd bought, she came out wearing something altogether different.

"Wow," I said, and it was no word of a lie.

She wore a half-cut red bra that cupped her breasts perfectly and the thinnest of red thongs. She turned, let me see that it formed a dark line dividing the two firm moons of her buttocks.

She turned again, shaking her head so her long hair curtained her breasts. Then she walked to me slowly, hips swaying, pulled me to my feet. Holding my gaze, she undid my shirt buttons and slid it off my shoulders. Then she unzipped my trousers, pulled them down and off. She stood back a pace, slowly sliding off her thong.

And yet again, I decided that if I was going to stand any chance with Santonaga, I needed to accept my situation and take control of it, instead of being caught in this guilt trap all the time. So I kissed her hard, pushed her on to the bed, bent my head between her legs, let my tongue explore there. She lay back, moaning softly.

After a few minutes, I straightened up and this time let my shadow self pound into my thrusts. She got into it too, pushing back against me. All my will went into the point where our sex joined, my hope being that it would be over too quick and leave us a little cold.

But a moment after she came, tears ran down her cheeks and she said, "I love you, Jack; I really do."

SEVENTEEN

Men, Blood, Women

I DIDN'T REMEMBER ANYTHING before the Bonding but it didn't matter. Whatever I was could not possibly match the incredible feeling of having finally joined up with people who understood me. I mean, *really* understood me. Being female and Asian just didn't matter here.

Sixteen of us sat in the air-conditioned training room, waiting for Rin to enter. I glanced around at the others and couldn't help smiling; everyone looked, not so much happy—because happy is for the empty-headed—as focussed, keen, alert, conscious.

Different races, half of us men, half women, different backgrounds, inclinations and probably astrological signs, but all united by the same thing: curiosity. Who am I? What can I achieve if I really try?

None of us remembered the Dead Life, as Rin called it. The one we'd come from. Whatever the details, we knew it was a life stifled by compromise, muffled by indoctrinated beliefs, compacted by family responsibilities.

Whereas here, all we were required to do was ask questions and with Rin's help work out the answers.

There was no technology in the briefing room, only a desk for each of us, a pad and pen and, at the front of the room, a white board that Rin would no doubt cover with drawings, symbols and phrases by the end of the day.

The door opened and Rin walked briskly in.

I wouldn't say I loved him. I didn't know enough about him personally for that. But I was totally inspired by his amazing concentration: that the watchfulness in his eyes never departed for a moment, even when he was laughing.

He put down a pile of books on the front bench and stood for a moment, his gaze lightly scanning our faces. I felt the atmosphere perk up with anticipation.

Rin was not a tall man but he held himself erect, shoulders square, and his slightly Oriental face lent him a natural charisma.

"So," he said, "how are you getting on without TV, iPods and mobile phones?"

I think I'd been shy in the Dead Life, but I threw up my arm at the same time several others did, and felt a thrill in the pit of my stomach when Rin said, "Meera?"

"I had a thought last night. I filled a whole book with notes about it. I suddenly realised why people in the Dead Life are so easily led."

"Okay," he said, "I'm sure we all want to hear about it. But you have to answer my question first: are you missing TV?"

As I began to answer, I had the familiar feeling that I'd once again fallen into Rin's trap. But it didn't matter; this was the best way to learn.

"No," I said, "but then I don't think I watched it very much in the Dead Life."

"Well, you should have," he said. "TV is the best way to monitor the minds of the people. And once your training is finished here, I'll expect you all to go out and buy a satellite dish, the more channels the better."

Rin said all this with a straight face.

"But," I said, "you've always told us that TV is designed to keep everyone stupid."

He nodded. "But you're not everyone now. You're becoming someone. Someone who can think for herself. Which means the usual rules don't apply. When you watch TV, you're looking for the truth. When Mr and Mrs Deadhead watch it, they're looking for oblivion."

Brice said, "So, we're getting TV?"

Rin laughed. "Try not to look so excited. I might think you've been faking the training. No, you aren't going to get TVs just yet. But I'm trying to prepare you for going back into the Dead Life."

I had no doubt the others felt the same hollow disappointment at this. We'd spent every day in the training room for the past week or so, and each had been an adventure into looking at the world completely new. So the thought of going back to a place where everything was always the same felt like a betrayal.

Rin nodded slightly, acknowledging our feelings, then said, "Okay, today's topic is: what are the true roles for a man and a woman today?"

Rin had an unpredictable way of approaching the subjects we explored. Usually, as he did that day, he first went around the class, getting us to express our views. We all knew this was invariably a prelude to him then tearing them all to shreds, but we also understood that the revelations that would follow only had their full effect if we gave this section all we had.

Again my arm shot up, this time before anyone else's. Rin looked around briefly, possibly to give someone else a chance, then nodded at me to continue.

I hadn't planned what I wanted to say but had been prompted to speak by the nagging of an old memory at the back of my mind.

"I think the roles for a man and a woman are the same, in that they should support each other, but the kind of support is very different."

The memory almost took shape then. I felt energy gather around my body, as if some man was trying to protect me. Not against violence—although I sensed that had been part of my previous life—but to help me be myself.

"Earth to Meera," said Rin.

I smiled. "Sorry. I think the support a man can offer a woman is to trust her instincts. Whereas the support a woman offers a man is to believe him when he says he'll never leave her."

As soon as I said this, I knew it was wrong. Tears surged through my closed eyelids, and I sensed the others' spirits retreat a little, embarrassed at this sign of weakness from the Dead Life.

When I opened my eyes, Rin looked at me with a firmness bordering on kind.

"That's an old myth still active in your subconscious," he said. "It's okay. We all have them to deal with. Anyone else?"

I seemed to have broken some taboo about expressing outdated views, because the others tripped over themselves then to talk about men and women, everyone feeling oddly secure to be part of such a mass admission to ineptitude.

Some talked about how a man should protect a woman physically, while a woman should nurture the family. Others went on about how there were no meaningful differences between the genders; all such divisions were just the remnants of ancient reactions from times when roles had more effect in the pragmatic.

And so on.

By the time Ellisa talked passionately about how far women's rights had progressed since the Suffragettes, we were all laughing as if this was one of those sitcoms where everyone is stupid but doesn't know it.

Rin laughed, too. He even offered, deadpan, another stupid view which we all took seriously for about a minute before the slight curve at the corner of his mouth alerted us.

"Woman enjoy sex," he said, "because men do. They don't often feel directly turned on."

We laughed even harder, revelling in the sheer relief of being able to admit that the world's views—and ours—were just plain stupid. And in feeling totally free to open our minds to new views, real views.

After we'd finished throwing all our old opinions onto the class moral bonfire, Rin said, "So, given that you all have no idea what a true role for a man or woman is, why don't we start with the basics, with what's true for both genders?"

"Blood," I said. "Blood is the key."

Rin smiled. "Blood is a neutral base material, surely, otherwise how would we be able to give someone a transfusion of another person's blood without it changing their character?"

Everyone was looking at me. I guess they could see the shadow of fascinated disquiet on my face.

"But if someone had the power to energise blood," I said, "they could control the signals back to the brain. The blood-brain barrier prevents foreign chemicals in the blood getting into the brain but it doesn't prevent energy—thoughts—put into it by someone with the power to."

"So, what are you saying?" said Rin.

"I think I'm talking about vampires," I said. "But they died out centuries ago, didn't they?"

"Well, that's what history tells us," said Rin. "But that shouldn't stop the brave from studying the systems they used."

And then, unusually, he called a break and told us to meet him in half an hour, out on the lawn. Which was when I realised he'd never intended to answer the question of what are the real roles for men and women, just wanted us to open our minds to whatever he'd show us next.

We wandered into the small canteen, helped ourselves to hot drinks and biscuits.

I sat with Ellisa, probably because her normally open face looked deeply thoughtful for once.

"That was pretty weird," I said.

She smiled, gaze not quite focussed on me. "It's also pretty weird that none of us can remember anything of our previous lives."

"But we've been through that," I said. "We all agreed it doesn't matter what we did before; it's what's ahead that counts."

"Bullshit," she said. "How can we possibly not care about our lives up to a week or so ago? Any of us could be married, have kids, parents who are wondering where we are."

"I just want to know the truth," I said. "I want to know what I'm really capable of achieving."

"They've done something to us, Meera. All that stuff about blood—didn't that give you a clue?"

"Yes, about vampires. But what's that got to do with us?"

She took a deep breath, apparently deciding not to continue with this theme. I sipped my coffee, content that she appeared to have chosen to return to the exciting here and now.

Yet, when we gathered on the lawn, Ellisa was not amongst us. Oh well, I thought, maybe she's decided to return to the Dead Life.

I didn't know where exactly we were, other than a country house set in large grounds, with sweeping lawns and a lake, willow, oak and silver birch everywhere.

Rin asked us to face the lake then raised his arm. The silvery water was about a hundred yards long by eighty wide. Swans and ducks dotted the surface but they rapidly made for the shore when the centre of the lake began to send out large ripples. Something was rising to the surface. Something big.

My heart thudded in anticipation as great slews of water rose alongside the huge shape that surged upwards.

It was circular, stealth black with blackened windows, around fifteen yards in diameter, bell-shaped and hanging above the surface of the lake completely silent and still.

As silvery rains of lake water slid off its smooth sides like mercury, the top of the bell retracted and a stream of black shapes flew out.

"Bats?" said Brice but Rin didn't reply.

They certainly flew like bats, in jagged arcs, circling over our heads with disturbing synchronicity before dropping into a line about ten metres from us. Except that when they landed, it was a row of humans facing us, half men, half woman, sixteen in total.

"Show them," said Rin.

The man at the left end of the line stepped forward and pointed his right arm at a nearby tree. Orange, yellow and blue flames spurted from his fingers to ignite the branches. Burning wood and charcoal filled our nostrils, but before we had time to take in this amazing event, a flush of power, lights, crashes and booms spread along the line. People flew, froze water on the lake, spun violently to tunnel under the grass and reappear yards away; one disappeared, one became a blurred streak fading through the distant trees . . .

And then they turned back into bat shapes, flitted into the hovering craft and sunk once again beneath the lake waters.

In amongst our stunned silence, we swapped looks and I could tell others had the same thought as me: is this what's going to happen to *us*?

Rin let the tension build for a few more seconds then told us to gather round him, to sit on the grass and get our breath back.

"Just to put your minds at ease," he said, "or maybe not: you aren't scheduled to take on abilities like the people you just saw. But you will be given learning enhancements."

Maybe it was because he'd timed the display so well—at a moment when we were most open to his teaching—but none of us even questioned then the morality of him giving us 'enhancements'.

"The people you just saw are going to be pathfinders. But you're going to be leaders. World leaders."

EIGHTEEN

A Right Royal Do

MEERA HADN'T CONTACTED ME in over a week, since leaving a message at Bellers' HQ that she wanted to work under cover for a while so would stay off any comms links. Which I admit suited my current state of guilt.

I'd spoken to the boys a few times. Mostly, they were frustrated. Santonaga was still too quiet, basically. Or if not quiet, hidden. Other than that, all they had were some isolated bits of possibly strange events in the news, including one or two murders in maybe unusual circumstances.

But then I woke up one morning with that awful feeling in my gut, when you know you've failed to spot the obvious.

Meera was in trouble. I just *knew* it.

Sandra was still asleep and I made as little sound as possible getting dressed. I'd packed a small bag and was just about to leave the room when her eyes opened slowly.

"Where are you going, Jack?"

"Got a text message from Ambrose. He's discovered something important. I didn't want to wake you."

I put down the bag and walked in front of it, sitting on the edge of her bed, stroking back her hair.

"What's in the bag?" she said.

And right then, every bleedin' thing hung on the next few words I spoke. If she suspected I was doing a runner, her dark side could flood back in and re-possess her; she might even kill me.

"Dirty washing. I'm giving it to the landlady to clean. Anything you want to add?"

"No. You never let me keep anything on long enough for it to get dirty."

The duvet slipped off her breasts and she leaned forward slightly, accentuating their shape. I kissed her on the forehead and said, "Hold that pose for when I get back."

I dropped the bag with the landlady, just in case Sandra checked, hoping she wouldn't notice the dirty washing I'd given her was as clean as I wished my conscience could be, then ran to Ambrose's place.

He invited me in and while he made coffee I asked him how the cure was coming on.

"Nearly there," he said.

"You'll have to send it to me in London," I said.

"Why, what's happened?"

"Meera's in trouble."

"How do you know?"

"Got a feeling."

He handed me a mug of coffee and we went to the living area to sit.

"Are you sure this isn't your guilt trip finding an out for you?"

"The feeling's in my blood, not me imagination. The boys have been monitoring the news. It's been pretty quiet but they picked up a police report about a murder in a Surrey mansion. But there was hardly any details given out, as if the security forces were keeping a lid on it. Could be nothing or it could be a deep betrayal."

"And you think Meera might have been involved?"

"Maybe. Santonaga has been turning toffs, so she might have been following up a lead then had to fight one of his followers."

He stood up. "Okay, looks like I've got a race on my hands. I need to finish that cure before Sandra works out where you've gone. I'll tell her I sent you somewhere to collect ingredients for me, but she won't buy that for very long."

I took out my phone. "I'll tell her in a minute. Thing is, Ambrose, I've mostly been treading water here, whatever we needed Sandra to believe."

He held out his hand and I shook it. "I'll send on the cure as soon as I can," he said. "Keep using your instinct for now, Jack. Don't over-think everything."

"I hear you," I said, dialling Sandra's number.

The Atlantic was royal blue flecked with white, the horizon darkening as the sun set behind me. I had the jet in stealth mode, not wanting anyone to know my location. The only call I'd made was to the yanks, to set up a mid-ocean refuel, and I just hoped they'd keep it secret like I asked. If not, well, I'd be in London soon enough anyway and I didn't plan to be kicking my heels any more.

I had plenty of thinking time in flight but after re-fuelling, and with the Scilly Isles flicking into view beneath, you know what? I finally got fed up with blaming meself for everything.

Fuck it. Fuck fuck fuckety fuck it. All that bleedin' guilt had just wasted time. I needed to get stuck into Santonaga, and stop waiting around like a spare dipstick at a wedding.

Because, he would know only too bleedin' well that our silence wasn't down to us putting together some master plan like he no doubt was. No, our silence was confirmation that we didn't have a clue how to stop him.

I told Jeeves to prepare a helicopter at the Rainham Marshes base. London was in darkness by the time I flew over it, hoping the stealth cover was holding.

I landed the plane, leaving it to the rozzer ground crew.

In the helicopter, I followed the Thames as it silver-snaked through London, on to Surrey. Jeeves gave me the address of Lord Stratton, the murdered toff, and I landed on the far side of Richmond Park, the place empty at night apart from herds of deer and the odd scallywag who would receive a nasty shock, literally, if he tried to lay a hand on my chopper.

I ran through the park, barely noticing the moon's soft glow upon the grass and the tree-tops. My handheld locater guided me to a high wall under some trees.

I was about to climb it when something had me switch the handheld to sweep and wave it slowly around.

Bingo! Me moped, and the trace of a Beller's suit, from about a week or so back. So, it *was* Meera.

This gave a spring to me feet as I ran and jumped up the wall. I threw meself over the top, twisting in the air to land on my toes in thankfully muffling leaf mould.

Through the trees, the lights of the mansion. I ran onto the lawn and made straight for the centre windows. If they saw me, they saw me.

Dressed in my black Bellers' suit, face covered by its mask, I used my universal pick to open the lock then wrenched open the French windows and ran into the house.

Accompanied by screams, I stopped in the centre of a large beige carpet. There were three women in the room and two men, all clearly toffs. The older woman had stopped screaming but trembled at the sight of a masked intruder.

Right then, I realised I had no idea how much had been covered up about the murder; how much she really knew, for instance.

I had to bite back my anger. These people knew *some*thing. These people had a long history of ripping off the working man. These people—

—oh, sod it; these people just needed to tell me what they knew. And fast.

I picked the most matriarchal-looking dame and pushed my gun into her neck.

"I want to know what happened here recently," I said. "All of it, including the stuff you kept from the police."

The police they'd probably bought off anyway.

"Or I'll blow this woman's tiara off, and her head along with it."

Interesting thing about toffs: as soon as they hear your accent isn't quite as glass-shattering as theirs, a lot of the fear in their eyes is replaced by naked contempt.

I pulled back the hammer on my gun, which made a very loud click, even though in fact it didn't do anything, since the gun fired sonic blasts. But I'd reckoned that folks were well programmed by TV to wet their knickers at the sound of a cocked gun.

"Look," said the young, be-suited cove who held out his hands in a placatory gesture. "Please, put down the gun and we'll tell you what we know."

"Well, since you said, please." I took the gun from the woman's throat. "But you sit down again, and I'll take this seat over here where I can keep a bead on you all."

I sat, watching them closely for signs of anyone pushing a panic button or fingering a mobile phone in a pocket.

"What's your name, son?" I said to the one who'd had the balls to stand up to me.

"Tom Stratton," he said. "Lord Stratton's grandson."

"The Lord who was murdered?"

They swapped a few 'careful what you tell the oink' looks at this before young Thomas continued. "We told the police that Grandpa was shot by a burglar. But the truth is, he was executed by a woman wearing an outfit not unlike yours."

"You discovered something about Lord Stratton after he died, didn't you?" I said.

The old dame—probably Lady Stratton—looked away with self-denial steel in her gaze, but young Tom shuffled uncomfortably. After getting no nods of approval from the others, he fixed me with a manly stare.

"Who are you to ask these questions?" he said.

"I'm employed by the government," I said. "Just like the young woman who shot your granddad. We're currently engaged in trying to save the country from vampire shape-shifters."

Their expressions told me all I needed to know. If they knew nothing about vamps, I'd have been facing sneers and ridicule, despite the gun in my hand. But what I saw was a bunch of faces filled with sheer, bone-deep dread.

Mind you, one of them didn't look quite as fearful as the rest, and I decided to find out why real soon.

Tom ran his hands through his hair, then nodded as if to tell himself it was time to come clean. "Before she ran off, the woman who shot grandfather told us to check out the basement, where he had his private den. We assumed he kept his best claret down there and ran a train set or something. But when we went down there, we found . . ."

Lady Whatever took a deep sigh then and, to give her credit, decided to come clean.

"We found a semi-naked young woman," she said, "dead from a deep bite mark on her neck."

She stopped, clearly upset despite the stoic expression on her face.

Tom took over again. "We explored the basement and found a computer. Which was strange for Granddad, since he hated modern technology; wouldn't even have a television in any room he used. Anyway, there were some disturbing films on the computer, including ones he'd made of what he did to that poor woman."

"Nasty, but hardly unusual," I said. "Perverts like to film themselves."

"But he wasn't a pervert!" said Lady Stratton. "At least he wasn't before something happened to him."

"As we checked his files," said Tom, "they started to delete themselves. I'm pretty sure Grandpa wouldn't have the technical knowledge to set up such a process. We think his computer was controlled by outsiders."

"Don't tell me: you couldn't get any names or details before the files went splat."

Tom shook his head then turned silent, looking at the others to pick up the story.

Well, I didn't have time to wait.

"You," I said, pointing my gun at the other bloke—in his late thirties, chubby, oiled hair. "Stand up."

He glanced at the others but they didn't respond. He stood.

"What's your name?" I said.

"Jim Harrington-Bulwar."

I continued to look at him, waiting for his gaze to change. Ordinarily, someone with a gun on him and being stared down by the owner would start to look a little nervous. Jimbo looked increasingly arrogant. Which told me what I needed to know.

"This gun," I said, "doesn't fire bullets. It issues a concentrated beam of high-frequency sound. I can send it into a solid object, like a human head, then have it fan out, spreading hundreds of bits of brain around the room." Which is of course what I should have had it do when I shot Santonaga, but back then I didn't know what he was and just wanted to save the Princess from getting blood and brains all over her face.

Whatever, that reduced the arrogance a little. A bullet he could no doubt recover from, but not something that would redecorate the walls with his noodle juice.

"Your husband," I said to Lady Stratton, "was turned by a bloodjacker, a super vampire. He would have felt like a million dollars and probably needed to satisfy his sudden powerful hungers."

"Why would this 'bloodjacker' want to do such a thing to my husband?"

"Why don't you ask Jim hyphenated here."

She frowned at Jim and he looked away.

"Go on, Jim," I said. "Tell her. Or do you want your brain to pebble-dash the ceiling?"

I'd forgotten how fast those things could move. Jim hurtled toward the French doors, all folding and flapping black, no longer looking so unfit and flabby.

Before I could get a line on him, he was out of the house. I ran after him but by the time I reached the lawn he'd disappeared into the night.

I returned to the woods, climbed the wall and dropped back into the park. I could see no point in interrogating the Stratton family further. They'd told me all they knew and I could do nothing to comfort them. I mean, it wasn't as if the government or anyone else was on top of the problem.

I sat on a tree trunk, planning my next move. Before me, the ancient trees and grassland glowed dull silver in the moon light. Some deer passed, slipping between the shadows of bushes and trees, unaware they were not likely these days to get an arrow up the Jaczzi, unless from a local hooded youth on crack.

Santonaga was turning only toffs. Did that matter? Weren't toffs already turned, at least in terms of having little grasp on reality. What would he gain by creating a load of toff followers?

Even if he took over all their land, what would he do with it, that wasn't already being done? After all, existing toffs had to work fairly hard at raising money to support their estates. How would that situation change with Santonaga installed as top toff?

If he infiltrated the government—turned a whole barrel of MPs and ministers—he'd still have to get laws through the usual processes, and these days most of our laws came through Europe anyway.

No, he must have something bigger and quicker in mind. He wouldn't want to take decades to change the country through the legal route.

Come on, Jack lad, *think*.

What would you do, if you was a super-powered, shape-shifting toff?

Well, Toffs believed in breeding. They arranged afternoon dances in their stately homes, where parents matched up their children with a view to preserving the strain, the genes, the family pile. What mattered to them was inheritance, and nothing else. Centuries back, they'd stolen the land from the people and only their contempt ever-after for their victims allowed them to justify the fact.

. . . And then I thought I knew Santonaga's plan.

Simple but effective. He wanted a return to a feudal country. Only this time, instead of the peasants being enslaved physically, the chains would be in their minds. Other toffs would be chained to him, too, but at least they'd have their rewards.

The facts appeared to be: Santonaga could either kill people by biting them or turn them into his blood lackeys with powers of their own. They in turn could bite to kill and possibly turn others too, though I didn't know if they also got powers. Presumably, this caused a dependence chain, with Santonaga at the top of the line. Did that mean if he was offed, the whole structure collapsed, or could he simply be replaced with a new head?

I walked back to fetch the moped. After switching off the cloaking field, I opened the storage box and felt as if I'd been punched in the stomach at the sight of Meera's things. I held up her jacket; God help me, I even sniffed it, and I swear her essence made my head swim. I was about to fold it up again when I felt a sharp outline in the pocket, reached in and swore softly.

A rozzer-authorised gold card. A ticket to anywhere. She must have planned to use it to track down Santonaga's turned. The irony was, she hadn't got to use it before she disappeared.

But right then, it gave me an idea of what to do next.

I rolled the bike to the chopper and stored it behind the pilot's seat. Then I took off into the London night sky.

In flight, I pushed the gold card into the onboard computer.

"Jeeves?" I said. "You there, mate?"

"Where else would I be—mate."

"You sound a bit pissed off."

"Maybe it's something to do with that gold enema you just thrust into my back passage."

"Giving you heartburn?"

"I'm having to use 93% of my intelligence to stop it squawking to its masters that it's incarcerated in a machine that's smarter than anything they have. Fortunately, 7% of my mind is more than enough to talk to you with."

"Were you this rude to Meera?"

"No, but then she's a lady. You, on the other hand, are a two-timing casanovanuts. At least that's what I deduced from the calls you made with Ms Nath from Halifax."

"Not that it's any of your business, but Meera's the one I care about the most."

"So why have you been banging someone else so enthusiastically?"

"You know why."

"Oh—because you believe Sandra has to be kept happy otherwise her controller will know something's up. How convenient."

"Yeah, well, you would think that. Because I programmed you to. What I didn't do was give you much of an emotional quotient."

"I don't need a high EQ to know you're heading for the lonely sad old git home."

"Fine, but right now I need you to re-programme that gold card. Make me the lawful owner."

"Done."

"Thanks. Mate."

"No problem, Jack No-mates."

He had a point but I didn't have time to think about it then. I had a gold call to make.

"Hello, Mr Stapleton. This is the control room at Buckingham Palace. How can I help?"

"First, I need clearance to land this helicopter on your roof."

"I'll send you the co-ordinates, sir."

I landed and two guards with beefy looking rifles met me at the door leading down into the building.

"May we ask the purpose of your visit, sir?" said the older looking one.

"I need to speak to Princess Marion," I said. "Urgently."

They swapped conflicted looks. Evidently, the card's power hovered somewhere between total access and *you* can tell her, not me.

"The Princess is indeed in residence," said the same guard.

"Well, that's dandy then, isn't it? Why don't you show me the way, gents."

More swapped looks, then the younger guy made a decision and dialled a number on his mobile.

"Ma'am, this is Thompson . . . Yes, I did, thank you. We're speaking to Jack Stapleton, on the roof . . . No, ma'am, he's not a burglar; he's a — ?"

He raised his eyebrows at me.

"Tell her I'm the ding-donger she met in Oban."

Reluctantly, he told her, then his eyes widened at her response. "Yes, ma'am; we'll bring him to you straight away."

Down the stairs, into a most cushty top floor corridor, all thick red carpet and walls bulging with paintings of starchy old royal coves glaring at you as a doubtless inferior. Round a couple of bends then on to a set of doors bordered by a couple of wimpy looking dudes in white leggings.

My two guards nodded at the other dudes, who opened the doors for me and in I went.

I guess I'd expected a Princess's quarters to be packed with antique furniture and grizzly bear rugs. But Marion's place had a stripped-out feel to it: bare, polished floorboards, a few modern looking bits of furniture, and not much more, truth be told.

The armed goons withdrew, closing the doors behind them, just as Marion walked out of another room to greet me.

"So, I know your name at last, Mr Belter."

"That's Beller, ma'am. As if you didn't know."

She wore a red dress, cut well to accentuate her figure, just on the right side of tasteful; her hair loose over her shoulders.

"Seriously," she said, "I didn't have the chance to thank you properly for saving my life."

She took my elbow and steered me toward a chair, then walked to a table full of bottles and glasses.

"Drink?" she said.

"Whisky, please."

She frowned. "I've only got malts from the east coast; had all the west coast makes thrown out after my kidnapping."

"Don't you have servants to do that for you?" I said, immediately regretting it.

But she just laughed. "No. They tend to get in the way. And they listen to one's conversations all the time. They pretend they don't, of course, but they rely on the ancient royal practice of supreme indifference to get away with it and, well, I'm out of practice."

She handed me a crystal tumbler inscribed with the royal crest, ice cubes clinking merrily, then sat with her own glass opposite me.

"Actually," I said, "I'm here to cash in again on your gratitude. And thank you for the info you authorised for my colleague recently."

She smiled. "Refreshing honesty, Mr Stapleton. What can I do for you?"

So there it was. I had no idea how much she knew about Santonaga. The royals tended to give the impression they kept their heads in the clouds about worldly events. But she was no blue blood dreamer. I suspected at least one of her rooms in here would be stacked out with IT and comms, making use of all sorts of specialised and widespread systems.

"Well, the first thing we both have to do is to agree not to bullshit each other."

"Everything that goes on in monarchy and politics is bullshit."

"Believe it or not, ma'am, I didn't come here to speak to a Princess. I came to speak to a gutsy woman who's prepared to do anything to protect the people of her country."

"You forgot the bit about my resources."

"You've never given much indication before that your wealth means an awful lot to you."

"Oh, it means everything, Mr Stapleton."

For a moment, my spirits sunk, but then she grinned. "You should see your face! You look like a child who's just dropped his ice cream on the pavement."

"Where I come from, ma'am, a kid would pick it up again."

"Really? I'd just order a butler to get me another one."

As we'd been talking, she'd kept her gaze on me, letting me see that her eyes showed something different to what her words implied. And right then, I realised royalty worked different to the hoi polloi, even rebellious Princesses.

They needed to be asked.

"Princess," I said, "will you help me save this country from what I believe will be the worst fate possible?"

"And what would that be?"

"No one—commoner or royal—will be able to think for himself. We'll all be tied to the will of one man."

"I know all about one's will being tied."

"But this is different: no one will have a choice."

"And you think they do now?"

I didn't understand why she was resisting. She knew first hand what Santonaga was capable of, and that he clearly would have no trouble going after royalty again at some point.

Had she been turned? I didn't think so; reckoned I'd be able to tell if she had. Besides, if she was turned, surely she'd have been trying to lull me off my guard—ah! that was it: she didn't know if *I'd* been turned!

"Princess, I don't know how to convince you I'm kosher. I mean, these vamps ain't necessarily the kind what hide from the sun, or break out in boils at the sign of the cross; they don't even seem to mind eating garlic flavoured crisps."

"There is one way, actually, Jack: you could mix your saliva with my blood."

"But that's—I mean, if I've been turned, then you will be, too."

"And if I've been turned, you'd know I was then unturned."

I wondered how she knew a Beller's saliva had the power to unturn, but right then that was the least of my concerns.

"But why would you take the risk of being turned, ma'am?"

Her shoulders slumped a little. "Because I don't know who to trust anymore. Half the Palace could be turned by now; the government too. And you're right: the Bellers and my resources are probably the only chance the country has to resist this curse. But we have to be able to trust each other, Jack.

"The point is, if you've been turned, then I can't trust the Bellers, and if that's the case, all's lost so I might as well join Santonaga anyway."

I was stunned at her logic, and the bravery or callousness it required for her to come to such a blunt conclusion. Anyone else would have wiggled into whatever moral middle ground was available. But this woman had faced the only two options she had and chosen.

"I see your point, ma'am," I said.

She nodded. "If you don't mind, I'd better finish this drink first."

I did the same. Then she stood, reached up to tie back her hair. I took a small blade from a suit pocket, and a vial of sterilising fluid; cleaned the blade then went to her. We smiled awkwardly.

"Do you always draw blood on a first date?" she said.

She leaned to one side, exposing her neck. I took a moment to gather myself. No good dithering. The cut had to be deep enough to draw blood but not so deep as to be fatal.

"It has to last about a minute, ma'am," I said. "So my saliva has a chance to mix with your blood."

"I'm ready," she said.

Sandra had been unconscious when I'd unturned her, but Marion was very much awake. Her eyelashes trembled slightly and her chest heaved more quickly than normal. Yet she held herself steady.

I drew the blade quickly across her neck, dropped it to the floor, then covered the wound with my mouth, once more feeling warm blood on my tongue. I worked saliva into the wound then almost stopped when I heard the Princess moan softly.

She moved her body in to mine, put her arms around my neck, drawing me closer.

I sucked a little harder, and she moaned deeper. I knew it was just the blood and the whole vampire myth working in our systems but that didn't lessen its power.

"Mr Stapleton," she said, surprising me with the formality of her tone, especially in amongst a whole lot of very informal groaning. "This is simply necessary. We must be intimate for a while in order to maximise the efficiency of your effect in my blood. The fact that I'm enjoying the process does not mean anything personally."

She reached behind to unzip her dress, let it fall to the floor. The fact she was naked also surprised me but I kept my mouth on her neck, even though it had been longer than a minute. Her hands explored my suit, but she wouldn't know how to get it off. My decision, then. I decided to trust her notion that this was simply us doing the necessary.

I hit the release sequence on my hip pad and the suit fell away in five separate pieces.

Marion stood back, and I took my mouth from her neck. She had a fantastic body and stood straight and proud, not hiding anything.

This time, I stuffed any guilt right under the mental carpet. All I needed to do was be a man; be a hundred per cent. If having sex while making sure she weren't turned helped, then so be it.

She took my hand and led me into her bedroom. She lay on the bed and opened her legs, impatient. I kneeled and she turned her head to one side. I licked the trail of blood that had run across her right breast, sucking the hard nipple as I did so. Then I put my mouth to the wound once more.

She groaned loudly, now animal-like. I pushed into her, still sucking deep on her neck.

"Magnificent!" she cried, as if admiring a new horse, reaching behind to grab my buttocks, pushing me in further.

"Come, goddamit!" she yelled.

I took my mouth from her neck. "Since you put it like that, ma'am—" And concentrated on matching her release point.

I rolled off her and we lay side by side, breathing heavily.

"Well, Mr Jack Stapleton, I know that was required, but I won't deny I enjoyed it immensely."

"Required?"

She turned to face me. "Didn't you know? The effectiveness of a Beller to unturn is increased significantly if his sperm enters one's body as well as his saliva."

"Oh, I thought you—I mean, I figured you just wanted to—"

"Then you mean you . . . Oh, that's just hilarious!"

"Well, I'm glad you find it funny, ma'am."

"And you also plainly didn't know that when a Beller drinks someone's blood and they receive his saliva, chemical lust is rapidly escalated."

"I'm wondering how you know, actually, when I don't."

She laughed some more. Then smiled at me, not unkindly.

"You must have someone you think you've just betrayed."

"Well, I hadn't had time to think about it yet, but thanks for reminding me. Sex seems to be like London buses; you go years waiting for one then three come along all at once. Trouble is, I only wanted the one."

"Jack—really: we had no choice in this matter."

So, that's why she'd been naked under her dress. "Jesus—we didn't even use contraception."

"It's okay; I take the pill. Just another bunch of chemicals swimming around my systems."

"And how long do our lust chemicals last?"

She propped herself on one elbow, reached across with the other hand, lightly stroked my penis with the backs of her fingers.

"Is that a chemical reaction," she said, "or are you just pleased to see me?"

I frowned, wondering if a more delayed decision to have sex wasn't more of a betrayal.

"Seriously, Jack," she said. "We have to make sure."

I don't know if it was right or not, but when I kissed her long on the lips, I realised I'd actually made a separation in myself. I didn't love Marion, and she certainly didn't see me as anything other than 'required', but we had a duty. And nothing in any rule book said we couldn't enjoy it too.

And in fact, half an hour later, we were sitting opposite each other again, in the main living room, drinking coffee that some pantomime-outfitted servant had brought with a right irritating wisp of a knowing smile on his powdered face, as if there'd been no break in our conversation.

Marion had dressed in trousers and shirt this time, business like and professional, duty done. Funnily enough, I actually felt the same way too. Royal responsibility must be contagious.

"I need to take you into the basement," she said. "And show you what I've learned about Lord Santonaga."

"And the Bellers."

She frowned. "Yes, I must apologise in advance there, Jack. The monarchy has extensive archives on the origins and development of the Bellers."

I struggled to keep my temper down. "But you granted us access to your archives just a while back, so I could find out where Ambrose was; I didn't see nothing about the Bellers in 'em."

"As with most ancient institutions, the Palace has archives it lets only a few see and then it has archives it doesn't even admit exists. I gave you what you needed to find Ambrose. In fact, it was Ambrose who contributed greatly to our secret archives, when he was the court wizard."

"So, why didn't he tell me more; like about the lust thing, for a start?"

"You're a decent man, Jack. I suspect he knew if he'd told you, it might have prevented you doing your duty at some point."

I took a deep breath. Much as it was mighty frustrating to be mixing with people who wouldn't just tell you the truth up-front, I had to admit that my pesky sense of right and wrong would indeed have stopped me going to Marion if I'd known we was likely to be bouncing around together on her royal mattress.

"I guess he's right," I said. "If I'd known, then my conscience would have stopped me coming here, which means we wouldn't have formed an alliance, which means Santonaga would be facing no real opposition. But now, I can see my sense of duty needed to expand its world view."

"Don't think just because someone's born royal, it's any easier. Nothing I do is ever just for me. Sometimes I think it must be wonderful to simply go to work, come home, do anything you feel like doing; watch the television, go out drinking, whatever."

"You really think you'd enjoy that kind of life?"

"Of course not!" She stood. "I wouldn't swap all this for anything."

"But what about all them interviews you did, criticising the monarchy, making everyone think you'd probably abdicate the second you get to be Queen?"

Her gaze misted over. "I'll be Queen," she said, "but there'll be changes." She smiled, back again. "However, there's no time to talk of such things now; we've work to do."

We left her rooms, she pounding along the corridor as if the whole damn world was getting in her way. I followed smartish, a little awed at the mass of contradictions duty seemed to have filled her with.

She hated the idea of an ordinary life, yet didn't believe the monarchy should continue in its current form. She lived in a toff's world of privilege and luxury yet appeared to have no problem with helping me bring down Santonaga and his army of toffs.

We entered a wood-panelled lift and she tapped in a security code on its number pad.

"If we beat him," I said, "where does that leave the monarchy?"

"Why don't you answer that for me, once you've seen our files."

I suppose I'd expected the basement to be all brick walls and cobwebs. But this was Buck House, weren't it, so what we stepped into would not have looked out of place in a Harrod's show room. Thick maroon carpet giving a bounce to our steps, more paintings on the walls, presumably of minor royals this far from the gander of anyone important.

But there were a couple of differences to the main building. First, I couldn't see any guards or servants. Second was what I saw when Marion tapped in another code on a door that swung back to reveal a room looking about as at home in the Palace as I did.

"Wow," I said and Marion grinned, leading me further in.

Three of the walls were covered by large screens, some blank at present, others showing a collection of camera views from around the Palace and London streets, others various television news programmes.

Toward the back were three computers and a few control gizmos. Now, I knew all that input, which I suspected was mighty flexible, would need more processing facility than appeared to be available.

"I know what you're thinking," said Marion.

"So, how's it done in here—smoke and mirrors?"

"Close. It *is* magic, but the real thing."

She pointed to a chair in front of the central computer and I sat down. She took a cable from a drawer then opened a bottle of sterilising fluid. "Ordinarily," she said, "only father and my brothers and sister can work this room, not that they ever bother to. But now that you and I have shared fluids and blood sonics, I'm hoping it will work for you, too."

The cable ended in a needle that she now cleaned. She nodded at my arm and I pulled back my sleeve. She pushed the needle into a vein then turned on the computer.

Straight away, I knew it had worked. Having a lot of smarts, I'd figured Marion must have known the comms in my suit would link to her archives. Which meant I could now access anything that took my fancy. On the other hand, her system could no doubt pick-pocket Bellers' comms too.

High ho, well at least after several hundred years of peasants and royalty being separated by class and privilege, their blood was finally mixing and hopefully to mutual benefit.

The blank screens all around us hummed into life. Those that had been showing other programmes blacked out, joined the others.

"I'm guessing," said Marion, "that our two systems can extrapolate some real knowledge of Santonaga's whereabouts."

I felt a line of fire along my vein as Marion's systems drew in my blood. "Jeeves," I said, "allow the connection being sought."

In my deep earpiece I heard Jeeves say, "The amount of information that's proposed by this union, sir, may overload my storage capacity."

"Jeeves?" said Marion.

I shrugged. "Inside every Beller is a would-be toff trying to get out."

To Jeeves I said, "Make the connection anyway."

The screens were still black. Marion frowned. "We should have had something up by now."

"Does this system have 3D capability?"

"Yes, but why? I've never found it necessary."

"It could be the sheer intensity of the two data sets is overloading two dimensional expression."

She nodded, sat at another computer and typed in an instruction.

"Bloody hell!"

The screens seemed to disappear and we were in a plush living room, probably of some stately home, judging by the tall windows with sight of distant trees. I could no longer see Marion but assumed she had the same view as me, from a point against the opposite wall to the window.

A door opened and a man walked into the room.

Santonaga.

Until that moment, I hadn't realised how much raw hatred I felt for him. He'd killed most of my friends, ruined the mind of a woman I cared for and was apparently bending the entire country to his will.

But I could feel no body around me to do anything about it. Our systems appeared to have the power to put our consciousnesses into a virtual restructuring of an actual place, but we could do nothing active within it.

Santonaga stood with his back to the window, apparently sensing the atmosphere in his room. For a worrying moment, his gaze appeared to rest directly on me, but then I saw his focus was actually closer in.

His face seemed to tremble and melt slightly, and I wondered if the system was failing. But then his features resolved themselves, now showing a different man's face, one I didn't recognise.

I had to admit, if I didn't know it was really Santonaga I'd have thought this guy was a decent sort: twinkle to the eye, open face. Which made me wonder how Santonaga's shape-shifting could ape qualities too; surely that wasn't possible?

He moved to the door and our point of view followed, remaining about three yards behind, and just above his right shoulder.

He walked down a wide marble staircase, along another corridor, out a back door, on to a terrace then onto a wide lawn, toward a lake, to a group of people.

"Please face the lake," he said to them, then raised his arm in a signal. The surface of the water swelled and rippled, sending ducks and swans scurrying toward the shore. A huge black bell-shaped something ripped out of the water to hover perfectly smoothly about ten yards above the lake.

Then me absent heart was in me absent mouth when a whole litter of black shapes flicked and flittered out of the top of the damn thing. Their flights looked co-ordinated and sure enough, they landed in a straight line, facing the young people.

The black shapes swelled into people, men and women.

Santonaga said, "Show them."

The geezer at the end of the line pointed his arm and multi-coloured flames shot out of his fingers, setting light to a tree. One by one, the others showed off their powers, too; then they turned back into bats and returned to the bell-shaped craft which finally sank beneath the lake's surface.

Santonaga said something else but I didn't catch it on account of the fact I'd just recognised one of the awe-struck people facing him: Meera. I struggled mightily to get the system to take me to her but my anger only seemed to pull me away from the scene.

The last words I heard from Santonaga just made me even madder.

"The people you just saw are going to be pathfinders. But you're going to be leaders. World leaders."

I blacked out for a few moments, and when I came round again, felt like I'd just been involved in a particularly vivid dream; didn't at first know where I was.

Then Marion's concerned face appeared in front of me. She handed me a glass of water, told me to drink.

I realised I was breathing hard and forced myself to slow down. I took a long swallow of the water then met her gaze.

"Meera was there."

Marion nodded. "Your emotions dragged me with you. I felt what you feel for her. It'll only get in the way, Jack."

"He must have turned her. I need to get her back."

She reached down and took the needle from my arm. "We can't return just now. The system works through neural resonance; once your emotions get involved, it overloads."

I was about to insist we went back anyway but saw a flicker of fear in her eyes; something that hadn't been there even when Santonaga had her in his grip in that castle near Oban.

"What's the problem, ma'am?"

She didn't answer immediately; instead, rushed around shutting down the system. Only when all the screens were black and every light gone from every monitor did she sit down again.

"Your concern for Meera has temporarily clouded your perceptions, Jack. Now: tell me what we just saw."

She was right. All I could think of was getting Meera back, both in body and mind. But we needed to work out what exactly Santonaga was up to.

"Well, unimaginative though it is, he appears to be planning on world bleedin' domination. He's got two armies to do it with: the heavy squad for the initial roughing up, followed by his brainwashed whiz-kids to run the show for him once he's bashed everyone else into submission."

"Three armies, in fact. Don't forget all the influential people he's already turned."

"But who's he actually going to bash with those super-bat-kid things?"

"The army, the secret service—anyone who tries to stop him."

"But stop him doing what exactly? We're an elected democracy in Britain; he can't just take over parliament without being voted in."

"He'll destroy parliament," she said. "Maybe literally: use his super-powered people to smash down both Houses. Then he'll replace the King with a new monarch and swear in his turned lords and ladies."

Which was pretty close to what I'd concluded in Richmond Park.

"All he needs to do," she went on, "is co-ordinate everything properly: hit the key points at the same time."

"Hang on though, Princess. You're forgetting something—and don't take this the wrong way—that you royals have a tendency to forget: the people."

She flushed, probably annoyed that I'd pinned a snooty rap on her when she'd always seen herself as the royal with a difference.

"The people of Britain," I went on, "ain't going to take kindly to been re-toffed, not when it took us centuries to yank 'em out of power."

"You have a point. He'd need thousands of super-powered troops to dominate sixty million people, and I suspect that's beyond even his ability. Perhaps we need to work out *why* he's doing this before we can understand *how*."

"He just wants to be king vamp in a world full of vamps?"

"Who would they feed on if they're all blood-drinkers?"

"Okay, so he needs to keep most of the population as a vamp herd. Which means he ain't planning to turn us all. But that still leaves the problem of how he's going to control the unruly mob."

She sighed. "Well, whatever his plans for the common people, it doesn't alter the fact we have to stop him somehow. And we need to do it before he puts his new system in place, whatever exactly it is."

"What do you mean?"

"Despite his powers, there's a fundamental weakness to his plan. Yes, once he's set in place a new system of rule, with himself at the head of it, he'll be home and dry. But before that, everything depends on the blood link he's made to his people."

"Take him out and the whole house of cards collapses?"

She still looked worried. "We have to hope so, Jack. Palace archives don't contain much information about previous bloodjackers. For all we know, if his victims are turned long enough, they retain their powers and their hunger forever."

"Which would be another reason for him to act fast."

"Yes, to be proclaimed before his own people lose their psychic link to his will."

"Well, we know how to use royal and Beller's blood to unturn people."

"But we have to find and subdue them first. There won't be time for that."

"Professor Paul invented a vamp sensor, and the lads have been tracking down turned toffs; only found a few, though, locked 'em up where possible, shot them where not."

"Okay, but I can't help feel that also plays into Santonaga's hands, to keep us separated in chasing his pawns, when we should be concentrating on the main attack."

"So, what do we do? And how do I rescue Meera?"

"If Meera's been turned, it's too late; and if she hasn't, then she can wait a little longer to be rescued. After all, Santonaga appears to find her useful to him at the moment."

I thought about patterns again. And what the Prof had said about electrical patterns in the blood of Santonaga's victims. And Pete talking about a change in the language matrix of the country, started some time in the 60s, around when the Bellers were born. And Santonaga. And Ambrose rigging Bow Bells to change us forever . . . But I couldn't quite grasp it. I needed to—

"Jack? Are you all right?"

"Sorry; I was trying to get me head round the bigger picture."

Marion was standing now, ripping off her clothes.

"Ma'am?"

"As it happens, Mr Stapleton, I am still feeling exceedingly horny, but we really don't have time right now." She pulled open a cupboard and took out a black one piece suit. I have to admit the sight of her pulling on the tight latex, breasts bobbing with the effort, hair falling around her arms, was more than enough to take me mind off the current crisis.

She saw me looking and smiled. With the suit just up to her waist, she walked over to me and straddled my lap.

"You have the same look in your eye my terrier gets when he hears the opening of a can."

I sucked gently on one of her nipples and she tipped back her head, moaning softly. I sucked the other but then she shook her head and climbed off.

"We really have to go, Jack."

She pulled up the rest of her suit, then I was frowning.

"That looks mighty like a Beller's suit, ma'am."

"It does the same job, that's why."

"Maybe, but I have to say it looks a lot better on you than those hairy, lumpy guys I normally knock around with."

She had her mouth open to answer but closed it again as a deep booming sound from above made the walls seem to shake slightly. Then another, and another.

"The Palace is under attack!" she shouted, running for the door.

I ran after her, grabbed her arm before she could pull it open.

"You'll just get yourself killed, ma'am."

"But I can't leave the staff unprotected."

A whole flurry of muffled explosions, followed by alarms, hit our ears.

"Marion, you have a duty—"

"Fuck my fucking duty!"

She turned away, opened the door and ran into the corridor, me following. Outside, the sounds of destruction were much louder, punctuated by screams and shouts.

Marion reached the stairs but stopped before climbing them. She turned to face me, expression full of furious self-loathing.

"You're right," she said. "I can't help them any more than the police and ambulance services can. It's important that you and I live to carry the fight."

"Does the elevator go to the roof?"

She shook her head. "The elevators will have shut down because of the emergency. We'll need to take the spiral stairs."

We ran back along the corridor; she opened a small door leading into a dimly lit stone room with a narrow spiral staircase winding up from it. Without pausing, she hit the stairs, me following, telling myself I might have to push her on, once the noises of death got closer as we moved up the levels.

And although the walls of the staircase looked pretty thick, they didn't keep out the crashes and crunches of rooms folding in on themselves. We ran through choking smoke and more shouts and screams. No one else appeared on the staircase, so I figured it must be some kind of royals-only escape route.

Then we were running into chaos. Smoke billowed around the edges of the roof, and flames everywhere below sent violent shadows dancing across the surrounding trees. Police sirens cut through the crackle of fires and crumbling woodwork.

The helicopter stood like a shadowed admonishment, but I didn't let guilt stop us now. I bundled Marion into the passenger seat and locked her door, then ran round to my side and jumped in. As I flicked on the controls, I nodded to the set of headphones hanging next to her ear, reaching for my own.

The blades whumped into life then we were bumping up through the turbulent air. Deliberately, I took a route away from the Palace, so she wouldn't have to look down at the carnage.

Her voice crackled into my headphones. "How did he do it, Jack? And so fast—we'd only just pulled our minds out of his base."

"Might be a coincidence," I said. "He could have been planning to hit the Palace right at the same moment." But I knew that didn't hold up as soon as I said it. And she didn't bother to reply.

Five miles from the Palace, London oddly calm below us, I said, "So, where do we go from here, Princess?"

She looked down at the slow-moving traffic, winding through the black-topped buildings and the pockets of green, her gaze somewhere else again.

"We go to fight," she said.

I was reading a history of psychology when someone knocked on my door.

"Come in!" I yelled, expecting one of the girls to want to borrow something, although they rarely bothered knocking.

"Hello, Meera; do you have a minute?"

"Rin—of course. Please sit down."

I tried to read his face for clues, since he never visited our rooms. Perhaps he looked more serious than usual and I frantically tried to work out what I might have done wrong.

He smiled. "It's okay, relax. This is a friendly visit."

"Can I get you some tea?"

"No thanks. I won't be long."

He sat on the edge of my bed and I stayed in my study chair.

"There's been an important event in London."

I nearly suggested that if he wanted us to be world leaders, we really should have some kind of connection with the outside world, but decided it could wait for later.

"Buckingham Palace was hit by several rockets; half the building has collapsed and fire destroyed just about everything in the other half. Nineteen staff died and another ten are seriously injured."

"Rockets? But who would fire on the Palace?"

He shook his head. "No one's claiming the hit and it's too early to tell if the government and police will be able to get much from the rubble."

"Oh, God—the King . . ."

"He's in Windsor; at least that's what his people are saying. Only Princess Marion was in the Palace at the time. They haven't found her body, so it's assumed she got out somehow. A couple of witnesses saw a helicopter leave the roof, so she was probably in that. I happen to think she had prior knowledge."

I didn't know if I felt shocked because people had died, or because someone had dared to attack the symbolic heart of British life. And while I thought this, and wondered about Rin's curious statement that Marion had perhaps betrayed her own kind, I felt one of the mind-sways I'd experienced a few times since being here.

Rin carried on looking at me, as if he could tell what I was going through.

My mind settled again, and with it I felt once more the profoundly deep sense of purpose that had accompanied my time here.

"What do you want me to do, Rin?" I said, perhaps the tiniest moment before I'd intended to.

He smiled warmly. "You've got a great attitude, Meera; which is why I've chosen you for a mission."

My heart accelerated like a love-struck schoolgirl's, but I forced myself to remain calm-looking.

"I need you to track down Princess Marion for me."

I should have asked him why he wanted to find the Princess, and what it had to do with the attack on the Palace. But all I cared about right then was that he'd chosen *me* for a mission.

NINETEEN

A Blood-Spattered Poncho

"LOOKS LIKE MILLWALL'S ground back in the 80s," said Sam.

"Yeah, a real shame, when before it looked like Arsenal's today," I said.

Marion's stately home's main lawn had turned brown and rutted over the past few days. Rainwater had collected in the mini craters left by the guys' various machines and powers.

"Think it's going to be enough, Jack?"

I shrugged. "We don't know what he's going to do or where or when. But at least we can now mobilise fast with force. Which is better than the bunch of manky loners we used to be."

We walked toward the main house, through the rain that had been falling all day. If you didn't look down, the warm, evening yellow lights in the windows of the great white house could have you believing that all was right with the world.

"Do you really think anything will change," said Sam, "even if we beat this Santonaga bastard?"

Through the windows of the long dining room, I saw Marion, still in her muddy battle suit, moving along the table, helping the guys put out dinner.

"Actually, I do."

"Well, I grant you that one at least knows how to fight."

I blushed, hoping he didn't see. Marion and I had decided to disguise the super strength she'd developed after mixing my saliva with her blood, backed up with my sperm, by telling everyone it was all down to a special one-off suit that had been developed by a Palace scientist who'd died in the attack. We'd only told Pete and the Prof the whole truth, mainly because they were the two most likely to find a cure from it.

The reason we wanted to hide it from the rest was we didn't want the Bellers to know just yet that mixing their saliva with someone else's blood might instigate powers in the 'victim'. Best if they made that decision, where their partners were concerned, in the cold light of day. Although, of course, we might have to force the issue if the fight went badly against us.

I'd said to Marion that it seemed odd this hadn't happened with any Beller before, if only by accident. She'd just looked at me in her toffly pragmatic way and said that of course it would have happened before. Therefore, either the transference ability had only switched on recently, maybe the same time as Santonaga's did. Or it only worked with royal blood. Or the recipient had to want it to happen.

Sam and me entered the dining room, pulled off our wet boots and left them on the mat. The pattern of the days had found us wanting to eat immediately after training; later, to go shower then meet in the ballroom to talk tactics, swap stories and news.

I sat between Dan and Pete, waving at Sarah dishing up food on one of the serving tables at the back of the room.

Marion sat in front of us with a plate of Irish stew.

"Nice work today, ma'am," I said. "That suit really lets you bash the bongos out of tree trunks and ugly statues of your ancestors what you presumably needed an excuse to pulverise."

She smiled. "I'm just pleased I'll be able to add some muscle when he finally strikes. And yes, it was rather satisfying to permanently crack the smiles on a few smug forebears who've been spoiling the views around here."

I said to Dan, "What did you do today?"

He didn't look up and though he spoke quietly, his tone cut deep. "Why won't you let me help, Uncle Jack?"

I was about to tell him that he'd been helping a lot—in the kitchen, working with the comms team in Marion's basement, running errands—but I knew what he meant. He wanted to be turned, by a Beller into a . . . well, he believed he'd be a Beller too.

One night, needing to talk it through with someone I trusted, I'd told Sarah most of what had happened recently, including the bit about Beller's now having the power to turn others. Unfortunately, Dan had been eavesdropping and ever since kept on at me to let him join the big boys for real.

Besides, I wasn't so sure he actually would get powers. Yes, Marion had developed some after I blooded her, not that Dan knew it, but then she already had royal blood. Blood that centuries of court wizards had worked on, including Ambrose, the father of the Bellers. Sandra seemed to have developed tremendous strength, too, although it was difficult to test for it to make sure, not without reviving the wrong memories in her.

There was also the matter of the sperm back-up thing, too.

Pete saved me then by saying, "I could do with some help tomorrow, Dan."

Dan looked at him sceptically. "But what do you *do*?" The smear of contempt in his voice was plain, and I was about to admonish him, but Pete just smiled. "Actually, I think I'm on the verge of finding out where Santonaga's base is."

Before moving the lads to Marion's stately home in Sussex, I'd had Jeeves run an extrapolatory diagnostic scan of the UK, meshed with all the details Marion and I could remember of Santonaga's place. But either he'd had that country pile shielded or Jeeves didn't have enough information, whatever— we still didn't know where he was. Marion's basement in the Palace had been devastated by fire, so we only had her less powerful and less connected home comms to work with; that and the version of Jeeves we'd brought with us, spread around several laptops.

Dan looked at Pete with a little more respect. "How?" he said.

"I've been using a new language extrapolator," said Pete. "I get Jeeves to randomly sample phone calls from across the country then look for small inconsistencies in word usage or tone."

"But how the bleedin' 'ell can that tell you where Santonaga is?" said Dan. Pete and I shared a wry smile, recognising Sam's influence in his tone.

"We're all affected by tiny changes in the electromagnetic field around us," said Pete. "But we aren't aware of it most of the time. Santonaga has been training super-people, and while he's probably surrounded them with shielding signals, he can't stop their powers getting into the general ghost field."

"Ghost field? Like dead spirits and stuff?"

Pete ran his hands through his hair, not used to explaining his weird mind to a kid. "Well, it's mostly full of dead words: things people have said that still resonate in the ether. But, yes, there are a few conglomerations that could be more than the sum of their echoes: real ghosts, in other words."

Oh bugger it. I knew that look in Dan's eyes; knew what he was thinking. His Dad had been his biggest hero; died when the kid was only five.

I caught Pete's eye, about to shake me head. But then I let duty guide me: we needed Dan to be useful and stop pestering me to turn him Beller. Therefore, even if his interest in Pete's work could only lead to shattered hopes, it would at least keep him out from under.

"Okay," he said. "When do we start?"

Pete, who never seemed to eat much, pushed aside his half-full plate and said, "Now."

After eating, I took a shower in my room then went to the ballroom. We weren't due to meet up for another thirty minutes but I felt restless.

The huge room was dustier than when we'd first arrived. But Marion had given all her staff an indefinite holiday, not wanting them in the line of possible fire, and we didn't have time for dusting around. Also, I suspected this was probably the first time in its history that it over-flowed with computers, wall maps, whiteboards and paper-strewn tables.

"Was Pete serious, Jack; is he really close to finding Santonaga's base?"

Marion's heels echoed on the sprung floor. She'd changed out of her black suit, now wearing slacks and a simple white T-shirt; most unprincess-like.

We sat either side of a table.

"I'm sure he's serious," I said. "The only problem is Pete runs on Pete time; so when he says 'close', we could be talking the Christmas after next."

"Well, it doesn't really matter anyway."

"Because you think Santonaga will attack us here?"

"He must know we're here, and this place is easier to breach than your headquarters—at least now you're ready for him."

I winced at the memory of how easily we'd let him crash Bellers' HQ, and she was right, he wouldn't do it again.

"Are the families comfortable there?" she said.

Most of the Bellers' nearest and dearest had opted to sit out the fight at HQ. We figured Santonaga wouldn't waste resources trying to kidnap them, not at this late stage. A few others, like Sarah, had insisted on camping out here, to help the cause.

As if reading my mind, Marion said, "Your sister is a remarkable woman, Jack. She works non-stop and never shows her fear; keeps up everyone's spirits. Yet she must be terrified inside."

"She used to be a quiet kid when we was young, and I suppose I took that for weakness. I mean, she was always good at school and stuff, but kept her own counsel. When Dad left, for instance, she just got on with life like he'd never been around; which actually was probably a brave thing to do, now I think about it. And when John, her husband, died of cancer, she kept Danny going."

"I envy the relationship she has with her son. My family isn't so close. We like each other well enough but there's always duty."

I recognised her expression, or perhaps my blood read hers. "You have a mission for me, ma'am?"

"Yes, I know it's your third this week, but the Professor and I are determined to wipe out as many links in the chain as possible."

The mission always took place at night, always alone, just like the other Bellers on their missions, too. "It's okay. It needs doing."

At that moment, the Prof entered the room. "Sorry, Jack," he said, handing me a data pad for my suit comms.

"Any news from Ambrose?" I said. "Last I spoke to him, he seemed to think he was just a few days from finding a cure for the turned."

He shook his head. I'd hooked the two of them up a few days back, figuring they'd speak the same language. "He's got a lot to concentrate on, and he's not as practised as he used to be in finding solutions. Brilliant mind but not always one I can find common ground with. He can be a little arrogant with his world view."

I smiled. "The old magic vs science scenario, eh?"

"More like stubborn old git vs stubborn old git," he said.

I headed for the main door. "Try to get some sleep you two," I shouted over my shoulder.

The fact I found him feeding just made it easier for me. His head turned at the sound of my footsteps, and he made no attempt to conceal the rivulets of blood on his chin, or the pointed teeth still warm from the neck he'd just pierced.

A large office for a larger than life man. Head of umpteen companies; tolerated if not exactly loved by the British public, because of his full beard and trademark white poncho. I wondered what they'd make of the red-spattered version he wore now.

For all I knew, he really was a good man before he'd been turned. Apparently, he used to do a lot of charity work and the photo on his sparse but highly polished desk showed a family shining with normality and health.

Then again, he hadn't shown much charity to the young man dying in his arms. Judging by his woolly cap and dirty clothes, I guessed Sir Brian Hopkins had picked him off the street. Untraceable and probably unmissed. Certainly, Sir Brian wouldn't be turning such riff raff. Just feasting on his life essence before disposing of the body.

"Who the hell are you and how did you get in here?" he said, dropping said body with just a quick reluctant glance at all that as yet untapped sustenance pouring out of the ragged wound.

"You're not going to let your food get cold are you, Sir Brian?"

For a moment, he looked undecided at this geezer in a non-descript overcoat not appearing as shocked as he should have been, and apparently with the ability to get into a locked building then a locked office, but at the same time clearly not one of his own.

Well, that was the only moment I needed.

His vamp strength, augmented by fury at being interrupted during feeding meant I'd never get close enough to unturn him, even if I wanted to. So I pulled the sonic gun from behind my coat and fired a beam into his forehead, programmed to scatter on impact. His head exploded all over the deep blue carpet, the Picasso on the wall and the family photo.

His victim was dead too so I just sent a message to MI5 and left the scene. They could clear up the mess and tell Sir Brian's wife whatever they needed to.

I slipped out of the door, then headed for the general lift rather than take Sir Brian's in case it was booby-trapped.

As I waited for it to arrive, an electronic throb pressed itself against my thigh. I opened the pocket in my Bellers' suit and took out the Prof's little sensing device. The screen flashed dull blue, indicating a vamp was in the vicinity.

But I'd just killed the vamp, hadn't I?

The screen now flashed yellow, telling me it was less than ten yards away.

I looked both ways down the corridor. Nothing.

The screen flashed orange just as the lift arrived. The vamp was in it!

I had time only to raise the gun, ready to shoot the moment the doors slid back.

I just managed to stop my trigger finger when I saw who was inside.

TWENTY

Sounding Out a Princess

"SANDRA?"

She wore soft coloured clothes—grey coat, pale blue dress under it, simple shoes—and her eyes full of joy to see me.

"Oh, Jack, I've missed you so much."

She stepped out of the lift, put her arms around my shoulders, pulled me to her. Her perfume hinted at roses and just for a second, I forgot to ask myself how she could possibly know I was there.

Which was the same second, as it happens, in which I lost consciousness.

My name was Meera Nath. A graduate from Manchester University, first class honours in Political History. Thirty six years old; joined MI5 a year after leaving university. Rose quickly through the ranks but was frustrated at not being promoted fast enough. Then Lucilla Hammond-Parker, head of the agency, offered me a fast-track to the top.

As the hired car glided through the Sussex lanes, summer hedge dust swirling through the open window, sluggish herds of cows chomping on emerald grass as if on another planet, one where world-changing events never happened, I recalled the now necessary details of my Dead Life. Rin had given me a file to read before leaving on the mission. The details were interesting enough but assimilating them felt like wearing someone else's coat: functional but just not *me*.

He didn't tell me how the information in it had come into his possession. I didn't care; suspected it came from someone in the agency who was working for the real world to come.

The file included a copy of a note by Lucilla to say my profile fitted perfectly with the romantic aspirations of a very important Beller. The Bellers, as she had told me, were not a myth, as many believed, but a group of East End men, all born on the same day, all affected dramatically by the sonic patterns of Bow Bells ringing out when they weren't scheduled to, mixed, some believed with a little magic.

By and large, the Bellers were friends to the government, despite their general rebelliousness toward any kind of authority. They had undertaken many dangerous missions, mostly successfully, using their unique powers.

Jack Stapleton was the main contact point between the agency and the Bellers. But he had a habit of going incommunicado. Lucilla also suspected the Bellers had contingency plans that did not involve the government. The agency had invested a lot of time and money in the Bellers, so it didn't want them to suddenly go off and do their own thing, or worse, side with the enemy. The agency wanted to be forewarned.

My own Dead Life recollections were hazy: a buzz of pleasure from helping Jack Stapleton, in amongst plenty of irritated periods when he wouldn't do as he was supposed to. Somewhere in there, having sex . . . but Rin's data was insufficient to tell how much that had been part of Ms Nath's agency brief, and how much she might have actually felt something for the man.

But it didn't matter anyway, because that was all Dead Life stuff that happened before I knew the truth about the future, and just how many deluded people were dedicated to making sure it never occurred.

A mile from the gates to Princess Marion's estate, I pulled the car off the road and took a syringe from my bag. The contents looked like ordinary blood. But in fact, this was Rin's programmed blood. It would keep me strong, help me to not die back into my Dead Life.

I injected myself then dropped the needle into a nearby, very thick hedge. I drove on and in a couple of minutes found myself passing alongside a long wall heading towards the central gate.

I turned in and stopped the car in front of a new-looking barrier. I waited for a guard to approach me, hands in lap, trying to look non-threatening.

A black man with a friendly face but cautious eyes leaned into my window. Nath's memory pinged and I said, "Hello, Al, how are you?"

"Meera? Hey—where have you been?"

His tone was light but I knew he'd have switched his suit comms to transmit this conversation to the main house.

"Well, that's top secret information," I said.

"Sorry, but I have to ask you to step out of the car."

"No problem."

I climbed out of the car, letting him see my ordinary jeans and T-shirt, handing him my bag to check.

He looked through the bag quickly but efficiently and gave it back to me. Then he apologised again before running his fingers lightly, expertly over my body, not finding anything, of course.

Finally, he asked me to look into an iris-scanner.

We stood awkwardly together while he waited for the result. Then he grinned and said, "Good to have you back, Ms Nath. I'm afraid you'll have to leave the car here; one of the guys'll drive you to the house."

Another Beller, one I didn't recognise, drove me in a Land Rover to the main building. The drive must have been nearly a mile long, surrounded by ancient woods and open meadows with herds of deer grazing here and there.

Rin had talked convincingly about the absurdity of inheritance. Rather than use their incredible wealth to introduce better ways of living for all the people, the titled had surrounded their estates with walls, both physically and figuratively. Royalty had become remote, idealised, stagnant and violently resistant to change.

The main house appeared around a corner of elm trees and, despite my desire to see the country released from the stifling grip of royalty, I couldn't but feel a surge of wonder in my chest at the massive, white stone stately home, with its minarets, flags, turrets, moat and drawbridge.

People ran between buildings, doors flew open constantly, and as I stepped out of the car, I could hear from behind the house sounds that clearly issued from special powers being used.

The jeep crunched off through gravel, returning to its post, and I made my own way to the main entrance. Just inside the door, I smelt cooking, closer than the kitchens would normally be in this sort of house. Voices cracked through the electric air, both real and virtual.

I followed the food smells into a large room full of long tables: no ta-blecloths, more like an army canteen. At the back of the room, a man and woman were arranging bowls of food; the woman I recognised.

"Sarah?"

Her face lit up with delight and relief as she put down a pile of plates then ran down the gap between tables.

"Meera!" She hugged me tight, then let go to check my face. "Does Jack know you're coming today?"

I shook my head. "I wanted to surprise him. Is he here?"

"He's not around at the moment, love. Probably on a mission somewhere. They don't tell me where they go, which is just as well. Hungry?"

I nodded and she led me downstairs to the kitchen. I suspected she want-ed to save me from having to answer too many questions when all the others came in for lunch.

The kitchen was large, lit by slanting sunlight from high windows. Peo-ple washed pots and prepared vegetables. Sarah sat me at a pine table in the corner, then fetched a plate full of meat pie, cauliflower cheese, potatoes and cabbage.

"The food's pretty basic," she said. "But then we ain't cooks and the guys mostly just need bulk, what with all the training they're putting in. I'll have to get back upstairs in a minute. Are you here to stay?"

"This is delicious," I said, swallowing a mouthful of steak pie. "Yes, but I suppose I'd better speak to whoever's leading here first; let them know what's happened to me."

She smiled. "Well, there ain't no *official* leader, but it's dead obvious to everyone who really is."

"Her Royal Highness?"

She laughed. "Honestly, the guys moan about her bossiness, but secretly I think they was just waiting for someone to tell 'em what to do. Jack's sort of their brain box, but he's never been the sergeant major type. I guess it's all down to breeding in the end. Look—I really need to get back to the dining room. I'll tell Marion you're here, if she don't know already, and I'm sure she'll send for you soon."

After she left, I ate the meal, quelling the feeling of being a traitor in their midst. Clearly, these were good people, doing what they believed was right. It wasn't their fault that the system they supported had been rotten for centuries. Hopefully, we could re-educate them, once the cancer at the top had been dealt with.

About forty minutes later, a voice behind me said, "Watcher, Meera!"

I stood and turned to see a bulky, bald man straining out of his black Bellers' suit. I hugged him hard.

"Hey, Sam, it's good to see you."

He held me at arm's length, looking in my eyes. "Where the bleedin' 'ell have you been, girl?"

I gently broke his hold, tapped the side of my nose with a finger. "That's for the Princess's ears only."

"Understood. I'm to take you to her now, as it happens. Need a hand with that bag?"

He swung my bulging pack on to his shoulder as if it was made of marshmallow and steered me out of the kitchen.

"Seriously," he said, "I hope you've got a lead on Santonaga. We ain't been able to find nothing. Put plenty of his lackeys out of action, but without capturing a single one, to get information on their master. They're crazy as blood-sucking coots, so we've had to kill 'em all."

"I have got some interesting things to say to her, actually."

We climbed a wide, marble staircase to the first floor, then he stopped outside a set of oak doors.

"I'll take your bag to the women's quarters. Just knock and go in."

"Thanks, Sam. I'll come and say hello to the others after I've spoken to the Princess."

"You do that. And if Jack calls in we'll tell him you're here."

I knocked, took a deep breath and walked into Marion's rooms.

I'm not sure what I'd expected—something luxurious and chintzy, I suppose—but it looked more like a room that had been commandeered. While the furniture was plush, the carpet deep and so on, clothes were scattered everywhere, along with mugs, glasses, papers and muddy boots.

Marion herself sat behind a desk that looked as if it had been pulled into the middle of the room. She'd been typing on a laptop when I entered, but stopped to watch me approach.

Her hair was tied back, giving her white face more light from the window to her right. She wore what looked like a Bellers' suit, which seemed odd indeed for a royal.

She stood, held out her hand. I thought about kissing it as the proper thing to do, but the pragmatic look in her eye told me to just shake it.

"Take a seat," she said. "Please excuse the outfit but we've more training to get through this afternoon, so it hardly seems worth having a shower and changing just for lunch. Have you eaten?"

I sat opposite her. "Yes, thank you. Not the sort of meal you'd expect in a stately home, but very good."

"I realise you've signed the Official Secrets Act and should only be reporting to an MI5 senior officer, but I'd appreciate any news you can give us of Santonaga. We're sitting out here like suicidal ducks, waiting to be shot, but so far he's not taken a pot at us."

Santonaga. Rin had prepared me for their obsession with what most likely was a mythical figure. I had to play along for now.

"As you can probably guess," I said, "I've been on his track for some time. But it's been difficult to pin him down."

"Well, he does have shape-shifting powers; could look like anyone."

Something about her gaze warned me she may know more than she was telling. Certainly, she could have contacted MI5 about me, but they would have simply told her I was on a mission.

"This suit I'm wearing," she said, "is a combination of the best of Court Wizards' magic and Bellers' technology. It's actually connected to my nervous system, by sonic resonance meshing. It can detect the approach of a bullet and super-harden the point of impact before it arrives. Even if the bullet is aimed at my head, the mask will cover my face and protect it before it hits."

"Why are you telling me this, ma'am?"

"I'm just telling anyone who might be listening."

"You think I'm bugged?"

She shook her head. "Not conventionally. We've scanned you for that. But you might have been infected without your knowledge."

Her eyes moved once, slightly, sideways—perhaps a gesture to tell me that if I was worried about listeners, too, I should cease from giving her any more sensitive information.

Was Rin listening? He hadn't said he could. And I trusted him to respect my privacy. On the other hand, I'd seen people turn into bats and throw flames from their fingers. And this mission, he said, could not be more important.

Then I saw the trap. If I stopped talking, I could not deliver the exact form of words Rin had made me memorise; the ones that would subliminally draw the Princess closer to our side. Or if not, then at least show me that she would need to be eliminated.

Yet, if I carried on, the Princess, clearly alert to any deception, might sense the coded language and possibly resist before I could complete the sequence.

I decided not to proceed for now, figuring I could at least explain to Rin later.

"I'm really sorry, ma'am, but I just don't have anything to report. I'm glad to be back, though; is there anything I can do to help?"

She sighed. "Yes, you can help Peter and Daniel in the basement. They've been working on sonic and electromagnetic patterning. At least that's what they say they're doing. I suspect they're actually tapping into the Bank of England's computers and transferring large sums of money out. Which would come in handy, as a matter of fact, since this exercise is using up most of my assets."

"I'd be happy to help them."

She smiled, went back to her screen and I left the room.

It must have been the luck of the royals, but in just a few minutes she'd managed to stop me using the ensnaring words Rin had given me, shown me there would be no point in trying to kill her, and despatched me out of harm's way.

I could do nothing more about my mission right then.

Pete and Dan looked pleased to see me. Danny blushed too, which told me he'd grown up since I'd last seen him. I hugged them both, then listened to them describe their language matrix work, relieved that they didn't seem too interested in what I'd been doing since we'd last seen each other.

They'd set up a circle of computers in the basement, looking somewhat incongruous amongst the wine racks, and almost but not quite triggering a memory of somewhere similar I'd recently visited.

Pete stood in the middle of the machines, hands appearing to caress the air, while Danny worked one of the computers.

"Wait for it," said Pete, grinning.

A low rumble of sound enveloped us—words, musical notes, traffic noises: as if the world wanted to nudge in its sonic story.

Pete's hand movements increased in complexity, and as his fingers drew lines through the air, the sounds responded, rising in pitch, thickening in meaning.

"It's so tantalising," I said. "Like you could understand *every*thing, if you could only hear the pattern of it all."

Pete looked like responding to this but apparently changed his mind, concentrating instead on his hand movements.

And then all the sounds stopped.

Pete breathed heavily, hands now useless by his sides. "Can't take any more than that for now," he said. "We're getting closer, though. I nearly had a picture: water, burning trees . . . We've not found him yet, but at least we've made a discovery, ain't we, Dan?"

The boy grinned. "Can I show her, Pete?"

Pete nodded and Dan picked up a slim tube from the desk he sat at. "It's an improved version of Uncle Jack's sonic gun," he said.

Gingerly, I took it from him. The tube was only about four inches in length, ending in a small, round hand-grip.

"How does it work?" I said.

Pete said, "When you press the hand-pad, sensors take a matrix reading of your heart-beat and amplify it. You then speak a word—any word—and a pulse amplifies through your flesh and goes from the gun straight to the heart of whoever you're aiming it at. Stops it dead."

Dan said, "We're going to make some more for the Bellers, in case their powers don't finish off the enemy."

"And who is the enemy?" I said, before realising that I should know. I finished the question by folding my arms and smiling, hoping they'd interpret the question metaphysically.

"I know what you mean," said Pete. "Santonaga wants power over all of us, but how come our system allowed him to get created in the first place?"

I nodded, although I didn't really follow his drift. Before I needed to say something, Dan blew a raspberry, then said, "It don't matter how he got the way he is, does it? All that matters is stopping him."

Pete looked at me, expecting to share an adult look, which I duly gave him.

"Coffee?" he said. "We've got a kettle out back."

"No thanks," I said. "I'm going to shower and change."

They left the basement by the opposite door and I was about to put down the gun Pete had given me, thinking that I just about recalled how absent-minded he could be. And realised that she was simply too strong to be swayed.

If I was quick enough . . .

I half walked, half ran, to the door and up two flights of stairs, knocked then entered. Marion still sat at her laptop.

"Meera?"

I fired the gun and Marion's face crumpled in shock and pain. She slumped on to the laptop, head at an unnatural angle. I removed my shoe, peeled off the patch of fake skin under the bridge of my foot and removed the entirely plastic transmitter; pressed it to send the signal that I'd succeeded, then re-placed it and left the room.

I forced myself to walk normally through the front door, as if on my way to the women's quarters. Outside, I made for the east wing but instead of go-ing inside, slipped around the building, then made for the woods that led to the wall and beyond it the road.

Keeping to the shadows of the trees, I ran the mile or so to the wall. It was easy enough to climb the ancient bricks then drop to the grass verge beyond. My plan was to walk to a crossroads I'd noticed half a mile west. But I'd only gone about fifty yards when a fast engine noise rushed toward me. Turning, I saw a sleek, black machine approaching too fast to get away from. I con-sidered climbing back over the wall, but that would seal my guilt. Instead, I walked normally, hoping they weren't actually coming for me. After all, surely no one knew yet what had happened back at the house.

But the car ripped to a halt by cutting off my progress on the verge. A black window wound down and Pete said, "You'd better get back in, Meera. We need to talk."

Too shattered to speak, I let him lead me back to Marion's room. I tried to mentally prepare a story to cover her death but in the event I didn't need to.

"Sit down," said Marion, still at her desk, a dark bruise on her forehead.

She held up the sonic gun. "Doesn't do a thing," she said.

"How did you know?" I said.

"We've seen your lake and the bell-shaped ship—nice, ironic touch, that—and your teacher. He calls himself Rin but we know who he really is."

My gaze flicked to the window, to the door; no way out.

"We're going to cure you, Meera," Marion went on.

Cure? She meant return me to the Dead Life. I'd go back to walking around in a trance, believing that all these people smiling at me, saying hello, paying me a wage, making love to me, owned the real world, when in fact they just prevented it happening.

I reached under my foot, the other one, ripped off the patch there and removed the pill Rin had given me if it all turned hopeless. But before I got it into my mouth, Pete grabbed my wrist with surprising strength, making me drop it.

"But if you knew," I said, "why didn't you stop me trying to kill you?"

Marion looked very tired. "Because we wanted you to tell him I'm dead. We want him to send his people, thinking we're leaderless."

"You said he isn't really Rin."

"We'll tell you who he is after you're cured." She nodded to Pete who put his arm around me and led me out of the room, followed by two guards.

TWENTY-ONE

A Conversation with the Dark Side

AT FIRST, I THOUGHT THE DARK had taken me bleedin' eyes away. My mind struggled to get a grip on its surroundings but all I could feel was my hands tied behind me, my naked buttocks on hard wood.

I twisted me head slightly, felt tight cloth against my eyes. I forced meself to sit still, stay calm, listen, sense . . . the smell of candle smoke, muffled traffic noises, so maybe still London . . . maybe even the office where I'd killed the vamp. But no, because I'd met—

"Sandra?"

No reply, but you know what, I actually felt her presence pressing against my skin; prickly, alive, not natural, a bit like the buzz you get in your nerves just before a thunder storm breaks.

Ambrose hadn't called to tell me she'd left Halifax, so he probably didn't know yet.

"I can *feel* you," I said.

Still nothing. And I admit to getting right spooked then. There's nothing worse than not knowing what you're dealing with. When I'd seen her in the lift, she'd seemed just like the old Sandra—the one who'd been unlucky enough to go out with me.

Oh, bugger: had she taken me to Santonaga?

"Sandra, love—"

My skin burned; wrong word, then, but right person.

I sighed, pissed off if you must know. I might have had me bollocks on show for the world to see and in possession of about as much bargaining power as a bit of plankton that's just been sucked into a whale's mouth, but the fact was there were bigger fish to fry, pardon me mangled metaphors. If she was after retribution, then I just wanted her to get on with it.

"Either take me out the game or let me get on with stopping Santonaga," I said out loud, although I hadn't intended to.

The blindfold was ripped away by someone behind me.

I nearly laughed. Our surroundings couldn't be more ordinary: by the light of several candles, I saw a nice sofa with scatter cushions, a large flat screen TV in the corner, a couple of Impressionist prints on the walls . . . but then I twigged.

"This is *your* house, ain't it?" I said, me heart nearly breaking at the distance I'd taken her away from her home. Even though she stood in it now, she'd never actually be in it again.

"You brought me here because it's one of the few places no one's bothered to bug, yeah?"

Still no answer.

I tried to sound relaxed, not easy to do when you're sitting in front of someone who could probably rip your head off as easy as blinking.

I had no idea what to say, other than it better not be 'sorry'.

But at last she spoke, voice horribly cool.

"Santonaga figured Ambrose would get you to try half re-turning me. And that would have worked, if I'd actually lost my memory. But I never did. I just pretended to."

"Why the hell would you do that?"

My head jerked to one side, cheek burning from where she'd slapped me.

"So you wouldn't re-turn me. Oh, and to make you fuck me when you were in love with someone else. To spoil it for you with her."

And that's when I knew for sure she was still a turned vamp. Because the real Sandra would never be so cruel, even if she hated my guts.

"It was only sex, Sandra."

She walked around to face me.

"Jesus . . ."

She'd cut her red hair short, curving around her cheekbones, black-gold in the dim light. She wore maroon leather that seemed to have been melted on to her body. In fact, I thought I saw its surfaces move slightly, adjusting to her shifting flesh, remaining tight around her.

She saw my frown. "The sonics in my blood constantly react with the nano structures in the suit. Like it?"

The suit gripped her breasts, lifting them slightly; the nipples standing out.

"Oh, I see you do."

I knew she'd humiliate me but I could do nothing. Well, I could've closed my eyes but it was too late for that.

Part of her suit melted away, reformed into what looked like a corset, tucked under her naked breasts.

She didn't lubricate either of us, just rammed herself on to me.

"Does this hurt, Jack?"

As she raised her hips and lowered them again, twisting to increase the pain/pleasure, I realised she wanted to do this to me in her old house, inside her old life where, if what I'd seemed to promise her when we'd first met had been true, we might now be sitting together on the sofa watching The X-bleedin'-Factor.

We'd share a bottle of wine and kiss; make love, with kindness and care.

"Are you crying, Jack?"

She pushed faster and I felt my tears dropping on to my chest as I came. She carried on, used her fingers on herself then came too.

She climbed off me, the suit complete once more.

"He actually sent me to Halifax to steal the cure." She sat on the sofa, held up what looked like a data stick, presumably containing the sonics for the cure. "Our plan was for you to overpower me then—well you know the rest: all designed to give Ambrose an incentive to finish the cure quick and keep you out of action for as long as possible."

She smiled mockingly. "You'll be pleased to know he's finished it."

"Why does Santonaga want the cure?" I said.

She shook her head pityingly. "This device contains a sequence of resonance meshes that can be broadcast via national TV networks. The resulting signal will set up a similar resonance in the blood of every person in the country. If they've been turned by Santonaga, they'll be cured."

Oh, no.

"But of course," she went on, "what can heal can also infect. This signal can be adjusted to open everyone's blood, too. With it, Santonaga can prime the entire population so they'll comply easy-like with being turned, at his and his agents' leisure."

"Sandra, you can't—"

"I'm going now," she said, standing. "I have the satisfaction of knowing you'll need to face the real love of your life, your dusky agent maiden, and tell her what you and I did together. Or will you hide the details from her? Will you forget to mention how I dressed up for you; how I made you stiff even when I was raping you."

She walked to the door, then turned. "By the way, something funny happened to me half way over the Atlantic. The sum of the different parts of me—nice, ordinary Sandra, Santonaga's saliva, your sperm, plus all that walking the borderline between light and dark—is much stronger than anyone expected. For instance, I left my link open with Santonaga while you were forced to have sex with me just then. But I've switched it off now because, well, maybe I just ain't party to *any*one's plans no more."

She looked at the data stick. "Actually, I haven't decided yet who gets this. Santonaga thinks he's still working me, but you know what, maybe I'll just sell to the highest bidder."

I nearly begged then; tried to talk her into doing the right thing. But why the hell should she believe I knew what the right bleedin' thing was?

As she walked from the room, she said, "Oh by the way, Ambrose is dead."

The front door closed and sheer, raging anger filled me. I was just so fed-up of being used by everyone, of using everyone too. I liked to think I'd always tried to do best by people I cared about. But Sandra had shown me what a phoney I could be.

And she'd left me with nothing but more phoney crap to tell Meera about us, if I ever saw her again. It was a big enough ask already, that she accept I had to keep screwing Sandra to protect her from her dark side and thereby stop her using her powers to alert Santonaga about Ambrose, and prevent him developing a cure.

But now . . . Well, I'd have to tell her that in fact Sandra was Santonaga's all along, or maybe even just herself, whatever that now really was. And I should of seen it.

Hell, Jack boy, be honest: you did know it, really. You knew it weren't her illusion of loving you that you were keeping alive with all that rogering. You just wanted her; you wanted sex with dressing up, and just now, you wanted her to fuck you again, and you wanted to come when she did.

» TWENTY-TWO «

Broadcasts of the Blood

"MEERA, WE COULD BE ATTACKED any moment; there isn't time to properly de-programme you. You'll just have to trust me."

I made myself smile. "Of course I trust you, Professor Paul." I looked confidently around his basement laboratory, at the banks of monitors and the couch I'd just lain on, garishly lit by the lights he'd used to examine me.

"I mean *really* trust me," he said, causing me to look back at him, and for a moment I almost did sink into those sincere eyes.

But I had to be strong. Rin had warned me they'd sound convincing. Marion with her rebellious honesty, the Bellers with their misguided sense of right and wrong, and my agency's chief research Professor with his calm, reassuring tones.

He seemed to read something in my eyes then because instead of pressing me further, he turned to a small worktop and switched on a kettle.

"As you'll know from agency files, Santonaga's parents were head of a kind of rich person's inheritance mafia whose origins stretch back to the fifteenth century."

He poured coffee into a cafetiere, added boiling water to it. The smell was wonderful but I remained focussed on my task. Which was to escape as soon as I could.

"What our files don't show, and what Marion has been able to tell me, is that this group was responsible for the extraordinary growth of the vampire population during Tudor times. They infiltrated high office and royalty, turning those who could be of use to them, simply killing and feeding from those who weren't, mostly the peasant stock, as you can guess."

He poured just a little milk into one mug of coffee and handed it to me. I frowned and he said, "Sorry, do you want sugar?"

I shook my head. "It's okay; I was just thinking how easy it is to judge everyone from their file."

He smiled, as if not expecting me to make such an observation; and indeed, I hadn't meant to.

"Well, at least the Palace archives were written at the time—most of them destroyed the other day unfortunately. Anyway, the vampire population extended even into the Vatican; there's a strong possibility the Pope himself was one. The problem was that most of the important people in Europe were now vampires which meant the ones who weren't needed a plan for dealing with them, and fast."

His tone was quietly enthusiastic, like a history teacher who really wants his pupils to understand. But we both knew the actual purpose of this conversation was to make me betray my master, hence all these lies about vampires.

"It seems," he said, "that the unturned got lucky. Court wizards in Henry's employ discovered the link between sound and blood and, if you believe it, magic. Vampires, as you know, can turn their victims if they wish, or just kill them. But no one, including the vampires themselves, knew how this happened. The vamps, apparently, just willed it. But what Henry's wizards discovered was that in fact when they bit, their vocal chords emitted a different kind of grunt for turning as for plain killing. The right grunt set up a resonance wave in their saliva which in turn altered the gene ether matrix of the victim's blood."

He sipped his coffee waiting, I guessed, for me to add some thoughts.

"So, Henry's wizards found a way to use sound to re-turn vampires?" I said, playing along.

"Yes, it was in fact a fantastic piece of international co-operation that Henry organised. All across civilised Europe, churches rang their bells in a specific pattern prescribed by Henry's wizards. The resonance matrix that resulted re-turned every vampire within earshot, which was the great majority."

"Even the Vatican's bells?"

He smiled. "No, Henry was never a great friend to Catholicism and in any case, the Vatican was over-run by vamps at that time. We believe now that the Pope was a bloodjacker with the ability not just to turn others but also to have their wills thereafter controlled by him. So, it's not even certain the bells would have worked on him anyway."

"So, how was he killed?"

"We don't know. The current bloodjacker is a shape-shifter too, so if the Pope also was, it's likely he'd be very difficult to kill. A modern weapon could explode his brain, something that's obviously impossible to recover from. But back then—well, I think the court wizards used bells to create anti-vampires."

"Like the Bellers?"

He probably intended it, but despite retaining my guard, I couldn't help be drawn a little into this magical history which it was doubtful no more than a handful of people knew.

"Yes, and the fact there appears to be no record of them could indicate they were also drawn from the working classes who by and large couldn't write in those days, too busy surviving for the most part."

I sipped the coffee which was pleasant but more bitter than I'd expected.

"So, what do you think Santonaga has planned this time?" I said.

"Oh, ultimately I don't think it's very different to Pope Christopher Steven's plans five hundred years ago. Okay, Catholicism no longer exists, so he can't hide behind the respectability of that. Instead, I reckon he intends to maintain the power structures we have in place today: government, monarchy and so on. We'll still be a democracy, on the surface at least. Except that all power will lead back to him."

"But how can one man possibly control a whole country?"

I remembered Rin's super-powered, shape-shifting people, and the others like me he was training to be leaders. Surely, Rin could not be planning the sort of dominance they claimed Santonaga had in mind. And then I got it, at last.

"Professor Paul—thank you! Now I understand why you've been telling me all this. You wanted me to work out what's really been going on. And it's okay, I don't mind that the agency had to restructure my memory for it to work."

He looked uncertain and I realised he needed me to prove further that my mind was intact, that I'd worked out the truth.

"Rin works for the agency, doesn't he?" I said. "You've set up an alternate movement, to beat Santonaga and establish a more stable government."

"Er . . . if that's true, why didn't we just invite you to join; why remove your memories?"

I laughed. "You *know* why, but it's all right; I don't mind explaining. It's all been a test of my character, hasn't it? You had to see if I was capable of doing whatever was necessary for the cause, even assassinate a Princess. Of course, that was only because I'd been convinced she was actually part of the enemy, allied to Santonaga. But obviously I failed: you all knew what I was here to do from the start; which is why Pete was able to rig Marion's death."

"And why would we go to all that trouble? Why would this Rin send you on such a mission, and why would we make you believe you'd succeeded?"

I nodded, up with him now. "You have important plans for me. I needed to be tested."

He picked up a small device. "And do you think you've succeeded, agent Nath?"

"What's that thing you're holding?"

"I'm sorry, Meera. But this is the only way."

He pointed the device at me and pressed a button. A cacophony of tiny ringing sounds, like distant bells, filled my ears. Not just my ears but my blood, too.

"Oh, god," I said, "you put something in the coffee, didn't you?"

As I felt my blood leap and twist in my veins, consciousness hovering on the edge of oblivion, the last thing I heard was him saying, "Yes, I mixed it with some of Jack's blood. It's more effective if we use the same Beller's blood as the traces of sperm you still have inside you. I just hope the resonance of the sperm is still . . ."

I reckoned this was as low as I could get: tied up naked, just been raped, miles away from the fight, not a bleedin' clue as how to stop the end of the world as I'd known it . . .

And I did think about giving up then. Why not? What's the worse that could happen? Santonaga takes over the country? So what—pubs would still serve beer, and we already preferred it at blood temperature in this country anyway; the Hammers would struggle to avoid relegation most seasons; Hollywood action movies would get made, although I guess vamps might become the heroes instead of the villains. And if I just kept me 'ead down for a while, Santonaga would decommission or turn the Bellers. I might even be able to do a deal with him. After all, my powers were all about inventing things, and gizmos would still be needed in the new world. He'd probably even let me keep my old gaff. I could become a backstreet boffin; no more MI5 calls in the middle of the night; just days spent twiddling me screwdriver, nights contemplating Mum's roses, followed by a leisurely stroll to the pub. I might even meet a nice, ordinary girl there.

This cushty vision didn't evaporate as soon as I'd had it, like it always did before, when civilian life occasionally whispered seductively from somewhere inside me spiritual cardigan pocket. Maybe this time it would hold.

Maybe this time I really had had enough.

But then, I thought, *Oh, fuck it* and set about waddling in tight little duck steps toward the kitchen.

It took a long time, on account of me falling over quite a bit; that and the swearing breaks.

"Fuckety fucking fuck fucks and double bleedin' fucks," was the gist of it. Interspersed with an ancient Shamanistic mantra I'd picked up from a New Age geezer I once met in a pie and mash shop off Elephant and Castle, which went: "Come on, Jack, you old bastard; you can *do* it. Come on Jack, you old bastard; you can do it."

On the way, I planned how to open a kitchen drawer with me teeth. But in the event didn't have to, because there was a mighty sharp looking knife already out, on the table. Which might have meant Sandra actually hoped I'd try to escape. On the other hand, it could have been because she'd intended to slit my throat with it at some stage.

It ain't easy, slicing through rope with one of your bound hands having to hold the knife. And I suspect only my sheer self-loathing and need to do something about it worked that blade at the right angle.

Once me hands were free, I untied my feet and went looking for clothes. Fortunately, Sandra had just thrown them behind the sofa, so after washing meself down, I climbed back into the Beller's suit and ran outside.

"Jeeves—you there? I need to know where I am."

"Yes, I'm here, sir. Where are you? Well, morally, no doubt just south of Total Bastard and a few degrees west of Shit Creek without the proverbial. But I suspect you really want to know that you're in Hackney and how to—"

"It's okay, I've just hailed a taxi. There ain't no access points in Hackney so I might as well just head for home."

"Would that be where your heart is, sir?"

"Remind me to re-programme you if we survive this, to remove some of that great fat lip of yours."

"I shall inform Hilary to expect you. I take it you won't want her to pre-pare cocoa and a nice warm bath?"

"No, tell her to prepare weapons 35 and 39. And when you've done that, call Marion, tell her—is this line secure?"

I climbed into the cab before he answered, told the driver to head for Whitechapel.

"I'm sorry, sir," said Jeeves, actually sounding it for once. "But I can't guar-antee this system has not been compromised."

"Okay, well just tell 'er I'm heading for the source."

"What's that, mate?" said the driver.

I cut off comms, said to the driver, "Sorry, mate, just talking to meself."

"No worries, I do it all the time. Passengers think I'm talking to them but, hey, they're just part of the continuing story, know what I mean?"

"Actually, I do."

I didn't know then, exactly what powers the other one like me had received—Sandra, the former barmaid and object of Jack's domestic fantasy. But I could see what the two bloods had caused in her psychology: the horribly realistic appraisal of others, rooted in insight but unleavened by compassion.

For myself, I don't believe what saved me was a purer heart. Only very young children have one of those and even then it's quickly corrupted.

No, I think what saved me from becoming like her were two things: first, that Santonaga—or Rin as I'd known him—had tainted my blood more mild-ly than hers. He wanted me mostly to have my own thoughts, since I was to be one of his leaders. Oh, ultimately, I'd follow his policies and plans, but he needed his leaders to have enough self-ness to fool the masses and the media.

The other thing that helped save me, at least to begin with, was my love for Jack.

I was there when she said, "I have the satisfaction of knowing you'll need to face the real love of your life, your dusky agent maiden, and tell her what you and I did together. Or will you hide the details from her? Will you forget to mention how I dressed up for you; how I made you stiff even when I was raping you."

Almost as if she knew I was there. Or at least sensed this scene would in some way be monitored maybe by Santonaga. Whatever, she hurt me with those images, even though it was Jack she wanted to hurt most.

And the fact she'd never met me said that Santonaga had told her right from the beginning about Jack and me.

I saw her tight, tight body suit, and how she shaped it just so. I saw Jack's erection. I saw her impale herself upon him. I saw him come. I saw him cry.

Of course, when I say 'I', I mean my powers. My powers sent my soul, or essential self, or inner feeling, wherever I wanted to go. Not that I wanted to see a man humiliated like that, left trussed up naked, drops of semen on his thighs glistening in the candlelight.

I wanted to see Jack.

And after Sandra left, I saw Jack in despair for the first time ever.

And he *had* betrayed me. I understood why and even encouraged him to have sex with her. But he hadn't fully told me.

Well, no time to think about the implications of all that right then. Jack hadn't moved for several minutes and we couldn't afford for him to give in to failure.

Without a body, I didn't know what I could do. I could return to mine and get the agency to rescue him, but that, I suspected, would be a humiliation too far.

So it was I gathered up my own anger at what Santonaga had done to me and shaped it as best I could into the sheer desire to stop him; then breathed that into Jack's ear, hoping it would somehow affect his mind.

And a few seconds later, he started to hobble in his chair toward the kitchen. I stayed long enough to see him cut through his ropes, then willed myself to return to my body, and to the fight.

"Hilary! Code: Pie and Mash."

I ran into the kitchen, pulled a can of soup out of the cupboard, ripped open the lid, stuck it in the microwave.

"Code: Daisy Roots. Thank you, Jack. As you seem to have guessed, my main systems have been compromised. I'll work from the deep back-ups to fix it just as soon as I've serviced you, pardon my French."

"Yeah, well, I reckon I've had enough servicing for now, thanks. Weapons ready?"

Although she didn't like my code checks, it was a simple but effective system. I'd programmed her to respond to 'Pie and Mash' with her instinct-simulation software. This took a reading of my current chemical signature and sent a wireless signal to my suit sensors, of which there were five. Hilary was programmed to shut off this wireless effect the moment she was breached, and the breacher would be none the wiser. Sensor three had throbbed against my chest, and three was to give the Cockney for boots.

"Yes," she said, "but at the rate you're gulping that soup, you'll have severe heartburn interfering with your aim."

"Jeeves: I need you to make sure there's a very fast car waiting for me at our Glasgow base."

"Certainly, sir; would it help if I order one with go-faster stripes down the sides?"

"Hilary: I need you to go into deep coma mode after I leave. If Santonaga kills me, I don't want him ransacking you for information on the Bellers."

"How do you know he's in Scotland?" she said. "Jeeves and I don't have any data on his whereabouts, and neither does Princess Marion's systems."

"Because up until now, I've not wanted to admit we're alike in a lot of ways. Ever since I saw the light—saw the dark, actually—I've been able to smell him. Same way he smelled me out and stole Sandra from under me bleedin' nose. He's got bases all over the shop but he's in Scotland now, for the end game."

Silence for a few moments, which told me they was colluding. Then Jeeves said, "Sir, the weapons you're taking could kill a herd of elephants in a nano-second. But Santonaga can shift forms around anything you throw at him."

"Well, you know what they say about the kitchen sink."

"You have another weapon in mind—one we don't know about?"

"Yeah—it's called keeping the faith."

"Is that Cockney rhyming slang for you're going to get your arse blown off, sir?"

I finished the soup, took the guns from the priming cabinet, then dropped into the tube shaft.

"No comms in the tube, Jeeves," I said, hovering above the pod. "Don't want him picking up anything."

"Mum's the word."

"Which reminds me: if I don't come back, can you get one of the guys to water the roses every now and then?"

"Consider it done, sir."

The journey north by tube gave me a bit of time to wonder what the hell I was doing. Okay, revenge mixed with guilt is the human equivalent to rocket fuel. And Santonaga knew how I felt; he'd probably even engineered it. Expected me to go charging in, guns blazing; so he'd be prepared.

But sometimes you have to do what's expected because there's no other choice. All you can do is work a kink into the line of expectation, and hope it's enough to trip the bastard up.

The reason I had no choice was Sandra. She was no doubt on her way to Santonaga with Ambrose's resonance pattern doohickey. I was sure Santonaga would indeed know how to hijack the national television broadcasting system. Once he sent out that reversed pattern, the entire country would be primed to offer itself up to any famished vamp as meek as those what ain't going to inherit the earth after all.

The Bellers and Marion needed every able and super-powered body they could muster to fight Santonaga's shape-shifters. But even if they could spare troops to help me, I couldn't tell 'em where to go in any case. I could sense he was in Scotland, but he could be moving around and I'd have to track him.

The strength of a bloodjacker is that everyone tied to him has to do his will. The weakness of course is that if you take him out then all that's left is a bunch of purposeless vamps ripe for unturning.

If Ambrose was dead, Sandra must have killed him; another death that could be chalked up to my mistakes. But my feelings were split about Ambrose. He'd created us Bellers, right enough, yet I couldn't help wonder if he'd only done that because he felt guilty at making Santonaga, albeit he delayed his powers coming on.

Guilt again. It seemed to drive most folks. Except the vamps, of course. And come to think of it, toffs were not exactly famous for feeling guilty. I guess it's hard to sit on a great fat pile of wealth if you've got any doubts about your entitlement.

In other words, toffs and vamps were always a match made in heaven. Except heaven had been abolished, at least the Catholic kind. Which meant hell must have been too. Whatever, the point was I needed to bury my guilt under six feet of garlic to stand any chance of beating Santonaga. And Sandra.

I didn't know how she'd get up north, but the Bellers' tube couldn't be beaten for speed. Unless that is, she had a private jet warmed up and ready to go, but that seemed unlikely in Hackney somehow. So, I might get a couple of hours on her if lucky. Though she would of course have phoned ahead to tell Santonaga about Ambrose's device.

I didn't believe her for a second when she'd said she still hadn't made up her mind whether or not to help Santonaga. That was just part of my torture. He might be a little pissed that she didn't kill me but then if he had any sense he'd think twice about arguing with what she'd become. In fact, I guessed the only thing stopping her taking over his entire enterprise was whatever subservient hook he'd managed to keep in her blood.

The pod slowed and drifted up to the docking port at the Glasgow base. I took the nondescript Renault we used when working undercover and drove three miles to the pub where Jeeves would have arranged for the new car to be delivered.

A man in black suit and shades leaned against the bonnet of a Ferrari Grand Tourer. Not exactly discreet but then I didn't need to be: Santonaga was going to smell me coming anyway.

He nodded, handed me the keys then walked off without even a backward glance.

"Meera? Are you okay?"

My body felt strange, even though I hadn't been out of it very long. Its rigid skeleton and heart that could not stop beating, and the nerves that could only be on or off, all seemed so restrictive.

Then again, I also sensed the danger of being away from it too long—because that very fixation of form was what made my essence safe.

"I think so," I said, sitting up on the couch in the basement, Professor Paul holding out a glass of water.

I drank, the sheer physical touch of the cold liquid exquisite and real.

"I don't think my powers are going to be much use in the fight," I said.

"What happened?"

I told him about suddenly finding myself, minus a body, watching Sandra humiliate Jack. And about Ambrose's device that she intended to take to Santonaga.

"I'm pretty sure Jack's gone after him," I said.

"Yes, we received a cryptic message from the Bellers' comms system, and figured that's what he's done."

"I've been out for hours?" I shivered. "I don't know that I ever want to do that again. Apart from the danger of just drifting off forever, I didn't enjoy seeing Jack so down, especially when he didn't know I could. Why have I got this weird power, Professor?"

"I don't know, but I once read something in an agency archive, about Tudor wizards who believed the answer to controlling evil forces lay in the astral worlds. The problem is that only the soul can travel there, and the soul is very comfortable in its nice, safe body. It needs a compelling reason to leave—"

He stopped because right then the main alarm went off.

"We're under attack!" said a voice over the house speaker system. "Take positions!"

We ran from the thick-walled basement, hearing crashes and shouts from above. Up the stairs to the main lobby and I choked on all the smoke and brick dust. Flames ran up the curtains, furniture had splintered into jagged heaps; smashed vases littered the floor. Worst of all, three people lay still, blood swelling around their bodies.

The Professor ran to one of them, opening the bag he'd brought with him. I ran to the others, felt for pulses, found none. I recognised one of the Bellers and felt a searing loss, enflamed by anger. The other dead person was a wife, a tray of food scattered around her.

Sam ran into the lobby, carrying a huge gun.

"We've been hit by a couple of missiles. Softening us up."

I ran after him, up the stairs to the long gallery that looked out over the vast lawns.

"My god," I said. Reflected flames stippled Sam's grim face. "They've set all the trees on fire."

Crackling light made the lawn into a kind of ruptured stage.

Sam used his gun to smash open a window, then handed me a smaller rifle he must have had in his suit.

"Can you shoot?"

"Shoot what?"

He nodded outside. "Bats. The Prof made a load of bullets that shatter on impact, spraying a mixture of his cure: garlic and everything else vamps are meant to die from—let's see if the fuckers work."

I didn't need a satnav, didn't even need a bleedin' map. Now I'd accepted my guilt, I could feel him pulling at my blood. Whatever the link between the Bellers and Santonaga, it could do nothing but home itself, now I'd stopped fighting it.

I threw the Ferrari along the M8 at a hundred and twenty; then left the motorway, heading north east, weaving in and out of traffic on the dual carriageways, hurtling around country roads through silent black humps of the night hills. The car's lights made the bushes and trees at the verges leap out as if warning me not to go on.

But my blood just pulled harder. I had no doubt he knew I was coming, and that he couldn't avoid me any longer.

And then . . .

I got cut off. My blood stopped tugging. Nothing. I pulled off the road, stopped the engine, climbed out to sit on a rock.

This was *so* stupid. I'd come so close but without the blood link, I might as well stick a pin in the map and head for that.

Santonaga must have cut the connection. Must have known I was on the way; waited till I'd moved several hundred miles from the main fight then left me stranded.

Jesus wept, he'd played me for a sucker. Fired up my testoster-bleedin'-one so I'd zoom up north without considering the obvious: that he'd learned to control the signals his blood gave out.

I must have sat in the dark for twenty long minutes, frantically trying to come up with another plan but failing miserably.

Then I heard a voice in my ear.

"If you'll allow me to interrupt your self-pity fest for a moment, sir," said Jeeves, "I have Peter on the line. Once I realised that you had cocked up on the navigational front, I contacted him to ascertain what stage he was at with regard to finding Santonaga."

"Jack? Pete here. Look, I have to be quick. We're under attack. I'd got as far as narrowing down his location to three possibilities."

"Shit."

"No, it's okay. One's in Sussex, where he's got that brainwashing camp; another's the estate in East Scotland; the third is on the North West coast of Scotland, the direcetion you was already heading in, so it's got to be that one."

"Brilliant! Well done, mate. Let me have the map reference."

I drove for around another three hours, half way up a range of hills, on to a single track road where I gave no quarter to the occasional car coming the other way. I figured, if he had been moving around to confuse me, he'd stop now he believed I'd been disconnected.

Finally, I turned right, on to a gravel road winding through a dip in the hills. At its summit, I climbed out of the car and gazed down at an awesome and troubling sight.

About half a mile away and around five hundred feet below, the road ended at a castle. It sat on a cliff top, behind it the great dark grey Atlantic Ocean spreading to the horizon, a silver trail leading toward us from the full moon hanging just behind and to the side of the castle's tallest tower.

I wanted to use Jeeves to tell me about any weaknesses it might have, or even just the best undetected way in. But if I turned him on, Santonaga would pick up the transmission and know for sure I was close by. And with him having switched off our blood link, I could at least approach undetected.

Yes, I'd have to do this the old-fashioned way, which meant ditching the Ferrari for a start.

I walked down the winding road, looking for lights from the castle but saw none. He was there, for sure, but apparently he could see in the dark.

"There are dozens of them!"

"Shoot as many of the fuckers as you can!"

I lifted the gun, broke a window and aimed along the sight.

Sam let off a volley, tracer bullets hurtling fire through the flitting mass over the lawn. Five or six bats exploded, looking well dead.

I figured if I aimed at the centre of the flapping mass, I'd hit something. Other tracer fires flew out from other windows. I squeezed the trigger and destroyed two bats.

"They're retreating!" said Sam.

The remaining bat-vamps returned to the cover of the flaming trees.

"But now they've taken on human shapes," I said.

Sam jumped to his feet, ran to the stairs. "Keep yer 'ead down!"

"Why don't we just shoot them from here?" I said but he was out of ear-shot.

Then I realised why we couldn't just sit and wait for them: now they knew we had weapons that could destroy them in bat form, they'd come at us another way. It seemed incredible that Santonaga would sacrifice so many of his troops just to learn the extent of our weaponry. Whatever, now they'd use stealth and cunning to get to us. Which meant the best thing was to take the battle to them, fast.

I ran down the stairs after Sam, found him in the lobby with a dozen or so other Bellers in their black suits, all armed; Marion in her suit too.

I stood at the back as she gave orders; then they all dispersed—about two thirds of them running, crouching, out into the night, the others to take up various positions around the house.

Which left me with nothing to do but feel rejected and useless. But I couldn't expect much else: I'd only just been re-turned, and Marion didn't even know if I had any powers, let alone what they were.

I still had the gun though, so—

A crashing sound from the basement steps. I ran down them to see a hole in the corridor floor with a black-suited man standing next to it, brushing clumps of mud and wood off his body.

Oh no—Dan had heard the crash too and left the safety of the Professor's lab to investigate. Just as the Professor arrived to pull Dan back, the interloper saw them and ran their way.

Anyone strong enough to power through solid earth could no doubt rip them to pieces easily.

I ran after him, mind thrashing in desperation about how to help. He reached the door before they could close it. I caught up to see him bearing down on the Professor and Dan who'd put a bench in his way.

Dan saw me but to his great credit didn't call out my name.

I threw my soul out of my body and into the super-digger's. His blood network lashed at me, the essence of his master keen to capture and destroy me. But I closed my etheric fingers around his heart, tight around the little electric spark that made it beat. I used my own electric self to stop it.

He fell to the floor and I jumped out, back into my own body now collapsed on the floor.

The Professor rushed to me, helped me sit up. "What did you do, Meera?"

"No time to tell you; I have to go help the main fight. You two stay here."

Which was the moment I noticed Dan wearing a black Bellers' suit.

"Why aren't you with the partners and kids in the bunker?" I said to him.

"I'm going to fight," he said, with terrible certainty for one so young.

The Professor shook his head. "He tricked me; waited till my back was turned then injected himself with Bellers' blood. We don't know what his powers, if any, will be. He's got Bellers' genes in him as it is, so maybe that will have the same effect as saliva would. I gave him the suit anyway; at least it'll offer him some protection"

If there'd been more time, I'd have bawled him out. Instead, I just said, "Stay close to me, Dan, okay?"

He nodded, then we ran back along the corridor, up to the ground floor. As we made for the entrance, shouts, crashes, the zip-zip of bullets, the choking tree smoke, all smacked us with the fact we were about to enter a totally alien world. One where kill first or be killed was the only morality.

I stopped Dan, held his shoulders, looked into his eyes, glad to see some proper fear there now. At least I had agency training in martial arts; all he had was knowledge of how to use the damn offside trap.

"I'm only just discovering my powers, too," I said. "So we need to keep close to each other; understand?"

He nodded again, and we ran together through the ancient door, across the gravel parking area and into the incredibly fast and furious carnage beyond.

I won't deny me 'eart was thumping harder than a boxer's punch ball as I crept down that moonlit road. No guards intercepted me as I approached the wooden bridge leading over a long drop between the cliff and the castle outcrop. Crossing the bridge would mean leaving the shadows of the bushes and boulders. No doubt cameras would pick me up, if they hadn't already.

So be it.

I raised my suit's head mask, turned up the resistance setting to full. This meant my movements would be impeded a little by the extra tension in the nano-weave of the fabric, but better that than getting shot or impaled before taking a crack at the bloodjacker.

I stepped into the muted silver light and onto the bridge. Still no lights showed at the front of the castle; no signs of life at all.

I held a rifle in each hand, well aware that to stand any chance of taking him down, I'd need to fire both of them. A triangle of focussed sonic resonance, with Santonaga as the third vector would mean I could turn his blood neutral, like the rifle's two beams. But apart from needing to hold Santonaga in their range for around twenty seconds, which seemed unlikely, I also suspected the vector between my left and right arms would not be wide enough to make a proper triangular sonic matrix.

My boots sent faint echoes under the bridge, off the high granite cliffs. Which was when I noticed how quiet the place was. The Scottish coast is normally battered constantly by sporran-shaking winds. But even though I saw white-topped waves on the sea below, up here the air remained still. Could he control the weather, too?

I reached the main gate of the castle, the huge iron doors standing open. I hesitated before going under the dark arch. The suit could probably protect me from a stone dropped on me noggin, but I weren't sure about a whole bleedin' portcullis.

Well, I didn't have much choice, did I? Through the archway then, and into the vast central courtyard: cold, heavy stone, three-quarters in shadow, the rest vibrating slowly in the moonlight as if the walls had their own heart-beat.

About eighty yards ahead, the main building showed a light at last, in a first floor window.

Still no guards or defences. Which put the willies up me no end. How confident must this guy be, to let me come this far without challenge?

I could have crept along the shadowed wall but was convinced by now he knew I was here anyway. So, I walked right down the centre of the courtyard, trying to look confident, keeping my gaze ahead, on to the door to what looked like the living quarters.

I wondered why there didn't appear to be any staff around. His country pile, where I'd torched his motor toys had been swarming with lackeys. But this place seemed empty.

And as I paused just inside the lobby of the main house, making out the jagged silhouettes of stags' heads on the walls, a suit or two of armour, everything musty and dusty, I realised *this* was his real home. The country mansion was his outer face; the one he'd grown out of that day when he suddenly felt his blood kick up with new hungers and lusts.

Right then, of all times, my blood tugged me real hard towards a staircase leading down to what must be the cellars. And I should have ignored it, given the important job to hand, but then I was also painfully aware of being under-equipped to take out Santonaga. Maybe down there, I'd find something else to use as a weapon.

As it happened, I found something that got me angry, which was the next best thing.

I ran down the steps, to a locked door. I used my jimmy to open it, not convinced by the lack of an alarm going off that Santonaga wouldn't still be aware of my busting in.

The room beyond was the size of a tennis court, and very cold. As the door swung back, overhead lights flicked on to show rows of identical white cabinets. I lifted the lid of the nearest one. I picked up one of the plastic packets inside.

Blood filled it, and the others. Human blood, no doubt. I did a quick calculation: fifteen cabinets each containing the blood of around twenty individuals: Santonaga had drained three hundred people to stack up his survival rations or whatever the hell he needed all this spirit juice for.

This, more than anything else that had happened so far, convinced me he could pull off his world-beating plans. Because the deaths of those three hundred had been covered up, which meant he had extensive influence in the police, emergency services, government, the whole shebang.

I let the anger channel through my own red stuff. Then I decided the folks who'd given their lives to make up these supplies would sooner know their blood had been destroyed than help keep monsters alive. For this blood was already tainted by his spit, so it couldn't even be used in transfusions.

I ripped open my belt and took out a flat-pack of highly flammable chemicals. Then I ran around opening all the cabinets, pouring some in each. Finally, I threw a mini-lighter in to the nearest cabinet, knowing that the resulting flames would soon jump to the others.

A stench of burning plastic, packets crackling in the flames; roiling red-black clouds of burning blood filled the air, swarming towards me. I took a deep breath, to keep out the acrid fumes then ran back up the stairs.

Still no alarm sounded. The chemicals I'd thrown over Santonaga's supplies were powered by nano-accelerators. So it was that the clouds of blood smoke and stench already billowed up the stairs, and followed me on as I took the wide stone staircase up to the first floor, keeping a rifle fire-ready in each hand.

At the top of the stairs, a door stood ajar. Incongruous TV noises came through the gap; that and a man's voice talking over them. Either he had company, then, or he liked to talk to himself in the manner of nutty villains. Except this bloke was no nut.

Oh well, as Sam would say, *Geroni-bleedin'-mo*. I pushed open the door, just as the blood smoke reached me.

Now, I was more than au fait with all things techie, but what I saw in that long, large castle room had me wondering if I hadn't missed the plot. It wasn't so much the giant screens lining the right hand wall, or the computer consoles with 3D air screens, but the almost silent hum which impressed me most. For the quieter that machines hum, the more efficient and integrated they are.

Which showed me that this secret world of vamp toffs had the techno march even on MI5; and what did that say about our so-called national security? Unless the spooks had some of this gear up their cloak and dagger sleeves they weren't telling me about.

As said, all this flashed through me mind in less than a heart beat. Because my attention swung fully to the two people looking at me as I approached, a rifle pointed at each of them. Smoke and blood stench followed me but much to my dismay appeared to have little effect on Santonaga.

I glanced only briefly at Sandra, not wanting to give her the satisfaction of seeing me look disappointed to find her there.

When I focussed on Santonaga, he just smiled affably and said, "Hello, Jack. We expected you about now. Sandra got here a couple of hours ago but then she had the use of one of my private jets. As for setting light to my blood supplies: well, after today, I won't be short of more."

He must have triggered a circuit because I heard the door swing shut behind me, cutting off any more blood clouds.

He wore a simple but well-tailored white shirt, black trousers and plain black leather shoes. Nothing ostentatious on show unless you counted the rich gleam in his eyes. Because, while I had a rifle pointed at his head, we both knew I couldn't kill him. Yes, I'd caught him out with a sonic bullet once before but that was partly because he didn't expect me to shoot and partly because he didn't want me to know who he really was at that stage.

But he knew all about me now, and Ambrose's research, and so would have worked out that two rifles meant I was going for sonic resonance triangulation. And how could I possibly pull that off, seeing I needed to keep one pointed at Sandra too.

"You don't look like a blood-sucking pillock," I said. "But then it's always been the way of the toff to cover their shit in the best linen."

This also had no effect on him, unfortunately, proving to me he knew my game was up.

Then he did a weird thing. His facial features melted and went through a number of changes, all into people I knew.

Morris. Lee. Sam, Pete, Errol, Brian; even young Eric.

I suppose he wanted to scare me by showing how much he knew about my life.

"Nice row of mugs," I said, "but it's still the same turd underneath."

Santonaga's usual boat race returned, not quite so sparkly eyed now. He shrugged. "We're about to make our broadcast. Unless you want to try stopping me, of course. But I wouldn't recommend it. If you behave, like the well brought up Cockney oink I know you to be, I might just turn you instead of killing you."

He bent to a 3D console, glancing up at the screen showing a TV channel. Any second now, he'd jack the national broadcasting system and blast the whole country with Ambrose's cure/infect resonance matrix.

"Oh, by the way," he said, "right at this very moment, my people are beating yours to a pulp at Marion's estate. The Princess is already dead, killed by someone you know, actually. The Bellers should all be dead, too, about the same time we claim the country's souls."

≈

At first, I couldn't make out who was who, what with everyone wearing black. But very soon it was obvious: mostly, our enemies were the ones still flying, flaming, living.

Dan and I stopped in sheer hopelessness at the edge of the fighting. I saw a Beller literally cut in half by a woman who's steel-shiny arms moved so fast they sliced straight through him. Other Bellers grappled with enemies who changed size suddenly, or broke into electric flames. And although the Bellers were also taking out plenty of Santonaga's people, who seemed less organised than us somehow, there were just too many of them, with more still arriving from the trees and the air.

"Dan," I said, "I don't want to die just watching all this."

His smile was mostly fear but he ran forward, and I guessed, at the same time forced his will into his new blood.

I ran just behind him. A huge man, arms like marble columns, swiped Sam aside and made straight for Dan. I fired my gun at him but the bullets just chipped his face and bounced off.

He reached Dan and put a stone hand around the boy's neck. Without thinking, I threw my soul into Dan's suit, joining the nano mesh. This way, he could withstand a missile hitting him in the chest. But the hand around his throat was compressing the suit anyway, regardless of its strength. I could do no more.

But then the hand relaxed its grip. I rushed back to my own body, just before it fell over, in time to see the marble man literally melting. Dan must have used powers to beat him.

Despite this little victory, we were not doing well. In fact, the enemy backed-off just slightly then, to stand in an arc about fifty yards from us. Dan and I joined the remaining half-dozen Bellers and Marion. I took a quick glance at the Princess's face, her skin ashen, eyes bleak.

Around thirty of them faced us.

"Surrender or die," said a tall young woman in the middle of the arc.

Marion breathed heavily. We would go with her decision. But before she could speak, a hurricane of gun-fire flew into Santonaga's people, from the direction of the woods behind. A few fell dead, either because they had insufficient protection or they'd been caught with their guard down.

Blinding lights flared across the startled enemy, shapes ran from the trees, still firing.

They came at an angle, aiming to join us. But their surprise advantage lasted only a few seconds before the enemy turned on them, the rest moving toward us.

I guessed our would-be saviours were MI5 agents. Which made the pain all the greater, seeing them so quickly destroyed. Only a handful made it to our little group.

"Morris?" I said, recognising him, despite the blackened face.

He nodded. "Lucilla had been turned," he said. "We've got her in chains, put Lee in charge for now. Looks bad, doesn't it?"

In fact, it looked final. The enemy, now enraged by the surprise deaths, had clearly decided to finish us, whatever Marion might have said by way of surrender.

As they flew and ran at us, our bullets doing nothing to stop them, I reached for Dan's hand and squeezed it by way of saying goodbye.

In the end, it all came down to one look, and my interpretation of it.

Santonaga had pretty much dismissed me from his attention for the ultimately useless peasant I was. He worked his fingers through the hard air laser matrix operating his link to the television satellites and towers.

I raised my rifles, with the intention of trying to blast him anyway.

But first I glanced at Sandra to my right, sitting at a console but not actually working it, to see if she was going to lunge at me. Which was when she nodded very slightly at the rifle in my right hand, her gaze holding mine.

If I threw it to her and she was lying again, I'd have absolutely no chance of stopping Santonaga. And I'd face yet another humiliation.

On the other hand, if she was kosher, we just might pull it off.

In that second, I had to check for the tiniest touch of dark in her eyes; the smallest twitch of contempt on her face.

Couldn't see any.

But still.

Oh, fuck it—I threw her the rifle and the moment she caught it fired mine at Santonaga.

A horrible hanging moment in which he turned, murder in his gaze, and nothing came from my right.

Then, thank god, Sandra's rifle cracked with sonics, just like mine. Twin beams of intelligent sound wrapped around him, thrumming into his blood. He roared with fury, realising the danger. Sandra and I fought to resist the backwash of sound rattling our hands, threatening to shatter our bones.

In the invisible net, Santonaga thrashed through form after form, trying to escape. Men, women, wolves, lions and of course bats.

As I held on with every bit of strength my body and suit could muster, I gave praise that Sandra had been given super-powers. I was the one in doubt.

Then, just when I felt the shaking get to the point where my fingers opened without me having any will left to stop them, Santonaga's shape-changing slowed down and his outlines grew fainter.

Finally, he relapsed into just a man.

We turned off our rifles and approached him cautiously. Head bowed, he looked ready to pass out.

I lifted his chin. His eyes looked wearily human.

I swung back my fist and punched him hard in the mouth, knocking him over, a couple of his teeth shattering in the process, blood spurting from his nose.

"That one's for the boys," I said.

I turned to Sandra.

"Ambrose is still alive," she said, "and you bleedin' well *did* re-turn me."

"Then why on earth did you give Santonaga Ambrose's signal to broadcast?"

"We had to keep Santonaga believing I was still turned and that he could trust me. That was the only chance of you and I ever catching him off his guard."

"'We'?"

She reached out, touched my face gently. "I'm sorry, Jack, really. When I came round, after you bit me, I knew everything that had happened to me. But I also felt your mind in mine, desperate to get me to link back to that night, before Santonaga took me. So, I pretended I still had amnesia, till I could figure out what to do. Then Ambrose asked you if he could have a word with me alone. That's when we talked it all out real quick and came up with a plan that might just beat Santonaga."

I don't know why, but I laughed loud and full right then. "Bugger me! So, all that time I thought I was fooling you with sex and romance, it was the other way round: you were taking me for a bleedin' ride."

"In more ways than one."

She smiled too, but what I saw in her eyes was a million miles from romance.

"But what if I hadn't got here?" I said.

She shrugged. "At least I'd have been close to him; could try to do him in at a later date if possible."

There were a lot more questions to ask her but I made do with, "Why don't we clear up and go home?"

She smiled. "I'll help you with the first part of that plan, but I'll have to come back to you on the second."

"Strewth, I don't believe it," said Sam, the dried blood on his naked body glistening in the fire's light.

None of us did. We stood and stared in silence for several minutes before Marion acted.

The certain death that had been just a few feet from claiming us had stopped. Just stopped. The black suited people simply stood, expressions blank, like mannequins waiting to be given a job to do.

Marion walked to the nearest of them, a tall young guy who only a few seconds ago had flames curling around his hands, ready to throw at us. She took off a gauntlet and lay her hand on his cheek. At that, his focus shifted a little, taking her in, and when he smiled, it had all the charm of a child who's just received the exact birthday present they'd hoped for.

She returned to our little group just as Morris talked rapidly into his phone, requesting help with the aftermath.

Right then, Marion's own phone rang.

"Hello Jack," she said. "Yes, I guessed that's what had happened. Very well done to you . . . oh, right, and to Sandra too."

TWENTY-THREE

Ain't it the Truth

IT TOOK US A MONTH to work out exactly who'd died in the fighting. In that time, we also had several long meetings at the agency, filling in the details of Santonaga's activities. Agents dealt with over a hundred politicians, landowners and business people who'd been turned, but they were the ones who approached us, desperate to have their own lives back. The Professor gave them the cure, of course.

Jack could have broadcast Ambrose's general cure over the TV. But he'd figured, rightly, that would mean anonymity for the turned. Which would suit the toffs, no doubt, but the rest of us wanted to know who they were and what they'd done. Besides, the cure was designed to work on victims, not on those who'd chosen to be turned. Which meant a cure-all might also revert those of us who'd been turned, or re-turned, by a Beller; and not everyone in that position knew for sure what they really wanted just yet. Myself included.

But we didn't know about the ones who hadn't given themselves up. Without the bloodjacker, their powers had disappeared; so why they would want to continue as ordinary vampires was anyone's guess. Maybe they hoped another would come and activate them again.

Jonathan Lee took to the job of leading MI5 very well. Mindful that Lucilla had been secretly pulling strings for Santonaga, creating gaps between the agency and people who should have been friends, like the government and the Bellers, he introduced a lot of sweeping changes, all toward more transparency. We even put out public advertisements for new agents; whereas before, recruitment had usually been by word of mouth. And the trouble with chains like that, of course, is that they can be jacked. Lucilla was granted a pardon on the grounds she'd been turned, but was put on permanent 'gardening leave' by the agency.

Eventually, a memorial service was arranged. The Prime Minister told Lee that it should take place in St Paul's Cathedral, and he'd do his best to keep the press away. Although we and the Bellers had saved the country from a truly dark fate, no one wanted to go public about it. For one thing, we still hadn't decided if we should use at some stage Ambrose's resonance matrix in a national broadcast, to inoculate the population from anything like Santonaga happening again, even if that meant some of us losing our powers. It was a debate sure to rage internally for years: accusations of mass brainwashing on the one hand, claims for peace of mind on the other.

As for Santonaga himself, he was tried in a secret court and found guilty of murder on several charges, also of kidnapping and attempted genocide—enough for the judge to rule he would be locked up for life. He was an empty shell by then in any case. Jack and Sandra had drained him of his vampiric essence and with it the fierce, virile power of the dark side. All his assets were stripped from him; his houses and castles given to the National Trust so the public could enjoy them on days out to the country—an apt and awful fate for the trappings of the wealth he used to so nearly enslave the entire nation.

At one of our meetings, there was some haggling between the agency and Jack for Santonaga's technology. And I smiled when Jack gave in, just a little too easily. He smiled back, which told me I'd guessed right: he'd already stolen the good stuff and just put up a fight for the rest of it, to distract attention.

Ah, Jack.

He'd come back alone from Scotland after beating Santonaga. Apparently, Sandra had commandeered Santonaga's jet with crew and flown to Halifax. Jack figured no one was going to be too bothered about the odd missing plane, not with everything else going on.

He was right: the day after the battle, Marion's house still vibrated with the aftermath. Clean up crews scurried everywhere, clearing away rubble and burnt furniture from the rocket attacks. Food seemed to be constantly appearing on makeshift dining tables, to feed all the extra staff.

The lawn was cleared of the dead and other debris but looked as if it had been the site of a tractor-pull. For some reason, the sight of all that previously beautiful ancient lawn now full of burnt craters, scorched tracks and just lots and lots of mud, hit me hard. How much had changed forever now.

All of us who'd been directly involved in the fighting had been up most of the night, discussing how to handle the immediate consequences. Although Marion's house was several miles from the nearest town, the sheer scale of explosions, fires and flashing lights had not gone unnoticed.

When I finally made it to bed I couldn't sleep so got up again just before noon.

I found a cup of tea and took it outside. Bright sunlight showed up all the horrific details of the fight. And I was just about to turn back inside when I saw him, climbing out of a jeep in the parking area to the left.

I put down the mug and ran to him. He saw me just before I reached him, grinned like a boy and threw his arms around me.

While I'd been able to change into jeans and T-shirt, he still wore his Bellers' suit, dusty and a little ripe with battle sweat, but I didn't care.

We kissed, smiling like idiots, and at last I cried, because I knew the simple joy of *now* would soon fade in light of the more difficult task we had to face.

And he didn't shirk it. After a quick shower and brief catch-up with Marion, he came to find me and we walked around the other side of the house, away from the chaos. He looked handsome in plain but expensive clothes which I guessed Marion must have found in one of her guest room wardrobes. He also looked older.

We sat on a bench under a willow tree, watching ducks scurrying around on a lily pond.

We told our stories, most of which the other knew but the details had to be spoken and to be heard. Then, after a long silence, he said, "Do you reckon that Lucy had already been turned when she talked me into taking you on?"

"I don't know; it's possible. Why?"

"Well, she must have known I was about to ask Sandra out. And Sandra at that stage was an unknown; someone neither she nor, more to the point, Santonaga could control."

"Are you suggesting she could control me?"

"No, not exactly. But you worked for Lucy—she told me straight out that you'd be spying on me."

He looked at the pond, clearly having trouble with what he wanted to say. So I said it for him.

"Now I think about it, yes, Lucy rushed me into your house probably because she felt that if you were finally ready to go out with someone, better it was me. She must have thought that because our profiles matched so well, you'd abandon any feelings for Sandra before they really began."

"And that may well have happened naturally. But looks like when it went to a second date with 'er, Santonaga got impatient and took direct action."

"Which put crazy pressure on your feelings, so you transferred them to me?"

He shook his head. "No. I really fell for you, Meera. In amongst all the mayhem and killing, and chasing after the biggest monster since Hitler, the one thing I've been certain about is how I feel about you."

"Even though I'm posh totty?"

"Seems that damn profile was more accurate than I'd like to admit. Speaking of posh crumpet . . . The other thing I'm sure of now is me bleedin' duty, and how it's always going to come first." He nodded in the direction of the main house. "Marion taught me that."

"What do you mean?"

Oh no, his eyes were haunted again. More truth I had to hear.

"Marion and I had to have sex too."

"*Had* to? Don't tell me she needed to believe you were in love with her too. I can't buy that, Jack: royalty don't fall in love; they get their marriages and their affairs on the side arranged for them, with the 'right' people. They certainly don't ever fall in love with one of the working class."

He sighed. "It wasn't like that . . ."

And when he explained, it did make sense. Duty came first, of course it did. But then Jack only saw his side of duty. I could picture Marion in her room the night he came to see her. Making a decision.

Yes, they had to mix blood and saliva, and yes, his sperm would increase the efficacy. But why not simply get him to fill a cup, then use a syringe? Instead, she reached for a dress she knew would cling in all the right places. Dabbed the right perfume on her neck, her groin no doubt tingling at the thought he'd cut her there and suck deep and hard.

Oh, *Jack*.

After all the talking was finally done, we sat together in a full but troubled silence.

Eventually, I broke it by standing up and saying, "Jack, I don't know where we go from here, if anywhere. I understand why you slept with Sandra and

Marion, but understanding doesn't alter the facts. I have to think about it some more. Let's get through the next few weeks and maybe we'll talk again."

He stood, nodded, didn't try to stop me. We hugged and I nearly kissed him, wanting to skip all that thinking that still needed doing and just be with him.

But I walked away instead.

The service at St Paul's got to me in a number of ways. First, I kept raging inwardly, that all these great people had died and, yes, we'd been given the grandest venue in London to see them off from, but part of me felt the whole bleedin' country should see it too. So they'd know who to thank for the fact their blood had stayed clean.

As it was, the pews were taken up with families of the Bellers and MI5 agents, all mixing in together, grief I guess the best leveller, all told.

And although the remaining Bellers looked no different to anyone else in their black whistles and black ties, the fact only eight of us sat there kept the hole in me heart wide open. One of those eight was a newbie, too. Dan looked ten years older than when I'd seen him kicking a bit of leather around on Hackney Marshes not so long ago. When he'd told me he'd turned his blood to Bellers' vintage, I thought about bawling him out, telling him to get back to school and forget all that hero baloney. But then I realised he actually had played a part in saving the world. Which meant school and jobs and marriage to a nice, normal girl and even footy were not really going to cut it for him any more. Besides, our numbers were down to the bone.

Somewhere in the middle of all my mental churning over the talk with Meera a few weeks back, still looking for clues in her words that she might forgive me after all, Marion stood up to the microphone.

"Your Majesty," she begun, which was the first time I noticed that the King sat in the front pew, wearing a black suit like every other bloke present.

"Ladies and gentlemen. We are gathered here today to honour the brave men and women who died saving this country from a fate surely worse even than the one posed by German forces in the last world war . . ."

Had Marion changed? She certainly looked sombre today, dressed in plain black skirt and jacket, hair tied back. The very first time I'd seen her, in the grip of Santonaga, not flinching even when I shot past her head to take him out, her eyes were full of rage and passion. But today she was in duty mode and could have been any other royal speaker saying all the right words in the right accent. Oh, come on, Jack, admit it: she *did* mean what she was saying.

After the ceremony, I stood on the steps outside the cathedral, squinting into the bright summer sun. Sam had just gone over to the agency folks, to invite them all to a knees' up we'd planned at the Astro.

"Jack?"

I turned to see Marion with an old guy who looked a bit familiar; behind them, two impressively impassive security goons .

"I'd like you to meet my father."

He held out his hand and I shook it, which was the same moment I realised I'd actually met him once before, by his tent opposite the Houses of Parliament.

I laughed. "How's the protest going, sir?"

"Shhh," he said, nodding in the direction of his guards. "If they found out, they'd insist on joining me and that would do little for my street cred."

"That's what I meant when I said he was in a safe place," said Marion. "Who'd ever think of looking there?"

"Nice historical joke, too, sir," I said. "You shaking your first at the politicians."

"Well, we never forgave Cromwell, you know."

"The country owes your daughter a huge debt."

"As do I. Which brings me to ask you a favour, Jack: would you be willing to work as special advisor to the throne?"

"I'm not sure, sir; I'll need to think about it. But why do you need me to advise you?"

"*I* don't. Marion does." He leaned closer, whispered to me. "I'm abdicating. Been bugger-all use the last few years in any case. And now she's full of this super rocket fuel or whatever the devil it is, there'll be no handling her at all any more, so I might as well give her the old crown to keep her occupied."

I blushed, realising I'd been nicely trapped by Marion. If she'd asked me, I'd have refused. She grinned at me now, delighted no doubt that I'd fallen for it. Well, maybe: I'd only said I'd think about it.

≈

I wouldn't say the bash at the Astro was a happy affair exactly, what with just about everybody present having lost someone close. But I guess it was far enough on from the event; that and the feeling we all shared of having done good work in resisting Santonaga; and the families' kids playing chase around the big room above the main bar, the teenage girls dancing in a corner despite themselves to the Sixties sounds we older folk had insisted on. So, we drank a fair bit, and munched the sandwiches and chatted about the future.

And somewhere in there, two people arrived who apologised for missing the funeral, something about the yanks taking too long to refuel the jet in the middle of the Atlantic.

I took them each a drink; hugged Ambrose after a split second of wanting to hit him instead, and kissed Sandra on both cheeks.

"Funny to think I used to be on the other side of the bar here," she said.

Out of a battle suit, she didn't look much different to when she'd been a barmaid: stylish blue dress, simple but tasteful silver ear-rings. Oh, but the eyes belonged to a different woman altogether.

"I'll spend a few weeks here, Jack," said Ambrose. "Share what knowledge I can with the right people, make amends where I need to. Then I'm going back to Halifax."

"And I'm going with him," said Sandra.

I frowned, and she laughed. "No, we ain't an item. He's going to help me control what I've become but whatever that actually is, I reckon I got a sepa-rate destiny to the Bellers or the agency, or anyone else I know here."

"You never said what powers you've actually got, as a matter of fact," I said. "Apart from being mighty good at faking orgasms."

"Who said I was faking?"

I blushed; she just laughed then went to talk to some of the others.

"God, you do enjoy beating yourself up, don't you?" said Ambrose.

"Can you blame me? I ruined her life."

He shook his head pityingly. "You're no longer a factor in her life, Jack. She's embraced her destiny and is thrilled at the uncertainty of her future. Okay, you may have led her unwittingly to it, but now it's totally *her* life and her choices to make. So why don't you butt the fuck out of it?"

I laughed. "You planning a new career as a motivational life coach?"

He looked around the room. "Meera not here?"

"No, she didn't want to come."

"Ah."

"Ah yourself, old man. That's one I definitely don't want your advice about."

"Fair enough . . . Have you thought about how you're going to boost Bellers' numbers again?"

"I don't know. I mean, we could do what Dan did and turn some new ones. But it seems mighty intrusive somehow. And besides the danger's over now."

"Come on, Jack, you know danger's never over."

"Okay, but I still don't know how we'd find new people. We can hardly put an ad in the papers: 'Wanted, Cockney kids who don't mind having their blood pumped with mutating sound to turn them into something super but who the fuck knows what exactly, the only guarantee is that your life will be wrecked and you could end up dying for your country with no one even knowing.'"

"One of my regrets is that back in the early 60s, I didn't think women should be super-powered fighters, so I rigged the bells to affect only male embryos."

"I wouldn't let Sandra or Meera know that if I was you."

He didn't reply, just smiled enigmatically and went to get more drinks.

"Hilary, can you ask Jeeves if I'm needed at HQ today?"

"He says you should stay where you are and wait for a message from Ambrose in about five minutes' time."

"Ambrose can phone me at HQ."

"What part of 'stay where you are' didn't you understand?" Says Jeeves.

I shrugged. "Fine by me. I can just sit here and relax. Don't even have to take off my Superman bathrobe. Might even do some gardening. Cook myself a roast dinner. Do my tax returns. Just as long as nobody needs me."

"You're not going to start singing now, are you?"

The doorbell rang.

"Who is it, Hilary?"

"Someone else who doesn't need you. Go answer the door, Jack."

I tied up me bathrobe and opened the door.

"Nice robe," said Meera. "Does the 'S' stand for stud."

"Hey, I'm not ready to joke about all that yet."

I led the way into the main room and put on the kettle.

"Wow, since I left, even your gizmos have got gizmos."

"Well, I've been exploiting Santonaga's stuff. Have to move fast before your lot come and nick it off me."

"Invented anything useful, like a broken heart detector?"

"Isn't it blokes what are supposed to hide their feelings behind sarky banter?"

I made coffee while she stood at the window, looking at the garden.

I handed her a mug then sat, heart thumping.

"I've done a lot of thinking," she said.

"I've done quite a lot of drinking, meself."

She turned, sat opposite me.

"I've been promoted," she said.

"You deserve it. Do you get your own office?"

"We're strictly open plan these days. Lee doesn't want any walls between agents, literally. I think I get a mug with 'Boss' printed on it, though. That and a better pension."

I sprayed coffee at that. "Oh, like you and I are going to live long enough to collect pensions."

She smiled, a real nice, right with me smile. But then she said, "I'm not ready, Jack. I think we both have to adjust to duty. And when we do, we'll be different people."

"I'll still feel the same way about you."

"I hope I will, too, but—"

"What the hell is that?"

"Church bells? It's not Sunday."

"It's Ambrose's message," said Hilary. "Why don't you go outside and listen?"

I held out me hand and Meera took it. We went out to the street. A few others were there, too, just as puzzled as us.

"Know what?" I said, "I reckon that's bleedin' Bow Bells."

"Give the man a cigar," said Hilary, faintly from inside the house.

"But we shouldn't be able to hear them from here," said Meera.

"They sound amplified . . . he must have found a way to boost them."

"But why's he having them rung at all?"

I grinned. "Oh come on, Ms Meera Promoted Nath. Surely you can work that one out: the Bellers need new blood."

About the Author, T.D. Edge

T. D. Edge won a Cadbury's fiction competition at age 10 but only did it for the chocolate. He has published several children's/YA books (writing as Terry Edge) with Random House, Scholastic, Corgi and others. His short fiction has appeared in various places such as *Realms of Fantasy*, *Beneath Ceaseless Skies* and *Flash Fiction Online*. He has been a street theatre performer, props maker for the Welsh National Opera, sign writer, soft toys salesman and professional palm-reader.

Read more by and about T.D. Edge on his website, TD-Edge.com

And watch for more Bellers' adventures to come, as Jack and his mates battle all kinds of supernatural malarkey rather than fill in a load of government forms and become respectable geezers . . .

www.ingramcontent.com/pod-product-compliance
Lightning Source LLC
Chambersburg PA
CBHW020416180626
46812CB00003B/1002